ONCE

YOU'RE

MINE

Possessing Her
Once You're Mine
Now You're Mine

The Obsidian Order
Vicious Secret
Vicious Society

Dark & Dirty Vows
A Match Made in Hate
I Thee Lust
To Have & to Hurt

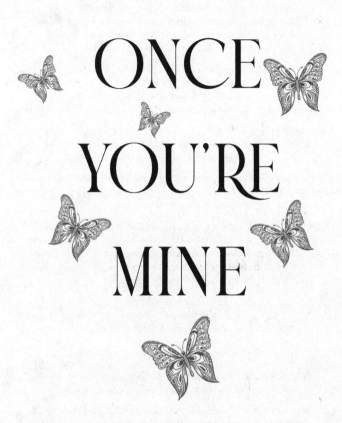

ONCE YOU'RE MINE

MORGAN BRIDGES

FOREVER

New York   Boston

Forever
Hachette Book Group
1290 Avenue of the Americas, New York, NY 10104
read-forever.com
@readforeverpub

Originally published in trade paperback and ebook in 2023
First Forever trade paperback edition: August 2024

Forever is an imprint of Grand Central Publishing. The Forever name and logo are registered trademarks of Hachette Book Group, Inc.

The publisher is not responsible for websites (or their content) that are not owned by the publisher.

The Hachette Speakers Bureau provides a wide range of authors for speaking events. To find out more, go to hachettespeakersbureau.com or email HachetteSpeakers@hbgusa.com.

Forever books may be purchased in bulk for business, educational, or promotional use. For information, please contact your local bookseller or the Hachette Book Group Special Markets Department at special.markets@hbgusa.com.

Character illustration by Skadior Art

Library of Congress Control Number: 2024938099

ISBNs: 9781538772164 (trade paperback), 9781538772157 (ebook)

Printed in the United States of America

CW

10 9 8 7 6 5

For anyone who thinks getting stalked by a fictional character is sexy, this is for you.

CONTENT GUIDANCE

The contents of this dark romance book may be triggering to some readers. It contains explicit sexual content and a morally gray hero who's over-the-top jealous/possessive, a stalker who falls first *and* harder and is willing to do whatever it takes to have the heroine.

Trigger warnings include the following:
Violence, murder, grief, stalking, death of a parent, mentions of involuntary drug use, mentions of assault (physical and sexual)

Welcome to the Dark Side.

CHAPTER 1

H ayden

I KILLED HIM.

The senator isn't the first, and he won't be the last. There's a satisfaction in this, yet it's fleeting, similar to a flame that's quickly put out. Dead and gone.

Like my victims.

Justice is a mistress that calls my name and pulls me into her embrace to fuck me. And leave me bereft. Empty. Wanting a closure I'll never possess.

Rain falls in a light but steady stream, landing on every surface in the cemetery.

The grass.

The gravestones.

The faces of the mourners.

Precipitation collides with tears to stream down the cheeks of those viewing the casket. Sorrow is everywhere, permeating the atmosphere like a dense fog. I let it cover

1

me, envelop me, bring me peace. It's rare to feel this serenity. The funerals of my victims are one of the few places I experience this, which is why I always attend.

To complete the ritual...

End a life.

Give justice.

Begin again.

I sweep my gaze over the attendees, a sea of black among the green backdrop, an ink stain on an emerald field. They congregate, huddling together to provide and receive comfort, some weeping quietly while others sniffle loudly. All of them broken.

Except for one.

The very person who should be shattered stands tall. But not for lack of caring. No, she loves the deceased. Deeply. Each of her breaths is a challenge as if she's being strangled, and she winces in pain every time her hazel eyes land on the mahogany casket.

Without a display of tears.

Not yet. But they all do eventually. Another part of the ritual I enjoy.

Although I still can't understand why people mourn evil. They should be relieved there's one less murderous individual in the world. One less man who preys upon innocent women and children. I suspect it's because they're not aware of the vile acts their loved ones committed. If they were, they'd express fear, not sadness.

Calista Green is exquisite in her melancholy.

This woman is the perfect example of what a politician's daughter should look like. Pristine and pressed clothes, flawless makeup, and her long, dark hair curled and piled atop her head in a way that accentuates the beautiful slope of her neck. What really sells the image is the string of pearls she wears, the ones she occasionally runs her fingers over to soothe herself.

As the only living relative, she's my focus. Not because the woman's young and attractive, although you'd have to be dead not to notice. Grave humor from me. How rare...and amusing.

Regardless of her beauty, Miss Green is the one I watch with bated breath, my chest rising and falling in time with hers, my body leaning forward whenever she moves. She's the one I'm connected to at the moment.

There's poetry, a sharp irony in taking the life of the man who's responsible for the vitality flowing through her veins. Making her heart beat. The subtle flickering of her pulse along her throat snatching my attention again and again.

Most women are delicate, in need of protection. But only in the physical sense. Emotionally, they are more intelligent, more in tune with the feelings that tend to dominate their lives.

The same ones I've destroyed within myself.

Specifically, the soft, tender ones: adoration and compassion. Whether that's caring for another, or even love. Whatever the name, they lead to weakness. Which results in pain and suffering.

And the arrival of darker emotions.

These are the ones in which I indulge, the ones that dictate my actions and fuel my ambition. Frustration. Anger. Disgust. Even desire, if it's through selfish acts; the gratification of it, both mentally and physically.

These things I understand and control, lest they take me over—as they try to do on occasion.

I'm not a perfect man. Only my intentions are.

The pastor asks everyone to bow their heads in prayer and they do. Except for me. And *her*.

Miss Green simply stares ahead, unblinking, her gaze sparkling with thought, her eyes becoming crystallized honey. I continue watching her. Scrutinizing her. The longer I do, the more piqued my interest becomes.

What is she thinking about?

And where the hell are the tears?

The petition to an unseen deity ends, and everyone lifts their heads. A middle-aged woman, the former manager for the Green household, covers her face with both hands. Her round frame shakes from the force of her sobs. Real or fabricated, I'm unsure.

Miss Green doesn't stop to question the authenticity of the tears. The young woman immediately embraces the older one, her full, pink lips whispering words of comfort while patting the housekeeper until the woman gathers her composure.

The pastor gestures to the casket, proposing everyone say their goodbyes. The first man to walk over is the family's driver. He takes his cap in hand and bows his head. His mouth moves briefly, clearly a man of few words, and then he's stepping back.

Before he can blend in with the crowd, the senator's daughter walks up to him and takes his hand. She gives the man a smile—a sad one, but a smile nonetheless—and says something that has the driver's shoulders straightening with pride. The interaction between them is familiar, comfortable.

I squint, not bothering to hide my skepticism. No one can see me at this distance, but I find myself wanting to get closer. It goes against my rules to get near my victim's loved ones, so I don't. However, rules don't stifle my want. My need to examine things more in depth in order to gain understanding.

Miss Green perplexes me.

She is the person most devastated by the senator's death, yet *she's* the one offering comfort instead of receiving it. And not just to anyone, but the staff. People she shouldn't acknowledge unless it's with a task for them to carry out.

I've met many men and women who come from the upper class, and none of them have a personal relationship with those on their payroll. They believe it's beneath them. A financial division that's been around since money and status became prominent in human culture.

But not Miss Green.

She treats each individual like a person of worth.

It's confounding...and refreshing. *If* it's real.

I don't believe her to be sincere. A funeral is the perfect excuse for a woman to gain sympathy and attention. For her to shine in the spotlight and be adored for simply being. Perhaps this is why she hasn't cried yet.

Miss Green is preparing her stage.

That is something I understand and have witnessed on numerous occasions. She'll be no different than the others. Just like she wears those pearls, she'll wear selfishness disguised as grief.

So, I wait.

My anticipation grows with every person who walks up to the casket. They leave shortly after, but not without the dutiful daughter greeting them farewell, a lily in her hand that she clutches like a lifeline. The rain falls harder and faster, scattering the mourners like a flock of ravens, the group quickly disappearing.

Until one person remains.

Miss Green stands there, a stoic expression etched in her features. Her hair, drenched by the rain, drips water onto her already soaked clothing. She doesn't move for a long while, despite the storm, despite the lack of audience.

Her continued stillness draws me, pulls me toward her. I adjust the collar of my coat to shield my face and gradually make my way in her direction. To a passerby I look like someone visiting the deceased. On any other day, that would be true.

I have mourned.

Once.

My steps bring me close enough to see the woman's bottom lip trembling, now tinged with blue due to the cold. Miss Green wraps her arms around her middle, flower still in hand, and sinks to the ground with a small cry of anguish.

Finally, the tears come.

She tilts her head back, her pale throat an offering, making my fingers twitch. Eyes shut and lips parted, the woman sobs. I don't possess empathy, but if I did, I'd be gutted at hearing such a forlorn sound.

Even so, there's a strange tightness in my chest.

It intensifies the longer she cries, the more tears she sheds.

There is no audience, no performance to be had. Just a daughter mourning the loss of her parent. In private.

Miss Green waited until she was alone to properly grieve, a revelation I didn't see coming. Her behavior is a deviation from the norm.

Disappointment surges along with confusion, and my brow furrows. For the first time, the joy I receive from funerals has vanished.

My satisfaction has been thwarted.

And replaced with an uncomfortable sensation that I refuse to name. Something I shouldn't be capable of.

It's there nonetheless.

Miss Green is the cause of this.

I run my gaze over the woman as she gets to her feet and slowly makes her way to the casket, grass and mud stains on her clothes and legs. Her perfect image is no more. The lily in her right hand shakes from the tremors wracking her body, dislodging raindrops that are quickly replaced by the storm. And her tears.

She brokenly whispers something I can't make out and kisses the flower's petals before placing it on the mahogany surface among the other blooms. Then she walks to the vehicle idling by the curb. I watch until she climbs inside and disappears from sight.

Then I head toward the casket. Peering down, I squint in disdain at the man hidden within, my lip curling. "You caused pain before and after your death. If I could kill you again, I would."

Reaching out, I trail my fingers over the lily that Miss Green held so tightly, the soft texture how I imagine her skin would feel. I pick it up and press my lips to the petal where she did moments ago, inhaling deeply. The fragrance of the bloom fills my nostrils, along with the scent of the woman who now invades my thoughts.

She's a mystery.

A problem.

One that I intend to solve and be rid of. No matter the cost. Or else the price I'll pay will be my sanity—what little still remains.

CHAPTER 2

C alista

"WHAT'S THE QUESTION *EVERY* WOMAN WANTS TO BE ASKED, AT least once in her life?"

I stop wiping the counter and look at Harper like she's lost her mind. Because she probably has. The things that come out of her mouth never cease to amaze me. And usually have me stunned into silence while blushing profusely.

I steel myself and guess, knowing I have a 1 percent chance of being right. "'Will you marry me?'"

My co-worker rolls her eyes. "I love you too, but no. Why can't a man simply ask, 'Do you want me to come over and eat your pussy till you come on my face?'"

"I think I'm having a stroke," I wheeze.

She grins at me, her green eyes bright and her expression feral. "All I'm saying is, if a guy ever asks me that, I'd totally marry him. *After* sitting on his face."

Harper gets me every time. I don't know why I even try to maintain my composure, but I suppose it's the way I was raised. You can't be a senator's daughter and *not* be aware of how you're being viewed by the public.

At all times.

I lift my hand to tuck a loose tendril behind my ear, only to recall I braided my hair to keep it out of my face. Still needing the mental satisfaction that comes from managing my appearance, I lower my arm and run my fingers over the pearl necklace hidden under my t-shirt. The smooth, round shapes, familiar and uniform, have me breathing out slowly, my flustered state dissipating.

Harper turns at the sound of the door opening and greets the customer as if she didn't just say something outrageous to me. "Hey there, Mr. Bailey. How's it going today?"

The elderly man nods once, shuffles up to the counter, and plants his wrinkled hands on the surface. He stares up at the menu, his forehead creasing in thought. As if he doesn't order the same thing every day. "I think I'll have the blueberry muffin and a coffee. Black."

Harper grabs a cup and scribbles his name on it. "Sure thing."

I walk over to the display and slide the glass door open. After grabbing the largest muffin with a set of tongs, I put it in a bag and set it in front of the register. A few keystrokes later, I give Mr. Bailey his total. He hands me the necessary bills, and I arrange them in the till, all facing up with the serial numbers in the same direction.

"If these muffins weren't the finest in the city, I swear I'd never come back here," the man grumbles.

He's not wrong. I think the pastries at the Sugar Cube are the best, and they're the reason I haven't starved to death. How can I when my boss lets me eat whatever I want when I'm clocked in?

"Here's your change," I say. "Have a good day."

Then I pump hand sanitizer onto my palm and spread it all over my hands.

Money is disgusting. And I mean that in every way possible. That doesn't stop me from needing it.

Mr. Bailey huffs and takes his items, heading to the corner seat, where today's paper sits on the table. As it does every day. He settles in the chair and takes the newspaper, but not before shooting me a glance. After a curt nod to thank me, the man's gaze leaves mine to absorb the ink on the page.

"So, where were we?" Harper asks.

I hold up my hands in mock surrender, the lemon scent from the sanitizer tickling my nostrils. "I don't want to continue that conversation."

"You're lucky someone else just walked in," she whispers. "Welcome to the Sugar Cube," Harper says at a normal volume to the newcomer. "What can I get for you this fine morning?"

The man's gaze zeroes in on me and I flag him down with a small wave. "He's here for me," I say to Harper.

"In what capacity?" She eyes the man without an ounce of shame, taking in his casual attire and blank expression. "Business or pleasure?"

"Business."

"Could be both."

I blow out a breath of exasperation. "No, it isn't. Hopefully, this won't take long."

"Don't worry about it," she says, waving a hand in dismissal. "It's all good until the brunch rush."

I remove my apron, signaling I'm on break, and wipe my

clammy hands on my jeans. "Good morning, Mr. Calvin. Right this way please."

The man follows me to the set of chairs that are farthest from Mr. Bailey. And Harper. She might be my best friend— my *only* friend—but the details of my father's murder aren't something I want to discuss with anyone. I can barely process the crime myself, and it's been four weeks since I buried him. And hired this private investigator.

"Did you find anything new?" I ask, lowering my voice and leaning forward.

The man shakes his head. "This case is turning out to be more difficult than I expected. With your father being a high-profile politician, I knew there would be a lot to dig through to uncover the truth. However, everything's been buried so deep I'm not sure I can find the person responsible for his death."

My heart cracks, and the fractured pieces fall, hitting my rib cage before settling in my gut. "My father was the only family I had. I need to find out what happened to him. Please, help me bring his killer to justice."

I blink back tears while the man scratches his chin. "Miss Green..." he begins.

"Call me Calista." I force a smile. My father always said that in order to humanize yourself to people, you had to break down social barriers and make them see the flesh-and-blood person underneath. "We've been working together for several weeks now, and I really appreciate all the effort you've put into this so far."

That "effort" has taken every single dime I own. My father's name might've been cleared in court, but his debts haven't. Between paying off his legal fees and hiring this man to look into his untimely demise, I'm one breath away from living on the streets.

Ironic, since I used to volunteer at a children's shelter.

"There is one avenue of inquiry I could look into," the man says, "but that would require you to retain my services for another month."

I smooth my features, struggling to keep my panic from showing. "Last month's payment wasn't enough to cover this? Especially considering you haven't discovered anything new?"

"Miss Green, I'm paid based on my time, not on results I have no control over."

"I understand. Do you think I could pay you at the end of the month?" When his brows lift and his mouth thins, I hold out my hands in supplication. "I've already picked up more hours at this place, and I've applied for other jobs as well. I just need time to get the money. That's all."

The man fixes me with a look that has my spine straightening. "You're aware of my policy," he says. "Payment up front. Non-negotiable."

His sharp tone cuts me like flint, sparking my anger. I narrow my gaze. "How do I know for sure you're actually searching for clues? Maybe you're just taking my money and doing absolutely nothing."

He gets to his feet. "Should you change your mind or obtain the necessary funds, you have my information. Goodbye, Miss Green."

I stare up at him, torn between begging for his help and letting him walk away. In the end, I bite my lip and stay seated. I simply don't have the money, and no amount of crying will change that. However, the idea of not making progress on my father's murder has a sour feeling growing in my stomach.

Whoever killed my father took everything from me. Not

just a loving parent, but my security, financial and physical. As well as my future.

Harper plops herself in the vacant chair across from me, her gaze clouded with worry. "That was definitely business, and not pleasure," she says. "Are you okay?"

"Honestly? I don't know."

"Do you want a cake pop? Those always seem to cheer you up."

I shake my head.

"Damn," she says, sucking in a breath. "Whatever you talked about must've been serious if you don't want a cake pop. Did that asshole threaten you or something?"

I shake my head again. "He didn't have the information I wanted, and I don't have enough money to continue hiring him."

"A private investigator. Figures. He's so cliché with the long trench coat and whatever." Her nose wrinkles in disgust. "As if that'll help him be a better detective."

I give her a sad smile. "It's the middle of winter and freezing outside. Most of the guys that come in here are wearing them."

"You won't change my mind. He's a loser." She reaches across the table and grabs my hand. "Forget him."

"I'll have to for now."

If only I could ignore my guilt as well.

CHAPTER 3

H ayden

I HATE SURPRISES.

They catch you off guard, force you to change your plans, and leave space for error. Not to mention the chaos that can follow. In my line of work, both personally and professionally, I can't afford that, which is why I research things extensively.

Senator Green is a prime example of this.

By the time I was ready to end his life, I knew everything about him, down to the names of his staff members. And of course, his daughter.

Miss Green has taken her father's place as the sole focal point in my mind.

I can't stop thinking about her, recalling and dissecting her behavior in order to understand it. Unfortunately, even while knowing a lot about her, I'm no closer to comprehending why she's different.

Or the reason her tears affected me.

I want to be rid of the problem, the confusion and lack of control she creates in my life. Except I won't kill her, because it goes against my code of ethics. However, invading her privacy doesn't.

In the last month, I've uncovered everything there is to know about her. And during that time, it's as though Calista Green has ceased to exist. She terminated all of her social media accounts, withdrew her enrollment in college, and her former residence is now owned by the bank. Without her having a cell phone, her digital footprint has shrunk and continues to disappear.

The scandal surrounding her father's trial, followed by his murder, will always keep her in the public eye. But not if she's untraceable. Fortunately, I prepared for this.

I can't let anything happen to Miss Green before I've had a chance to solve the mystery of her.

For this reason, I had a hand in getting her a job at the Sugar Cube. It's within walking distance of her apartment, which is convenient for her. But more importantly, it's close to my office building. That allows me to follow her to work every morning and to her home at night. Fortunately for me, Miss Green always commutes to work when it's dark.

All the more reason to watch over her.

"Zack, did you get a hold of that facial recognition software?" I say into my cell phone.

"Of course, Mr. B. I've always got the goods. You know me."

I repress a sigh and silently remind myself that this hacker is the best money can buy, not only due to his skill set, but because he's one of the few people I can trust. "Good. Hold on." I switch my phone to the camera setting and snap a picture. "I want this man's profile sent to my email immediately."

"This man" being the surprise that immediately pissed me off today.

"Sure thing, boss," Zack says, his voice too chipper for six o'clock in the morning. "It won't take me long."

"Excellent."

I end the call, my gaze still resting on Miss Green's face. As it has been for the last five minutes. Ever since she sat down with a stranger in the Sugar Cube. I shift my stance, letting my agitation flow through me like water. If it wouldn't alert her, I'd watch her from inside the coffee shop instead of standing outside.

After that day in the cemetery, I made it my business to know everyone she interacts with, and this person is unknown to me. He's of average height and build, his appearance forgettable, but he's in her life.

Which is why I commit him to memory.

Although I can't make out what they're saying, I can read Miss Green's expressions as if they were words written on paper in bright red ink.

Her shoulders droop, and the sparkle in her eyes dims while the man talks. Her bottom lip quivers, as it always does when she's distressed and trying to hold back tears. Whatever he's saying upsets her.

This adds to my intrigue.

I adjust my coat and maintain my post outside, not too far from the window. The city bustles around me, its soundtrack filled with honking horns and conversations of people. I only concentrate on the one.

My phone chimes with an email alert, and I reluctantly drag my gaze away from Miss Green. After a few keystrokes, the screen displays the man's face, and I quickly scan the information that Zack sent me.

The stranger is a private investigator by the name of Phillip Calvin. She must've hired him before the funeral, or else I would've known about him.

What are you searching for, Miss Green?

Is it your father's killer?

Are you looking for me?

I shove my phone in my coat pocket and return my gaze to the man. Calvin rises to his feet, and the woman's face takes on a stricken expression, her skin going pale. Her response to him only stokes my need for information.

As soon as the P.I. leaves, I take off after him, the edges of my coat flapping due to my brisk pace. Questions careen inside my mind, each one fighting for dominance while new ones manifest, creating a pounding at my temples. By the time the man enters a less crowded street, I'm vibrating with unspent energy and the need for answers.

"Mr. Calvin," I call out.

The man spins around, his brows lifting. "Do I know you?"

I shake my head. "No, but I know all about you. What's your relationship with Miss Green?"

Calvin narrows his eyes. "I'm not going to tell you anything. That's not how I run my business."

"You do now," I say. I step up to him and his gaze turns wary. "Give me all of the information pertaining to the senator's daughter. *Now*."

The man scoffs. But the sound is weak, airy, proof that his confidence is beginning to falter. "Get the hell away from me." He grips his coat and pulls back the material enough for me to glimpse the firearm resting on his hip. "I'm warning you."

I quirk a brow. "Are you now?"

My hand shoots out, fueled by my rising anger. I wrap my fingers around his neck, and the wheeze that puffs from his mouth has satisfaction streaming through me. With my free hand, I remove the man's weapon from his grasp and shove the nozzle into his side, wrenching a grunt from him. He stills, his arms extending in a show of surrender.

"Looks like I'm warning *you*, Mr. Calvin."

"Flash drive," he chokes out, "in my left pocket. Her file's on it."

"That wasn't so hard."

I release my hold on his throat. The man sucks in large breaths, causing the barrel of the gun to press deeper into his rib cage. I retrieve the USB, and once the item is in my possession, I lower the weapon, my grip on it still tight.

"Whatever agreement you had with Miss Green ends today. As of this moment, I'm taking over the investigation. You will not contact her for any reason. If I find that you've spoken to her or arranged a meeting of any kind, I will come after you. And that's when things will get interesting. Nod if you understand what I'm telling you."

The man's head bobs up and down, his gaze wide.

"Very good." I quickly remove the clip from the gun and any bullets resting in the chamber before handing the empty firearm back to him. "Remember what I said. Miss Green is off limits to you."

And anyone else.

Only until I discover why she affects me in ways I can't understand.

Or explain.

CHAPTER 4

C alista

Harper gives my fingers a squeeze. "Are you sure you don't want a cake pop?" When I shake my head again, she sighs and retracts her hand. "Fine."

The door opens. Out of habit, we swing our gazes in that direction. And my day goes from awful to complete shit.

I narrow my eyes while Harper's widens. "Who is that?" she asks, her voice near breathless.

"Another asshole in a trench coat."

The man is dressed in a tailored, navy-blue business suit that's perfectly fitted to his tall, athletic frame. His crisp white shirt accentuates his broad shoulders, while the silk tie knotted at his throat emphasizes the length of his torso. Over the suit is a wool overcoat that's dark gray and reaches his knees. Currently, the coat is unbuttoned, allowing a glimpse of the expensive attire underneath and adding a touch of casual sophistication.

None of the elegance he wears compares to the beauty of his face.

He stares straight ahead, giving me a view of his square, clean-shaven jaw and dark hair, styled with a purposeful disarray, a wayward black strand grazing his forehead. The man's lips are generous, forming a mouth that could easily slope into a smile or thin with disapproval. I've never seen the former, but I've had plenty of experience with the latter.

Harper grins at me, her gaze never leaving the newcomer. "I'm calling dibs."

"You can have him," I mutter.

But she's already gone, sashaying over to the register. "Good morning, sir. Welcome to the Sugar Cube. What can I get for you?"

"Black coffee. Large."

His voice fills the room like his presence. Commanding yet smooth, like silk on skin. I force myself to stare out the window despite my body urging me to look at him.

"And the name for your order?"

The man lifts a dark brow as if to tell Harper she's ridiculous for asking since he's the only one in line. Little does he know she has the fortitude of a Spartan. In terms of boldness, if anyone could give Gerard Butler a run for his money, it'd be her. I can easily imagine her shouting "this is Sugar Cube" in a customer's face.

My friend merely waits, her stare no less daunting, her smile losing none of its impishness.

"Bennett," he says, the syllables clipped.

My co-worker grins at him, the green of her eyes close to emeralds, alight with her small victory. "I've got you, Mr. Bennett." She whips out her Sharpie with the flourish of a showman and scribbles on the cup as though gifting him with her autograph. "Anything else?"

He shakes his head and a lock of his hair sways against his forehead. From the corner of my eye, I catch Harper's fingers straightening. She wants nothing more than to brush back the errant strand, to remove his devil-may-care appearance.

And his clothes.

If they were alone and Bennett was up for it, I'm sure Harper would let him bend her over the countertop.

I'd sanitize the hell out of it.

I still might. I swear her self-proclaimed "horny vibes" or pher*omoans*—yes, that's how she told me to spell it—are like the common cold: contagious and inconvenient. Just thinking about that has me eyeing my sanitizer from across the room.

"Your total is $3.50," Harper says. She waits for him to swipe his card before rushing off to get his coffee.

With the transaction nearly complete, I rise. Bennett's gaze flickers to mine. It's brief, hardly a full second, yet I freeze.

The coldness radiating from his blue eyes has always affected me this way, from my first encounter with him in the courtroom several months ago and every time thereafter.

I suppress a shiver and lift my chin, focusing my attention on the pastry display. Once I'm behind the counter, I keep my eyes downcast as though my apron is the key to my survival or a shield against Bennett's piercing gaze.

Just as he takes a seat across the room, the door opens, and a large group of customers walks in. A blessed distraction, cutting through the tension in the air. Those who arrive for the brunch rush don't trickle in, which would give us enough time to serve them without inciting their impatience. Nope, they herd themselves inside like cattle and immediately overwhelm the space with a long line.

"Welcome to the Sugar Cube," I say. "What can I get for you?"

After taking several orders, each person more growly than the last, I don't bother with the greeting. Even my "hellos" are less heartfelt and cheerful.

I stare up at the current customer to ask him for his order and the words melt on my tongue. The man resembles a grizzly bear with his unkempt hair and the wild look in his eyes. His clothes, a plaid shirt and ripped jeans, are riddled with stains. That alone has me leaning back, as if the filth on him will leap across the counter and taint me. Well, more than I am already.

I eye the sanitizer with longing.

If I thought I could squirt some on him without it being offensive, I would. Although I'm not sure it would make a difference. I know it doesn't help me feel any cleaner, no matter how many times I sanitize my hands.

"I want an Italian BLT panini and a black coffee," he says. "This better not take all damn day either."

His harsh tone combined with my already frazzled nerves has me shaking. The feeling of exhaustion is normal, but the apprehension is new. Harper hands me his drink, and I rush to put a sleeve on the hot beverage to keep from burning myself.

Only I miss the bottom of the cup. My sharp movement causes the coffee to spill all over my fingers. I jerk back with a yelp when the coffee sizzles against my skin, the burning liquid spreading all over the counter—and partially on the customer.

Harper peers over at me from the espresso machine as I

wipe my hand on my apron. The room doesn't go silent, but the conversations all around me becomes muffled, drowned out by the thrumming of my pulse in my ears.

The man slams his hand against the register and leans forward. I blink up at him. With every sweep of my lashes, the muscles in my body tighten until I'm a coil of tension, ready to spring.

Although I never held a job before my father's untimely death, I'd never been ignorant of how life worked outside of the estate grounds. People experience emotions, both high and low, and I've encountered them. However, this type of behavior isn't something I'm accustomed to.

"What the fuck is wrong with you?" he shouts in my face.

"I'm sorry," I say, the minor burns on my fingers already forgotten. "It was an accident."

"I don't give a shit."

Harper frowns and lifts her foot to march over while my bottom lip trembles. Anger churns within my gut at this man's disrespect, but what frustrates me the most is my lack of power. I won't say anything because I can't afford to lose my only source of income. But it's not just that. If this altercation shifts from verbal to physical, I will be in danger. Actually, I might already be in trouble.

"Apologize." The deep voice next to me is calm, yet dark and foreboding, like that of an executioner. "*Now*."

Everything goes quiet except for the sounds bleeding in from the street outside. It's like a vacuum has sucked the air from the room. My breath stills in my lungs, and my body trembles with the effort to breathe. I shift my attention from the threat in front of me to the one beside me.

Mr. Bennett.

He stands so close that the heat from his body sinks into my clothing, warming my skin. My blush is instant. Even so, I can't look away.

He doesn't glance at me. Not once. "If I have to repeat myself, things will become... *unpleasant.*"

The customer sputters, disbelief shining through his narrowed eyes.

Bennett shrugs off his coat and holds it out to me. Dazed, with my lips slightly parted, I stare up at him. His face gives nothing away. But his eyes...they're glacial, twin shards of ice polished to a lethal gleam.

I automatically grip the material of his coat, and the scent of him wafts under my nose. It's a combination of a spice and mint, refreshing and clean. It's intoxicating.

"What the hell?" The angry customer shifts his stance and leans further across the counter. "Who are you?"

Bennett drops his gaze to his cuff link. His long fingers work the metal through the tiny hole, the design a silver serpent with a ruby for an eye. His actions are precise but unhurried. He hands me the cuff link, and then the other before slowly rolling up one sleeve of his dress shirt.

I stand there, with his coat draped over my arm and his jewelry in my palm, watching him expose the skin of his forearms. It's akin to him stripping. Even Harper stands rooted to the spot, her gaze transfixed on Bennett's hypno-tizing movements.

With one sleeve in place, he begins to work on the other. My heart stutters in my chest, but I can't look away. Some-where, in the deep recesses of my brain, is the thought that I loathe this man. But it's been overridden by the woman in me.

The female that enjoys the sight of a beautiful and powerful male.

I suppose we're all animals at our core, always warring with our basic instincts. Similar to the way I've been fighting my attraction to the lawyer since I first laid eyes on him.

"What are you going to do?" The customer chuckles, the sound full of disbelief with hints of unease. "Hit me?"

"If it's necessary," Bennett says.

"She's just some chick."

"You're wrong."

Bennett fists his hands by his sides, his sleeves gathered at his elbows, and tilts his head. The lights shining overhead cover him in brightness, but the dark promise of his voice erases any indication that he's angelic.

Unless one compares him to Lucifer...

I clutch Bennett's coat tighter, pressing it against my chest as a wave of energy hits me. It rolls off of him and onto me like a breeze in winter, chilling me to the bone.

"Whatever, man," the customer says.

Bennett nods once. Whatever conclusion he's come to has me taking a step back. His eyes flash with intent right before his hand shoots out, snatching the man by the throat.

"Holy shit," Harper whispers from behind me.

I'd echo that sentiment if I weren't at a loss for words.

"What the hell—"

Bennett tightens his hold, cutting off the customer's airway, his fingers digging into the man's skin. He yanks the man over the counter, keeping him partially suspended in the air while the guy claws at his hand.

"If the next words out of your mouth aren't an apology, then you'll lose your tongue," Bennett says, his voice even despite the air of violence surrounding him. "Am I clear?"

I swallow deep, ready to obey even though he's not

speaking to me. This is what frightens me about the lawyer: my immediate instinct to do whatever he says. I ignore the urge, still too stupefied to do anything except watch this scene play out.

The customer thrashes about in Bennett's hold, and someone behind them mutters something about calling the police. The man's face turns a sickly shade, and his attempts to get free die down before Bennett loosens his grip. But only enough for the man to suck in a quick breath, as if through a straw.

He looks at me, eyes bulging and skin splotchy. I suppress a grimace when he parts his dry, cracked lips to speak. "I'm sorry."

It's hoarse, barely audible, but an apology nonetheless.

I nod, unsure if I'm acknowledging him or if I'm silently asking for Bennett to release him. Only he doesn't let the man go. Instead, Bennett pulls him closer.

"If I ever see you here again, it'll be for the last time."

Even though Bennett's voice is a low rumble, the threat rings loud and clear. Several people gasp and look at the door, contemplating their stay. The captive man nods vigorously, as much as possible with Bennett's large hand still gripping his throat. Only when the customer's eyes are bulging from his skull does Bennett finally release him.

The man stumbles back and makes his way past the group of people staring at him. Their gazes shift to me next, but my focus is on Bennett. He reaches for his coat and cuff links without a word. Once he's taken possession of his items, he walks from behind the counter and out the door, leaving everyone to stare after him.

Including me.

I believe that people have different facets to their

personality. But I never would've guessed that Mr. Bennett, the prosecuting attorney who tried to imprison my father, would be the same man who also possessed a degree of chivalry.

Or that he'd execute it on my behalf.

CHAPTER 5

C alista

"HOLY FUCK," COMES HARPER'S WHISPER. SHE TAKES UP THE space beside me, a poor substitute for the power that Bennett left in his wake. "Did that just happen?"

I nod, still unable to form words.

"You were right," she says. When I pull my gaze away from the door and look at her, Harper grins. "He's totally just another asshole in a trench coat."

I make a face at her, but she's already rushing back to the coffee machine to fill a previous order. It takes three deep breaths for me to find my voice and another one to actually use it.

"Welcome to the Sugar Cube," I say to the next person in line. "Give me a second to clean up the mess. And please tell me you don't want a panini like the other guy."

The woman in front of me, a college student around my age, giggles. The lighthearted sound fractures the tension hanging over me like a hammer to a mirror. I smile at her, clean the counter, process her order, and move on to the next customer as if the incident with Bennett never happened.

Only it did.

I can't stop thinking about it throughout the rest of my shift. Did he recognize me from my father's trial, and that's what prompted him to step in? Or did the lawyer come to my rescue because that's who he is as a person, a man willing to help someone in need?

Part of me wants to talk to Harper about it, to hear her perspective and see if it resonates with me. However, we're slammed, and there's no time to chat. Most importantly, I'm not ready to discuss the trial. If my friend watched the news, she'd already know about the scandal surrounding my father, but not the rest of the details.

I replay the recent events with Bennett in my mind again and again, trying and failing to answer my unspoken questions. The only indication that Bennett remembered me was when the customer said that I was "just some chick."

"You're wrong."

The lawyer's words flit through my mind like a caress to my psyche. No matter how much he attacked my father's character and made me feel uncomfortable in court, Bennett's voice never failed to stir something inside me. I'm not sure if it's the deep timbre of his voice or the way he speaks with such conviction that it leaves no question as to whether or not he's confident in what he's saying.

So why did he imply I'm not just some random woman? He and I have never spoken other than when I was put on the stand during the trial.

That was an awful experience. For me, at least.

"Whew," Harper says, blowing out a loud breath and

fluttering the copper strands resting on her forehead. "That rush was insane. There were way more people than usual."

I turn around to face her and lean against the counter, gripping the edge. "I thought the line would go down, but it just kept getting longer."

"Well, no one's here now." She gives me a pointed look. "Spill the tea before Alex gets here."

"There's nothing to say."

"Seriously?" Harper folds her arms over her chest. "You might be able to fool other people with your 'good girl' act, but I've worked with you almost every day since you got this job, and I know when you're hiding something."

"Mr. Bennett is a prosecuting attorney."

"And?"

I frown at her. "And I met him when my father went to trial."

"Oh."

"My father never killed his secretary and was found innocent of all charges," I say, my words rushing from me, tripping over each other in my haste to convince Harper. "I swear on everything, he was a good man."

"Anyone who raises a kind person like you has to be," she says, her gaze softening. "If you say he was innocent, then I believe you."

"It's not just my opinion. The judge declared him as such."

Harper presses her lips together. The nonverbal skepticism sets my teeth on edge. "I know people in my father's position could pay off someone to clear his name," I say, "but that's not what happened. I promise."

She nods. "I don't care about your dad right now. The only thing I want to know is why the hottest guy I've ever seen, a wet dream in a suit, walked behind this counter and acted like he wanted to kill some random customer for giving you a hard time. Care to explain that?"

"I can't. Not when I don't understand it."

"Fine. Just so you know, I hate you a little right now. Pure jealousy. I admit it."

"Don't be. That lawyer said the most horrible things about my father, and he practically bullied me while I was on the stand." I shudder as remnants of his accusations echo in my mind. "I don't hate Mr. Bennett, but I'm not far from it."

Harper tilts her head. "Was it personal, or was he doing his job?"

I open my mouth, close it, and try again. "It felt personal."

"I can't imagine a court case that wouldn't. Look, all I'm saying is, after what Mr. Hot-as-fuck Bennett did today, I wouldn't be so quick to judge him."

"Hey, girls." Alex, the manager and owner of the Sugar Cube, walks up to us. "How's it going today?"

Harper gestures to the nearly empty room. "Same old, same old."

I nod, but it's a lie.

It feels like nothing in my life will ever be the same again.

$\sim$

"Want to catch a rideshare with me?" Harper asks.

I inhale the evening air, letting it cleanse me from the inside out. "I can't. You live in the opposite direction, remember?"

"I haven't forgotten," she says, worrying her bottom lip

between her teeth. "I just don't like the idea of you walking alone at night."

"Well, it's not like I can sleep in your dorm room."

She shrugs. "You could. My hook-ups do."

"I swear you spend more time having sex than studying art."

"The human body is a canvas that I utilize at every opportunity."

A laugh bursts from me. "I'd believe that if you were a sculptor. Go on." I nudge her playfully. "I'll be fine."

"See you tomorrow?"

"Absolutely."

She smiles at me, the expression wobbly on her pretty face. I give her a little wave and shove my hands in my pockets, grabbing the pepper spray. The feel of it in my palm gives me the courage to face the trek back to my apartment.

Desperate times call for desperate measures, and I am beyond desperate.

I lift my chin, square my shoulders, and tighten my grip on the tiny canister before taking off. New York is a city that never sleeps, whether that be the good or the bad parts of it. The safe or the dangerous.

The only thing that gets me through is the lingering thought that this can't last forever. Eventually, I'll earn enough money to pay the P.I. to find my father's killer. Once that's done, I can lay this all to rest and begin to build my life. Or what's left of it.

I've made peace with the fact that I'll never live in the upper echelon of society or have access to that type of wealth again. It was never that important to me anyway. The only part of my former life that I miss was having a family. Even if it was only my father, some of the kids at the shelter, and the members of my household staff. It was improper to have friendships with them, but I never cared.

Family isn't defined by a number of people or the social construct. It's defined by the number of heartbeats, shared laughs, and a love that goes beyond borders or restrictions.

I sigh, the sound loud now that the noises of the city are beginning to lessen. Although my awareness increases. The buildings towering above encase me in shadow, the street lights weak against the magnitude of the darkness. The ground underneath my tennis shoes changes from the pale gray cement to the cracked asphalt found in less-cared-for parts of the city. The places I didn't know existed until I was forced to live there.

My instincts flare, sending a streak of alarm throughout my body. I don't stop walking, but it takes every bit of self-control I possess to keep from running. However, my heart has no such reservations. It races, the uneven cadence a reflection of my fear as it spikes again, ice filling my veins.

An invisible presence barrels past my defenses. The hair on the nape of my neck lifts and I fist my hand to keep from rubbing the area, to rid myself of the unwanted sensation. It lingers like a specter's fingers, gripping me tighter with every step I take.

I spin around, my gaze zipping from one corner to the other, searching every shadow and dark place in the vicinity.

That's where monsters hide. Not out in the open, but under your bed and in your closet. Within your home and other places where you're most vulnerable.

Where they can be close to you.

Finding nothing and no one, I turn around, no less frightened. If anything, spotting the source of my anxiety would lessen it and give me something to focus on. A target. Not that I would go on the offensive, but I could prepare my defense.

Maybe I should buy a gun.

I shake my head. I barely have enough money to buy food, let alone a weapon that costs more than I earn in a week.

Except...I won't need to eat if I'm dead.

I continue at my brisk pace, praying like I do every night that I'll make it to my apartment. That I'll live long enough to put my father's killer to justice. Then, I'll finally be at peace.

Until that day comes, I think I'm going to need a different kind of ammunition.

Like a short skirt and some high heels.

CHAPTER 6

H ayden

FOR SUCH A TINY CREATURE, MISS GREEN WALKS QUICKLY, HER
legs scissoring as if she can trim the distance to her home.

Is it because she's in a hurry? Or does she feel me
watching her?

The woman turns around so swiftly that her long braid
swings wildly, landing on her shoulder instead of resting
against the small of her back. She scans the area, her hazel
eyes wide with the panic she's desperately trying to conceal.
But she can't hide her fear from me.

Or anything else.

I study the woman from a distance, taking in the rise
and fall of her chest, the way her breaths come out in short,
uneven pants. She presses her full lips, refusing to believe
what her eyes are telling her. Although she can't see anyone,
she knows someone is nearby.

Smart girl.

Miss Green turns back around and walks up to T&A. It's understood that the name of the bar should read "tits and ass," but the owner claims it's "thirst and appetizers." I'd believe it if the female staff members didn't wear skirts short enough to expose the curves of their asses, and a shirt with a neckline that reveals more than it covers.

So why is Calista Green, a former senator's daughter who's used to wearing pearls and modest heels, going inside such a risqué establishment?

I cock my head, a frown tugging at my lips. It only takes me a second to make the decision to follow her inside. She has piqued my curiosity. Again.

The fact that she continues to do so is more aggravating and confounding with every passing moment.

The dimly lit interior of the bar is suffocating, the air heavy with the sour smell of stale beer and cigarettes. Dingy, mud-colored walls are adorned with old neon signs promoting various liquor brands, most of the letters in the signs burnt out. A haze of smoke lingers over the bar, visible in the fluorescent glow of the signs. The scuffed wooden floor is littered with crushed peanut shells, and the tables and barstools look grimy to the touch.

Rock music plays from an old jukebox in the corner, though most of the patrons are too absorbed in their drinking and low conversations to care about it. Behind the bar, an unshaven bartender stands polishing glasses with a rag, his stained apron and the shelves of liquor bottles behind him accumulating dust.

I immediately find Miss Green, my gaze locking onto her where she waits at the crowded bar. She stands out like a lamb among a den of lions. Pure and helpless.

The bartender freezes when he spots her. Then a licentious gleam lights up his dark eyes as he runs his gaze over her. His look is appreciative, lustful as I expected.

She's a beautiful woman. Rich, dark hair that reaches the small of her back, long enough for a man to wrap around his wrist several times. Her eyes are the color of honey, flaunting the sweetness inside, driving you to want a taste. Her body is not as curvy as most of the women here, but her tits are the perfect size to fill a man's hand.

My fingers curl, creating a fist as my thoughts thread themselves into my body, pulling a reaction from me. This isn't the first time. Another anomaly that's disrupted my thought patterns and wrecked the logic I've always employed when viewing any situation.

But only with Miss Green.

And I still don't know why.

Her gaze darts around the large space, before settling on the bartender. He says something to her, and she nods once. Then again, only with a little more conviction this time. Is she trying to convince him or herself? About what exactly?

The conversation is short, but to me it feels like an eternity of not-knowing. The second she walks toward the exit, I'm striding up to the bar, my need for answers the only thing keeping me from following her outside.

The bartender's gaze lands on me, and his pupils dilate. His immediate unease is a good sign that he recognizes I'm not someone to fuck with. At least not without consequence.

"The girl with the braid," I say, not bothering to waste words. Miss Green is alone, and I won't leave her unprotected longer than necessary. "What did she want?"

"Why should I tell you?"

"Because you want to live."

He jerks back, the drink in his hand spilling over the sides of the glass. "Look, man, I don't want any trouble."

"Then answer the question."

"Okay, right. She asked about getting a job here."

I narrow my eyes. "What did you say?"

"I said, 'yes.' She's young and pretty, which is what we want around here."

"No."

"No?" he parrots, his brow furrowing.

"No, she will not have a job here. No, you will not hire her. If you do, then I will burn this motherfucker to the ground. *With* you inside." I lean over the bar, letting him register my intent. "Do you understand?"

The man nods, his jowls flapping from the force of his movements. "Yeah, I got it. Damn, man. Chill."

I head toward the door, my long strides already shortening the distance between me and Miss Green. Little time passes before she's in my sights again.

A sense of relief fills me.

My lips thin at this. After weeks of study, I thought I'd understand her by now. While I do have copious amounts of information about her, it's not the same thing. I want, no, I *need* to comprehend why this woman draws me to her like no other.

Why I'm protecting her at all costs.

Today was a prime example. I threatened to kill a man in public, for fuck's sake. Despite the connections I have with the police and others who'd "handle" this situation, the attorney in me couldn't believe I acted so rashly. However, the man in me, the primal side that I keep concealed from the world? It didn't give a fuck.

Someone, another man no less, threatened what belongs to me.

Initially, I made sure Miss Green was safe because I was curious about her. Since then, I've done more than that, things I wouldn't do for anyone. I keep telling myself I'm doing it so she remains alive long enough for me to solve the puzzle that is Calista, that each new day offers me another piece, another clue as to why she's different.

And why I actually give a shit.

Except my morbid fascination is growing into something I can't identify. Something that's slipping from my control. This is what concerns me the most.

Miss Green walks up the steps to her residence, and I shake my head as she goes inside. The dilapidated building is more than an eyesore. It's a death trap. How she's managed to return to this place every night is unfathomable to me, especially after growing up in the luxury she did.

I run my gaze over the structure again, but this time, a fire heats my gut, burning me with the need to get her out of there. Would she even accept my help? Doubtful, after the things I said in court. Even so, I don't have any regrets. Everything I said about her father was true. And led to his demise.

At *my* hands.

Miss Green's silhouette appears in the window behind the drawn curtains, arresting my attention. Usually, I leave once she's inside with the door locked behind her, but tonight I'm lingering, wanting another glimpse of her.

What the fuck is wrong with me?

Even while berating myself for my lack of control, I watch Miss Green strip off her clothing. Her curves fill the window. Perky tits, slim waist, and nicely rounded hips, all begging for a man's touch. But when she undoes her braid, I suck in a breath.

She's Godiva, a nude temptress with her hair flowing around her shoulders, ready to seduce and prove the weakness of man.

Myself among them.

Damn her. And my fucking cock for getting hard.

This all-consuming lust is a surprise...and I hate those.

I run the heel of my hand over my erection. It jerks in response, wanting a tight pussy to sink into. But that'll have to wait.

I might've told the P.I. that Miss Green was off-limits to him, but the rule applies to me as well. Getting involved with my victim's family members is just fucking stupid. Which is why I never do.

That doesn't stop me from wanting her.

"Fuck this," I mutter.

I take off in the opposite direction, putting distance between myself and Miss Green before I do something rash. Something that I'll regret. But not because I wouldn't enjoy it.

On the contrary, I'd enjoy it *too* much.

CHAPTER 7

H ayden

BACK IN MY PENTHOUSE, FAR FROM THE DELECTABLE MISS Green, I pour myself a glass of cognac. The alcohol goes down smoothly. Unlike my cock.

It's still hard from watching my target.

That made the trek home irritating.

I take a deep breath as if that'll relieve me. It doesn't. There's nothing equal to the sweet cunt of a woman.

If I don't distract myself, I'll end up jacking off to the image of Miss Green. The woman has invaded my mind enough as it is. I don't want to give her more control over me.

After retrieving the hard drive from my coat pocket, I head to my office and sit at my desk. My computer screen flares to life with a keystroke. When I insert the USB, antici-pation slithers over my skin, making it itch.

The opportunity to learn more about Miss Green is a temptation I've never been able to walk away from.

I grip the mouse, my fingers tight with my excitement, and click on the files under "Calista Green."

Each one contains a bunch of notes pertaining to different parts of Senator Eric Green's life. Political, personal, sexual, etc...it's all there. Along with his trial, eventual murder, and everyone in his life.

Kristen Hall, his secretary.

Just reading her name has the need for violence flaring in my gut. Senator Green killed her. The evidence was there, a low-hanging fruit, ripe and ready to be picked. The woman was found dead in the senator's house, on his bed, and pregnant with his child for fuck's sake.

My case was solid.

Yet Green was acquitted.

Despite the overwhelming evidence, the justice system failed me. Therefore, I took the law into my own hands. Kristen Hall deserved to be avenged.

"May you have more peace in the afterlife than you did in this life."

I lift my glass in salute and down the contents before setting it on my desk. The burning in my chest is welcome, a reminder that I'm alive and the senator is dead. *I'm* the person who won in the end. No thanks to Robert Davis.

As the senator's campaign manager, and alibi, he made sure the senator was found innocent when the jury believed him. However, Davis was lying. I knew it that day as surely as I knew my own name. Which is why I visited him privately in the middle of the night.

It's amazing what people will admit to when you put a gun to their head.

"Tell me what I want to know, and I won't blow your

fucking brains out," I say. I press the muzzle of the gun into the man's temple, and he flinches, his tears falling faster, mixing with the sweat trailing down his face. Davis mumbles something unintelligible, and my mouth thins behind my mask. "This isn't going to work if I can't understand you."

"Before he left, the senator was with me that night," Davis says, his voice quaking like his entire body. The tremors snake along my fingers where I grip him by the throat with his back facing me. "I swear on my mother's life."

"What about the daughter?"

"He was with Calista like she said. Her testimony was truthful. She was baking in the kitchen at the shelter where she volunteers every week. For some reason, she felt sick and passed out. When she came to, she called her father for help. That's where he was at the time of Kristen's murder." Davis releases a sob. "That's all I know."

I scrub my jaw and blow out a breath. "Calista fucking Green."

The vision of her races to the forefront of my mind, providing an image of the woman who haunts me every minute of every day. She was beautiful on the stand, a constant distraction that I couldn't master, regardless of my efforts. As much as I hated to admit it, her testimony as an alibi also fucked me.

I scroll further down the document, my eyes absorbing the words at a rapid pace. The information in front of me is nothing I haven't already come across. My exhale is loud in the quiet, but disappointment screams within me, demanding answers.

There are none.

However, there's an image nestled within the file. Although I doubt the questions in my mind can be satisfied by a mere picture, I click on the icon, unable to stifle my curiosity.

Miss Green's beautiful face fills the screen. In it, she gazes straight at the camera, her expression defeated and vulnerable. However, it's her eyes that cause a pang to streak through my chest. The hazel within is lackluster and haunted. The ember within carries none of the light or fire that I'm used to seeing. There is one emotion present: stark terror.

My gaze drifts over her features as I search for clues for her stricken expression. The bruises on her throat have the hairs on the back of my neck rising. Splotches of blue and purple are spread across her delicate skin, nature's temporary tattoos.

Put there by a man's hands.

Ideas begin to take shape. Pressure builds inside my head as my thoughts trample each other, trying to make sense of what this means. The metadata on the image puts the date and time on the night of Ms. Hall's murder. Senator Green's hand, discernible by the Ivy League class ring on his ring finger, was the one holding Calista's hair back so the bruises could be visible in the photo. He *was* with his daughter that evening, documenting everything. What happened?

Miss Green is definitely keeping secrets.

This raises more questions: who's the motherfucker that attacked her? And *why*?

My intuition nagged at me all throughout the trial, bringing my focus to Miss Green again and again. I'd thought it was due to the fact she was fucking gorgeous. Now I know it's because there's more to her story than she told in court.

If her alibi was real, then I killed an innocent man.

"Fucking damn it!"

I reach for the tumbler, my fingers trembling with my rage, right before I hurl it across the room. The high-pitched sound of the glass shattering and the shards hitting the floor barely penetrate my consciousness. How can it when my soul is twisting with the injustice I committed? My moral code is one of the few things I value, and I fucked it up.

I only have myself to blame.

After pulling my cell phone from my pocket, I call the hacker on my payroll, who picks up on the second ring. "Yo, boss man. What can I do for you?" Zack asks.

"I need you to look into something for me. Calista Green might've been taken to a hospital on June 24th, and I want to know why and for how long."

"Sure thing. You want me to call you back?"

"I'll hold."

The sound of Zack's fingers striking the keyboard has me gritting my teeth. Patience is something I've exercised every day of my life, but for some reason it eludes me in this moment. Perhaps it's the foreboding that looms at the edges of my psyche. Or maybe I'm a paranoid fuck.

Whatever the reason, my rage is barely contained.

"Anything yet?"

"No," Zack says, sounding distracted. "You're not going to believe this, but I can't find anything."

"*You* can't find anything?"

Zack releases a sigh. "I know, right? Either this event never happened, or someone covered their tracks so well that I'll have to dig a lot deeper. That'll take me some time, assuming I can find it."

"Keep searching. If you find anything, no matter how insignificant, call me immediately."

"You got it, *el jefe*."

I end the call, my fingers gripping my phone so tightly the plastic elicits a creaking noise. There's a nagging doubt in my mind that Zack might not find what I'm looking for. And *if* he does, I'm not sure how long it'll take him.

Am I willing to wait?

Or should I break my rule and go straight to the source?

I've already fucked up my code of ethics, so why not continue to spiral downward into a pit of self-loathing? I release a sardonic laugh, the sound mocking me. The irony of it all makes me want to kill someone.

In the name of revenge.

How can I avenge Miss Green if I'm the cause of her heartache?

Her face rises to the forefront of my mind. Except in my mind's eyes, she's her normal self, not the battered woman from the picture. I can't think about that image without the need for bloodshed. Now, in my fantasy, her hazel eyes are like a beacon of light, the pureness of her soul radiating outward, so contrary to the darkness found in me. I've finally recognized this is one of the things that draws me to her.

I suppose opposites attract. A principle in magnetism. Except I should be repelled by her, not wanting to get closer. But I have to.

Even if it ends with her broken.

CHAPTER 8

C alista

"Good morning," I say to Harper.

She pokes her head out from behind the counter, a large bag of coffee beans in her arms. "Mornings are for losers."

I grin. "That's why Alex schedules us for the early shifts."

"True."

"Do you need help with anything before we open?"

She shakes her head. "No, just do your tidy up thing. I'll be ready in a moment."

"Okay."

I walk over to the hooks on the wall and grab my apron, tying the ends in a bow. Then I retrieve the newspaper I picked up on the way here and set it on the table for Mr. Bailey. Afterward, I wipe down every table and the countertops, although I'm sure my boss did that before he left for the night. Even so, I can't help it. I like things to be orderly and neat.

With the sugar, artificial sugar, and raw sugar packets arranged alphabetically in their containers, I place them on their designated tables. Lastly, I refill my hand sanitizer. The scent of lemon engulfs me, and I smile.

"Is that happiness on your face because of a man?" When I shake my head, Harper slaps her forehead. "Don't tell me it's because of the sanitizer."

I shrug. "I like the way it smells. Clean and fresh."

My friend clicks her tongue in admonishment. "Girl, we've got to get you a man. Wait." She snaps her fingers. "What about that hot lawyer from yesterday?"

"No way."

"Why not?"

"I already told you."

Harper plants a hand on her hip. "You don't have to like him. You just have to fuck him." She moans, closing her eyes and licking her lips. "I bet you'd need both hands to fist him and that he fucks like an MMA fighter on crack: hard, fast, and so, so good."

"I'm not interested in getting my ass whipped."

She bursts out laughing. "You actually cursed. Nice. But seriously, I'd be all over him if he weren't yours."

My gasp is loud in the coffee shop. I drop my gaze to the register and rearrange the bills inside. Alex never has them facing the same way like they should. "Mr. Bennett isn't mine. Honestly, what happened yesterday was a coincidence. I doubt we'll ever see him again."

"Maybe." Harper huffs. "If I'm right and he shows up here, then you have to flirt with Mr. Be-my-lawyer-daddy Bennett. If you're right, then you have to promise to go out with me sometime so I can find you a man."

I chew my lip in thought. I'm supposed to start my job at T&A tonight, and I have no idea what my schedule is going to look like going forward. The last thing I want to do is plan something with Harper and then bail. Or for her to find out why I can't go in the first place.

"I'm not in love with either of those options."

She glances at the clock. "It's almost 6 a.m. Bleh. To be continued."

I open my mouth to argue, but Harper dashes to the door and unlocks it to let the early birds in. She returns to stand behind the counter and winks at me.

"Good morning, Mr. Bailey."

The shift begins like it always does, and I settle into the workday by assisting the regular customers. Some people hate routine, but I find it soothing. Knowing what to expect removes the anxiety of the unknown.

"Phew," Harper says, wiping her forehead several hours later. "The brunch rush was worse than yesterday. We'll have to get Alex to hire someone else to help us. I'm not trying to get yelled at everyday just because the line is long."

"I know." I snatch up the dish rag and wipe the counter to remove a pile of crumbs. "At least we didn't have any issues like yesterday."

"True. Do you want to take your break now?"

I frown and look at her over my shoulder. "Why would I? It's not time yet."

"Oh, yes it is," she says in a sing-song voice. "Good afternoon, Mr. Bennett! It's great to see you again."

My entire body goes statue-still, shock paralyzing me. I didn't expect him to come back, but now that he has, I need to gather my composure. At least enough of it to avoid acting like an idiot.

"Welcome to the Sugar Cube," Harper says, her voice

49

carrying threads of impishness that makes me want to smack her. "What can I get you?"

After taking a fortifying breath, I slowly lift my head, refusing to cower before him—only to find his gaze is already on me. Whatever air I pulled into my lungs leaves me in a rush.

"Nothing," he says. "I'm not here for sustenance." The man tilts his head, his gaze boring into me. "I need to speak with Miss Green."

"Okay."

"No way."

With both of us answering him at the same time, the responses are a jumbled noise. I clear my throat and square my shoulders. "There's nothing for us to talk about."

Harper swings her gaze to me, her lips parted in surprise. But I ignore her. Bennett has my undivided attention. I'm not sure I could look away even if I tried.

"Are you telling me that you don't want to find your father's killer?" he asks.

I can feel all of the blood rushing from my face, bringing stars to my vision. When I sway on my feet, Harper throws her arms around my shoulders. Right as Bennett reaches across the counter for me.

My friend shoots him a dirty look, and he retracts his hand. Then she pats my cheek, her gaze clouded with worry. "Are you all right, honey?"

"I'm fine." After taking a deep breath, I give her a wobbly smile and step away from her supportive embrace to prove it. "Give me a moment to sort this out, okay?"

She nods. "Take all the time you need. And here..." Harper rushes to the display case and slides the glass door open before returning to my side. "Take this cake pop and eat it, before your blood sugar drops again."

I'd love to blame my response on something medical, but that's far from the truth. The real reason for my uncharacteristic display of weakness is due to the man staring at me from across the counter. The one who I'd hoped to never see again.

I take the dessert from Harper, unsure if I can eat anything while my stomach churns mercilessly, but for her, I'll try. "Thanks."

Without bothering to remove my apron, I walk from behind the counter and over to a vacant table that's far from the other customers. Bennett appears on the other side of the small table, his movements unhurried and refined as he seats himself in the chair across from me. This man doesn't belong in a coffee shop like this, sitting in a plastic chair like an ordinary person. He's too...everything.

Handsome.

Powerful.

Intense.

He belongs in a high-rise building, a courtroom, or even a mansion, but not here. And certainly not with someone like me who's powerless and so poor that it's embarrassing. We might've come from the same world of money and influence, but now we're oceans apart, two people whose paths should never cross.

So why is he here?

I sweep my gaze over his features, taking in every harsh line and smooth contour of his face, illuminated by the sun's rays streaming through the windows. In this light, he appears less severe, less menacing. Only it's just a trick, an optical illusion. This man wears darkness like a woman wears perfume, leaving a trail wherever he goes.

We continue to look at one another, and his gaze bores into me. Almost like a physical touch. It takes every bit of fortitude that I have to hold his stare. His light blue eyes are like twin ice picks, stabbing me again and again, searching for something deep inside me. Something I don't want to give.

Time becomes irrelevant as we sit like this for seconds or even minutes, each one studying the other. I refuse to be intimidated by him. Sure, he unnerves me, maybe even scares me, but my anger on my father's behalf is enough to keep me from running.

But, God, how I want to.

I nearly flinch when Bennett rests his hands on the table and steeples his long fingers. "Miss Green, what do you know of your father's...interests?"

The sound of his voice, deep and sensual, has my heart stuttering in my chest. Irritation causes my cheeks to warm. "Why are you asking me this?"

"I ran into a friend of yours recently," he says, his tone threaded with sarcasm. "Mr. Calvin, I believe?"

Hearing the familiar name makes my blood run cold. "And?"

"And he was very eager to part with some information pertaining to Senator Green's murder."

"Why would he do that?" I massage my temple with one hand while gripping the cake pop stick in the other. "Everything was supposed to be confidential."

"The man is an opportunist," Bennett says. "It's public knowledge that I was involved in your father's trial, and that case was one of the few I've lost in my career. Mr. Calvin presented me with your file, hoping to entice me with the things he learned. It worked."

I grip the stem of the cake pop so tightly my knuckles lose their color, becoming as white as the vanilla dessert. "I still don't understand what you're trying to tell me."

"I'm taking over the investigation."

"No." My denial comes out as a whisper, a mere puff of air, but it's all I can manage.

"Weren't you searching for your father's killer?" When I nod, Bennett quirks an ebony brow. "Are you telling me you don't want to bring the killer to justice?"

"I do, but not with you." The words rush from me before I can stop them, propelled by my unease. And something I won't acknowledge. "I'll do it on my own or not at all."

"Miss Green, I wasn't giving you a choice."

My lips part on a gasp, half in surprise and half in outrage. I squint up at him and lean forward, despite my body trembling. "I'm not giving you one either. There's no way I'll work with you."

"Even at the cost of never knowing?" he asks. When I nod, his lips thin with displeasure. "What if I were to tell you that I've already made headway, but in order to continue further, I need your cooperation?"

I shake my head. "I don't care. This conversation is over."

His gaze flashes with disbelief right before his hand shoots out and wraps around my wrist. The cake pop wiggles in my grasp as the heat from his touch sears me. I tug on his hold, but it's like trying to free myself from an iron manacle.

"Let go of me," I say between clenched teeth.

"Not until you've heard me out."

Bennett leans forward and pulls me to him at the same time. Everything within me screams for me to get away, to gain some distance, but like a flightless bird, I can't do anything except stare at him. Now he's so close I can see the flecks of ice in his eyes, the blue so hypnotizing I momentarily get lost in his gaze.

"Call it morbid curiosity, or blame it on my ego," he says,

his voice dark, laced with an uncharacteristic urgency, "but I need to uncover the mystery surrounding you." He clears his throat. "I mean, your family. I'm willing to do this free of charge. All you have to do is answer a few questions."

I yank my wrist from his hold, unable to think with his fingers on my skin. Then I plop the cake pop into my mouth in order to give myself a brief reprieve, a few seconds to gather my thoughts before I answer him. I twirl the stick, and the sweet dessert glides over my tongue as my blood sugar spikes and my mind spins.

If I let him help me, I'll have to converse with a man I dislike intensely. And divulge some personal information. While I've already done that with the private investigator, it feels different with Bennett. I can't explain why giving him access to my life unsettles me in a way that goes beyond mere nervousness. The idea leaves me feeling empty and vulnerable, as if I've sold my soul to the devil.

On the other hand, I can't afford to hire Calvin anymore, and having the lawyer work on my case for free is very appealing. Plus, Bennett has money and contacts that the P.I. doesn't. If anything, the man in front of me is a better choice overall.

Then why can't I bring myself to accept his help?

Because I don't believe him.

He's lying to me. I don't know in what way, or why, but he is. I've always relied on my intuition, even when I was comfortable and safe back in my old life. However, now that I'm constantly fighting to survive, I rely on my gut more than I ever did.

It's the reason I can sense danger in Bennett. The expensive suit and beautiful face are meant to distract, to lure unsuspecting prey. I might be in a precarious situation, but I can't let this man completely destroy me.

And he would.

I swallow the sugar coating my tongue in preparation to speak. Bennett's focus, riveted on my mouth, never wavers. My throat seizes at the glimmer in his eyes, the blue like fresh snow, bright and sparkling. I lower the cake pop, and it grazes my lips, leaving behind a trail of stickiness.

He follows my every movement with his gaze. His nostrils flare once, and he slides his hands from the table's surface to place them in his coat pockets. Then he stiffens, his entire demeanor morphing into that of a marble statue, hard and cold yet still beautiful to look at.

A masterpiece.

"What is your answer, Miss Green?" His tone is harsh, like a slap to the face. "My patience has come to an end."

"No."

He narrows his eyes, and I bite my bottom lip to keep from changing my response. "Are you certain?" he asks.

I nod and point at the door with the cake pop, the white outer layer nearly gone. "Thank you for your time."

He gets to his feet and adjusts his coat, bringing the ends together with a harsh snap of the material. "Should you change your mind, here's my information." He slaps a business card on the table. The letters and ink on it are like him: bold, harsh, and pristine.

I slide the card in his direction. "I won't change my mind."

He doesn't move to pick up the item, nor does he look away from me. Inside, I'm wilting under his intense stare. The man doesn't say a word, but it's like he's threatening me with his stance and his facial expression. That only hardens my resolve to be done with him.

I get to my feet, ignoring the shaking of my legs, and place the cake pop inside my mouth, a sign that this conversation is over. Somehow—which I highly suspect has to do with a sugar rush combined with adrenaline—I make it back to the register without tripping and falling. When I look up, Bennett is gone.

So why am I not relieved?

CHAPTER 9

C alista

EVEN THOUGH IT'S BEEN SEVERAL HOURS, I'M STILL NOT ABLE to put my conversation with Bennett behind me. However, as I stare at the door leading into T&A, my trepidation rises, giving me something to think about other than the infuriating lawyer.

Like the fact that I'm about to wear an outfit so skimpy I might as well be naked.

But, I'd rather work in this seedy bar than accept Bennett's help.

With that resolve firmly planted in my brain, I pull on the door handle and step inside. Just like it did the first time I walked in here, the place and its customers have my skin prickling with unease, and I nearly do an about-face. The music pounds through the speakers, and the numerous male voices make up the rest of the place's soundtrack along with the clinking of glass behind the bar. The lighting is dim, dark enough to hide the grime.

And hopefully, my disgust.

Gripping the strap of my backpack, I walk straight up to the bar and lean on the counter. The bartender does a double-take when he sees me, but then his mouth spreads into a licentious grin.

"What can I do for you, sugar?"

"I spoke to Jim last night and he offered me a job. I'm here to start my training as a waitress."

The man runs his gaze over me, his brow furrowing. "You're not wearing the proper clothing." When I tap my backpack, he nods. "Go get dressed, and we'll get you set up. The bathrooms are right back there."

I follow the direction he indicates, ignoring the stares of everyone around me. In the time it takes for me to change my clothing, I give myself a pep talk, recalling all of the reasons that led me to this. By the end, I don't feel any better about my choice, but I'm ready to take on the challenge. The only thought that comforts me is that this is temporary. Once I have enough money to pay Calvin to resume his investigation, I'm quitting this job.

Looking in the mirror, I don't recognize myself. The short black skirt ends mid-thigh, showing off my long, toned legs, courtesy of the many hours spent standing at the Sugar Cube. My top is a black t-shirt that ends at my navel, with a neckline that does more than hint at my cleavage. It puts it on full display. The mounds of my breasts sit snugly in the tight shirt, and the seam of my pink bra peeks out on occasion, depending on how I'm standing. In place of my tennis shoes are a pair of heels that my fiancé bought me, black with bloodred soles. They mock me now, as though he knew I'd end up needing them someday. He broke off our engagement when my father's reputation was in ruins.

If Adam had truly loved me, I'd be his wife, and there wouldn't be a need for these shoes.

After staring at my reflection until it sinks in that I'm actually doing this, I begin to unbraid my hair. The whole point of this outfit is to be sexually attractive to the customers in order to keep them happy, and in return, I would earn large tips. I'm not the most gorgeous woman to walk the earth, but I know I'm pretty. Pretty enough to forgo any makeup other than mascara and a bit of lip gloss.

No one will be looking at my face anyway.

I cringe at the thought. With my hair cascading down my back and my heels clicking on the tile flooring, I make my way back to the bar. Loud whistles and catcalls wash over me, and I steel myself against wanting to run. This is the price I agreed to pay when I stepped foot in here, and I can't back out now.

The bartender looks at me with an appreciative gleam in his eyes. "What's your name, sugar?"

"Calista."

"I'm Mack, the assistant manager. You spoke with the manager yesterday, so there's no need for anything else right now. As long as you're not a complete bust and make it through the night, you'll keep the job."

"Make it through the night?" I repeat, my voice nearly a squeak.

"We both know your type doesn't belong here. You're too sweet, sugar."

He's right, but I've come too far. Besides, my pride won't let me crawl back to Bennett for help.

"Too much sugar will make you sick," I say.

Mack chuckles and sets down a glass full of beer next to several of them already sitting on a tray. "That's true."

I hold up my backpack. "Is there somewhere I can put this?"

"Yeah, sure. I'll hold it behind the bar until you're done for the night." After he takes my belongings, Mack points to the collection of beers. "Okay, for now, I'll get these orders out, and you'll deliver them to the customers. Once you get the table numbers memorized, things will get easier. Later on, I'll grab one of the other girls, and you'll shadow her. Cool?"

"Sounds good."

"Great. Take this to table thirteen." He pushes the tray toward me. "It's the one in the very corner of the room."

I nod, no longer having the ability to speak evenly. Instead, I concentrate on lifting the tray while balancing the weight of the drinks to ensure I don't dump the contents all over myself. It's more difficult than I imagined but only because I'm in heels. I catch sight of a pretty blonde bustling about in a pair of heels that are twice as high as mine, and I mentally applaud her coordination.

Making my way slowly but surely to the designated table, I gain a tiny bit of confidence with every step. I stop once I'm standing beside a customer who nearly reaches me in height even though he's seated. He rakes his gaze over my body, making me inwardly grimace. I soothe myself by thinking that I'll get used to this in time.

The lie doesn't help.

"Hey there, pretty lady," he says, his voice carrying hints of a southern accent. "What'cha got for me?"

I force a smile, one that sits awkwardly on my mouth, and place the glasses on the table. Every set of eyes in the group trace the curves of my breasts every time I bend down, and I clench my teeth. "Do you guys need anything else?" I ask when I'm finished.

"Not unless you're interested in earning an extra-large tip."

The sexual innuendo isn't lost on me. I will myself not to blush, but it's futile. The man's friends laugh, only adding to my embarrassment. One of them slaps his shoulder while grinning. "Come on, Grady, can't you tell the girl is scared to death?"

Grady shrugs his massive shoulders, making his leather jacket groan softly. "Being scared isn't exactly a no."

I shake my head, hopefully not too emphatically that he's insulted and I get in trouble for being rude to a customer. The long tendrils of my hair glide back and forth across my back with my movements, and his gaze snaps to them.

"Have a good night," I say quickly. "Let me know if you need anything else."

Just as I'm about to turn around, Grady reaches out to grab a lock of my hair. I go still, like a wild animal caught in a trap. My heart thrums crazily in my chest and my breathing thins, panic rising with every second.

Unaware, or uncaring of my discomfort, he rubs the strands between his thumb and forefinger. "It's softer than I expected."

"Please let g—"

My plea is caught in my throat as a dark figure appears at Grady's side, instantly commanding my attention. Bennett resembles a wraith, clothed in black and encased in shadow. Faster than I can process, he snatches Grady's thumb and wrenches it back. The man cries out in both alarm and pain, but that doesn't deter Bennett.

If anything, he pulls back all the more.

With my hair free, I step away at the same moment the men at the table begin to rise.

"Stay seated," Bennett says, his voice danger in auditory form. "This doesn't involve you. Only this man since he foolishly touched what doesn't belong to him."

"What the hell are you talking about?" Grady shouts.

Bennett jerks his chin in my direction. His eyes are bright in the dim lighting, the fierce emotions within shining like diamonds. "She's mine."

CHAPTER 10

C alista

Everyone's focus shifts to me.

However, the only gaze I feel on my skin is Bennett's. It's brief, but in that moment, something shifts inside me, something bursting alive at his appearance. His eyes are glimmering with violence, and his body is taut with rage. I've never seen anything this magnificent, so fierce and primal.

"Apologize," Bennett says to his captive.

Grady's face is twisted in a grimace, but it slowly morphs into a sneer. "To her? Some random girl in a bar? Come on, man. It's like I grabbed her ass. She should've expected a little *friendliness* in a place like this."

"Why do people refuse to do what they're told?"

Bennett adjusts his hold on Grady's hand, wrenching it back until the man falls to the floor in order to keep his thumb attached. The loud bang jolts me, and I take another step back, my hip bumping into the table's edge. Out of the

63

corner of my eye, I catch the bartender watching the events with a scowl etched in his features.

A loud snap, followed by a scream of pain, arrests my attention.

I zip my gaze back to Grady, and nausea washes over me. His thumb dangles from his hand, not completely removed...but it's close. Bennett looms over the man like an executioner, his face a complete mask.

Except for the flash of emotion in his eyes.

It lights up his gaze with intent before he slams the heel of his shoe into Grady's palm. The man's wailing crescendos, making me wince, but Bennett doesn't stop. The attorney swivels his foot, grinding into the man's hand until the first streak of crimson appears. Even in the dimly lit room, the brightness of the hue is discernible.

A warning to everyone present.

An omen to me.

Bennett crouches, bringing his face close to Grady's and whispers, "Apologize to Miss Green for putting your filthy hands on her. Then apologize to *me* for touching what's mine."

Grady's words are a jumbled mess, but whatever he says appeases Bennett. The lawyer walks over to me with purposeful strides until he's standing close enough for me to smell his cologne. He removes his coat while I ignore Grady writhing on the floor in favor of watching his friends. They stare at Bennett. Every single one of them has wariness in their eyes, as if they're worried about garnering his attention.

I wouldn't want to dance with the devil either.

Yet he's right beside me.

Bennett drapes his coat over my shoulders and tugs at the lapels to cover me. I swing my gaze to him, unable to keep from gaping. Unlike me, his expression is void of any emotion. The warmth from his body still lingers on the material when it brushes against my skin. It's evidence he's human, but I'm having a hard time believing that.

He leans down, placing his lips beside my ear. His breath grazes the side of my neck, and I repress a shiver. "Come with me," he says.

His touch ignites my blood. It's nothing more than a simple brush of his fingers along the curve of my cheek before his hand settles at my lower back, but it has fire dancing across my skin.

Ignoring my body's reaction, I part my lips to ask about retrieving my backpack, then immediately press them together when Bennett narrows his gaze at me. With the feel of his hand imprinting itself into my memory, he steers me through the room and leads me outside.

The night air hits my legs, and I shiver, wrapping the coat tighter around me. Bennett's scent envelops me. I inhale, bringing his essence in my lungs, wanting this tiny piece of him in secret.

How can I be drawn to a man I dislike? Because it's the same man who rescued me.

Not once, but *twice*.

"My car is right there," he says.

There's no doubt as to which vehicle is his.

The sleek black sports car is low to the ground, giving the impression of a crouching predator ready to spring into action. Its glossy obsidian body gleams under the street-lights, flawless paint polished to a mirror sheen. Dark tinted windows hide the interior while maintaining the vehicle's mysterious aura. The chrome door handles are recessed into the body, parting to open the doors with the touch of a button.

I stare at it as though I've never seen a car. In reality, I've never seen a vehicle like this. Similar to Bennett, it's an image of status, wealth, and masculinity. Yet it's aloof and untouchable, an elusive fantasy to most.

Just like the man beside me.

I halt my steps and turn to look at him. "I appreciate what you did for me, but I need to go back inside."

Bennett's beautiful face tightens, a muscle flicking along his jaw. "No, you don't."

"Yes, I do. My stuff is still inside, but more importantly, that's my new job."

"You no longer work there, Miss Green. And you never would've if my instructions had been carried out."

"What?" I frown up at him. "Never mind."

I shake my head, trying to clear it. Bennett destroys my thoughts, scattering them to the wind with nothing more than a single glance. Confounding me further, he takes my hand in his, threading our fingers in a secure grip. I pull at our joined hands for him to release me, but my attempt is thwarted when he tightens his hold.

A breath of frustration leaves me in a huff. "You don't understand how much I need this job."

Bennett yanks me to him. I collide with his chest, my feet losing purchase as I stumble in heels. He's quick to wrap an arm around my waist and keep me upright while bringing me closer. His grip on my chin has me blinking up at him as he lifts my head, forcing me to meet his gaze.

It burns.

"You need *me*. Not this fucking job or anything else," he says. "Now, get in the car before I carry you."

"Please, just wait a second. I need to think."

"I've already thought about it. In fact, I've thought of nothing else."

He grabs my hips, his fingers digging into the material of my skirt. Right before he tosses me over his shoulder. After securing his hold on the back of my thighs, he walks to the car. My hair covers my face, the tendrils swaying in time with his steps, hiding my embarrassment from the people on the street.

Bennett stops, opens the car door, and then deposits me inside. I sink into the leather seat, my jaw slack. I've never been manhandled in my entire life, but from the way my heart pounds and my blood races through my veins, I suspect I'm not as opposed to it as I should be.

He takes advantage of my stupor and leans inside to grab the seat belt. His face is so close that if he turns his head, he'll kiss me. I press myself into the seat, my efforts futile when the man himself is an overwhelming presence, one that dominates my senses. The clean and crisp scent of him fills my nose, and the heat from him seeps into me. My body is painfully aware of his proximity, the nearness of his hands so close to my skin. His breath grazes my cheek as he secures the seat belt across my chest and into the buckle.

I'm drowning in him, without the promise of sweet relief in either deliverance or death.

"Don't try to run," he says, staring into my eyes. "I can see you want to, but don't."

"Why?"

"I will *always* chase you."

He pulls back and slams my car door before I can think of a response. Not that there's much to be said. Everything about this man confuses me. Especially the way my body responds to his touch, regardless of how my mind warns me about him.

Bennett slips into the driver's seat, filling the small space with his potent energy. My gaze stays locked on him while he fixes his seat belt, turns on the car, and grabs the steering wheel; his fingers moving deftly but with a grace that has my skin prickling.

"Stop looking at me like that."

I flick my gaze to his. "What?"

"Stop looking at me like you want my hands on your body." He inhales as if to keep a hold on himself, his knuckles turning white as he grips the steering wheel. "If I touch you, I won't ever stop."

I drop my head and lace my fingers, resting them in my lap. "I don't know what you're talking about."

"I'm talking about sexual attraction, Miss Green."

"You're mistaken, Mr. Bennett." I squeeze my hands together until they're shaking. "If I'm looking at you in any specific way, it's because you're scaring me."

"Fear is healthy. It keeps you from hurting yourself." He pauses, his gaze far away, distant. "But it doesn't stop you from getting hurt by others."

He puts the car into drive and pulls onto the busy street. I shift my focus to the city just outside the window. I can't look at him when I ask the question that's been in my mind ever since I saw him at the coffee shop.

"Do you want to hurt me?"

"Sometimes."

His answer, immediate and honest, steals my breath. I bite my tongue to ground myself, but also to keep from saying anything that'll provoke him. Maybe I should run, even if he promised he'll chase me.

"Why?" I ask, my whisper barely there. "What did I ever do to you?"

"You've ruined me, Miss Green."

"Calista. If you're going to say such things, at least use

68

my name. I think we're beyond formalities after the events that have transpired tonight."

"I agree, Callie."

I sneak a glance at him. "No one's ever called me that."

"And no one else ever will."

I ignore the way my heart stutters in my chest and the way my breathing goes shallow. Instead, I focus on the man who's taken me captive, both physically and mentally. There hasn't been a day that I haven't thought of Mr. Bennett. Possibly not even a night.

He invades my dreams.

Turning them into fantasies that I'll never admit to.

"Give me your address," he says.

I worry my bottom lip between my teeth. If I show him where I live, my humiliation will know no bounds. I'm not simply poor. I live in the dregs of society, the places someone like Bennett cannot even fathom. I know I didn't before my father's untimely death.

On the other hand, if I let Bennett see how dire my life truly is, maybe he'll be disgusted. And leave me alone. Because at the end of the day, that's what I want. I never asked him to interfere, to wreak havoc with my thoughts and to awaken my body.

"Give me your address, or we'll go to mine," he says. "Either way, you're coming with me."

CHAPTER 11

H ayden

CALISTA GIVES ME HER ADDRESS.

I'm not sure whether to be disappointed or not.

I slide my gaze to her. The woman infuriates me just as much as she arouses me. I don't think my cock has ever been this hard. And certainly not for this long.

My need for sexual relief only increases with each passing moment I'm around Calista. No, that's not true. It continues to grow even when I'm not around her because she's always in my thoughts, taunting me, tempting me with her beauty.

I want her more than I've wanted any other woman.

I'd be lying to myself if I didn't recognize there's more to it than that. My life would certainly be less complicated right now if all I wanted was to fuck her. I could do that and move on.

But with Calista, I'm not sure I can ever let go. Not with

how my curiosity has deepened into a full-blown obsession. She's not only gotten under my skin but inside my blood. A person can't survive without it, without that life force.

She is mine.

My reason for feeling alive.

My reason for feeling enraged.

My reason for feeling anything at all.

The moment I stepped into T&A after her, I knew the night would end this way. In violence, at my hands. I'd hoped to avoid any confrontations by speaking to the manager, but Jim decided to ignore my instructions. All it took was Zack tapping into the man's cell phone to confirm my suspicions. Not only did he text the assistant manager about Calista, but Jim told the guy he was planning on fucking her.

He signed his own death warrant with that simple text.

I'll deal with him, but she comes first. I need to get her home and behind a locked door. Where she should've been all along.

Her safety concerns me, even though there are times when I want to hurt her for making my life chaotic. I value control, the need for order and clarity. Yet with her, nothing I do is logical.

All of my actions are fueled by dark emotions.

Fury like I've never known swelled in my chest when she first walked into the room wearing that skirt and low-cut shirt. Every single man in the place looked at her. These weren't mere glances. They watched her with lust in their eyes, wanting to fuck her.

The fury morphed into an all-consuming rage when that man touched her hair. If Calista had not been present, along with numerous witnesses, I might've killed him right then. Instead, I fucked up his hand. Not nearly to my satisfaction, but enough to sate the bloodlust running through me.

When Calista looked at me with fear in her eyes, I knew I'd gone far enough. For her, *not* me. If I ever see that man again, I'll kill him. Without hesitation.

Just thinking about the entire ordeal has my blood boiling.

I park the car as close as I can to her residence and turn in my seat to look at Calista. She has her head bowed, hands in her lap with her hair draped over her shoulders and my coat. I enjoy seeing her in it.

It's a small way of possessing her.

The first of many.

"Are you going to cooperate with me?" I ask.

She slides her gaze to me. The hazel within flares with her inner fire. The woman is more stubborn than I could've imagined. I find it exasperating at times, but mostly I want to bend her to my will. Her submission would be all the sweeter if she fights me at first.

"Mr. Bennett—"

"Hayden," I correct.

She eyes me warily before licking her lips. My cock twitches in my pants, and I grit my teeth to keep from grabbing her and fucking her mouth.

"Hayden," she says, each syllable like a stroke to my cock. "I think it'd be best if we part ways," she says. "I'm grateful for what you did tonight, but I…"

"You what?"

"I don't feel comfortable extending our association. I'm sure you understand."

I scoff. "I'm sure I don't."

"Hayden, please."

Hearing her say my name in that sultry voice of hers

nearly undoes me. But hearing her beg me while saying my name? Fuck. Me.

I told myself to stay in control of my attraction to her, to stifle it while getting the information I needed, both about her past and the reason why I'm drawn to her. Now, I believe I was a fool. How could I ever think I'd be able to keep my lust for Calista from overriding my original goal?

"Listen, if you answer one question, you'll never have to see me again," I lie.

Her arched brows snap together. "What is it?"

"That picture in your file, the one of you bruised. What really happened that night?"

I keep my gaze locked on her face, which is why I catch it paling, becoming like the moon just outside. Calista's lips part, and she sucks in a breath. It causes her breasts to rise, nearly spilling over the neckline of her shirt. Although it steals my attention, whets my appetite, I don't look away from her crestfallen expression.

"There's something to that," I say. She startles at the sound of my voice, her eyes widening more than they already were, the hazel all but disappearing. "That event is significant. Tell me why."

She ducks her head and brings a trembling hand to the button to release her seat belt. Her fingers are shaking so badly she's unsuccessful. I lean over and place my hand on top of hers, stilling her movements. She jerks up her head to look at me, and the emotion in her gaze has my chest tightening.

If I thought I knew what fear looked like, this is something worse. Something disturbing.

I'm half a second from grabbing her and...what? Comforting her? The idea repels me but also calls to me. I suppress the conflicting urges.

"Callie, tell me what happened."

"I—I can't. Please let me go."

There's something in her voice that stabs me, going past my defenses and straight into my soul. It bleeds black. An oil spill that stains everything it comes into contact with. She'll be no different, ruined like me, but that won't stop me.

"I'm not going to do that," I say.

Calista must see the determination in my gaze and hear the ironclad will behind it because she stiffens. "You might think you can use your money and influence to get what you want, but you can't buy my secrets any more than you can force them from me."

"Is that a challenge?"

I run my gaze over her face, letting it trail along the slope of her cheek, across her full lips, and down her slender neck. She doesn't move, but her pulse ratchets up, flickering wildly underneath her delicate skin. I reach out and drag a finger over the spot, enjoying her heart's uneven cadence.

"I really hope so."

"Good night, Mr. Bennett."

"Wait," I say. "How are you going to get inside without a key?" I run my gaze over her body. "Unless you have it hidden underneath your clothing..."

"I have a spare hidden nearby. I took it from the manager so he couldn't get into my apartment."

Calista clicks the button to release her seat belt and pushes my arm away. After lifting her chin, she begins to remove my coat.

"Keep it," I say. "There's no need to draw attention to yourself when you walk inside. You've done enough of that for one evening."

She opens her mouth, most likely to argue, but snaps it shut when I raise a brow in warning. Then she gives me a curt nod and opens her door. I keep my gaze locked on her as she walks to her apartment building and disappears inside. Then I wait until I see her silhouette through her bedroom window.

Except tonight, it's not enough.

CHAPTER 12

C alista

H AYDEN B ENNETT IS GORGEOUS, DOMINEERING, AND AN
asshole.

I stand in the middle of my apartment while my
thoughts careen within my mind. Every one is centered
around the attorney and his actions. Not just those from
tonight, but all of them, since the day I first saw him. How
can I describe Hayden with mere words? They're nothing
but a combination of letters and sounds, unable to convey
the depth and meaning that goes with a man like him.

Calculating.

Cruel.

Cold.

Given his demeanor and the way he carried himself,
none of this was a surprise to me. Now, I know him a little
more. Well, enough to add to my original assessment.

Confident.

Chivalrous.

Considerate.

These things about him have forced me to reevaluate Hayden. Only, I'm more confused, more torn than I've ever been. How can the same person who defamed my father be the same man who demands that people show me respect?

My mind is quick to retrieve images from the past, things I haven't allowed myself to relive for fear I wouldn't be able to function. And I need to if I'm going to survive. Tonight, I can't hold them at bay. Like a cracked dam bearing the weight of water, I crumble under the pressure, and my brain is flooded with unwelcome memories.

The piney scent of the newly polished wood invades my senses, and my head pounds all the more because of it. Or perhaps it's due to the strained atmosphere in the courtroom? Regardless, there's no relief to be found. I clench my hands in my lap until nails dig into my skin. The pinprick of pain grounds me.

But it's nothing compared to the agony within my soul.

Like the rest of the people here, I sit in silence as the prosecution's lawyer, a tall man with blue eyes and glossy black hair, circles my father like a dog, ready to tear him to shreds.

And then he does. It's verbally, but from the way I flinch every time, it might as well be physical.

My father is on the stand, his back straight and his chin lifted. Considering he's a man fighting for his life and reputation, he holds himself quite well, a politician through and through. Like my father, the attorney displays no emotion, his handsome face a complete mask.

If only I was able to compose myself as effectively.

I failed miserably, and I blame it entirely on Bennett. When I saw the lawyer for the first time in the hallway, I hadn't been aware of his identity. All I could do was stare at the man in a complete haze of yearning. It wasn't just the beauty of him. I'd been drawn to the way he looked at me.

As if I were a woman and not the porcelain doll I'd been treated like my entire life.

Even Adam, my fiancé, had never gazed at me with such unconcealed lust. Sure, he'd been pressuring me to sleep with him, but it wasn't the same thing.

Adam wanted me.

Bennett would consume me.

"Senator Green," Bennett says, his voice as smooth as satin, "isn't it true that you were having an affair with your secretary, Ms. Hall?"

My father slowly nods. "Yes. I loved her."

Bennett lifts an ebony brow. "We have eyewitnesses who saw you with Ms. Hall on the day of her death. They also heard you two arguing. Is this true, senator?"

I shake my head as though to answer on behalf of my father. Deep in my heart I know he's a good person. Whether or not he had a fight with Kristen, there's no way he would've killed her. At the end of the day, that's all that matters to me.

"I was with Ms. Hall," the senator says, "but we were discussing campaign strategies for my upcoming election. The argument was merely a difference in opinion as to how we should proceed. In the end, she agreed with me."

Bennett tilts his head. "Did she really? So you're telling me it had nothing to do with her being pregnant with your illegitimate child? A scandal that could cost you the election?"

"I was planning to marry her!"

"Then why was she found murdered in your bedroom later that evening with handprints on her neck? With marks that matched the shape and size of your hands?"

The lawyer places a photo directly in front of the senator and taps the image, his long fingers directing my father's attention. He stiffens. And remorse flickers in his eyes.

Is it because he's guilty or due to the devastation of it all?

I have to believe my father's innocent, or nothing will make sense. But the thought of him going to prison for the rest of his life...

My chest seizes as my lungs contract, thinning my breaths until I'm wheezing. Stars appear in my vision, partially blocking out the scene before me, and I blink rapidly to clear it without any success. I close my eyes and press my fists against them while taking a long, deep breath to combat the rising panic.

My father is a good man. This will all be over soon. Bennett rattles my certainty with every silver-tongued word he utters, and I haven't even taken the stand yet...

Do I have the fortitude to relive that night? I might not reveal all of the details, but my father needs me as his alibi, and I won't fail him. I can't.

"Look at her," Bennett says, his voice like the crack of a whip. When my father's skin pales, the lawyer continues. "Do you see the way she's looking? Her final moments were spent staring up at her attacker. Do you see how her eyes are lifeless but even in death the terror remains?"

The ruthless interrogation of the prosecutor continues. And if it wasn't damaging my father, I'd think it a thing of beauty. Bennett's words are like daggers, employed with merciless precision while drawing blood with every sentence. Not enough to kill, but to slowly weaken and maim. And then there's his body language. His forceful energy permeating the room like a fog, making it hard for me to see a favorable outcome.

His voice commands my attention, causing my panic to slowly subside.

I pull in a large breath through my nose and blow it out through my mouth to continue ridding my body of the anxiety pummeling it from within. The last thing my father needs is for me to have a panic attack in the middle of the court hearing. Although I might lose my fucking mind if he's declared guilty.

I'd definitely blame Bennett for that.

I shift my gaze to the lawyer, his words a low rumble that my brain refuses to translate. Mentally, I've checked out and no longer want to hear the things he's saying about my father. It's torture.

Except watching Bennett is a different kind of agony.

A sweet longing that I wish didn't exist.

He walks to stand in front of the jury, his tone more insistent, more passionate than I've ever heard. It sparks something in me. Something I've never experienced, even with my fiancé.

Desire.

I groan at the memory, in both frustration and arousal. Hayden took up permanent residence in my mind that day, and I'm ashamed to admit that he never left. It's more accurate to say that I never got rid of him.

Even when my dislike for him grew throughout the trial.

But now? I'm not sure whether or not I still despise him for his past transgressions. Is Harper right in saying that Bennett was just doing his job in the courtroom and I've been over-sensitive on that front? Or is my intuition right when it comes to him?

Hayden is a conundrum.

He's violent, but he uses that violence to protect me. Until he walked into my life again, I didn't realize I'd been missing that security. Sure, I experienced it with my father growing up, but it was never to the level of intensity that Hayden showed.

Does sexual attraction heighten the effect? Or do I feel this way because of the man himself?

I have no answers. The only thing I know is that, for whatever reason, this man makes me feel safe even though I shouldn't. And his displays of violence don't shock or frighten me.

They seduce me.

CHAPTER 13

H ayden

I RETRIEVE MY CELL PHONE FROM MY POCKET AND THE SCREEN flares to life, illuminating the interior of my car. After a few keystrokes, the inside of Calista's apartment appears, the cameras allowing me to watch her closely.

I installed them the same day I found out about her hiring that private investigator. My rationale for my actions was to blame it on my need to keep her safe. In truth, it's the only way I can be near her without giving in to the temptation to do more. Regardless, over the past month, my fortitude has started to crack like the stones of an ancient church.

Except there's no redemption to be found for the sins I wish to commit.

She draws my gaze with her simple movements, each one sensual and enticing. I swear the woman could merely put lipstick on, and I'd be ready to thrust my cock between her lips, if only to stain my skin with the rosy hue. I shake my head at my wayward thoughts.

This always happens when I'm around Calista.

She kicks off her heels and removes my coat, her breasts nearly spilling from her shirt. I'm graced with the view of her delectable body in that revealing outfit. I wouldn't care if she always dressed that way, as long as I was the only one to see it. She takes things a step further and removes her clothes until she's standing in nothing except her bra and underwear.

It's a matching set of light pink, the color feminine, innocent, and sweet like her.

I suck in a breath and hold a fist to my mouth, nearly biting my hand to keep from groaning aloud. It's better than I imagined. Her body is a temple I want to be inside and worship until the rapture comes.

Then I'll go straight to hell.

Calista leaves the space to walk into the bathroom. I switch from one camera view to the other, never losing sight of her. She turns on the shower, and I grip my phone tighter with anticipation swimming through my blood. It travels straight to my cock, engorging the fucker until I squeeze it with enough pressure to cause pain.

The agony of that is nothing compared to seeing Calista naked with me not able to touch her.

She's quick to step inside the shower and yank the curtain, almost as if she senses that someone's watching. But I saw enough.

It's only a matter of time until I take her body. I just need to make certain that I've discovered her secrets by then. After that, I'll have to walk away.

Something I should've done the day of the funeral.

I've already put myself at risk by interacting with her.

Now I'm completely on her radar. Keeping Calista from finding out the truth about her father's murder will only become more difficult with time. I've always loved a challenge, but not one that could end with consequences I can't get out of.

I place the phone in its holder on my dashboard and drive onto the street. As much as I want to be close to Calista while she's wet and naked, I only have so much willpower. And if I give into the lust I feel for her at this moment, I'll lose control.

Over myself.

My goals.

My sanity.

That doesn't mean I won't keep watching, waiting with heavy anticipation for her to show me her body once again. Which she does. I groan and slam my hand against the steering wheel, hard enough for my palm to throb.

My gaze darts back and forth between the road and Calista's figure on my phone. Then my eyes widen when she pads across the floor in a towel and removes it to put on my coat. Along with those fucking pearls.

And nothing else.

The white color instantly takes me back to the time at the cafe where Calista put that cake pop in her mouth. The way she twirled it around made my cock as hard as it is now. But when she removed the dessert from her mouth and it left behind a strip of white? All I could think of was my cum on her pretty lips, leaving behind a streak the exact same way.

This woman fucks with me when she's not even trying.

A horn honks behind me. I reluctantly pull my attention from the video feed and notice the light is green. After putting the car into motion, I look back at Calista's image, somehow managing to stay in my lane.

She turns off every light except the lamp on her nightstand and crawls onto her mattress, lying on her back. Closing her eyes, she drags her hand down her chest until it settles between her legs. Her thighs fall open, and I stop breathing.

Such a pretty pussy.

It's even more pink than her undergarments. I bet it's sweeter too.

She entices me further by stroking her clit. I curse myself for leaving her place. But this is exactly the type of thing that would cause me to lose sight of my personal objectives. And I can't give in to this woman just yet.

No matter how much she entices me.

The neighborhood on either side of my car is familiar as I get closer to my residence, but I hardly notice, my focus unwavering as Calista dives further underneath the waves of pleasure.

She arches her back, her nipples pointing at the camera, taunting me. Her movements become frenzied as she draws closer to her orgasm, and my cock pulses, pre-cum leaking from the head. I could come from just watching her.

But when she moans my name, I nearly explode.

And almost crash my car.

Angry drivers and honking horns break through the haze of lust clouding my mind. Flipping everyone off, I turn on the next street and speed down the road until I find a spot to park, uncaring about anything except the woman on my phone. I watch Calista and grip my cock, angry that I've let her get me so worked up I can't do anything except fuck myself.

"Damn it!"

I unzip my pants and free my length, wrapping my hand around it. It's already hard, ready for me to take care of the ache that Calista has put within me. I'm so fucking pissed at myself, at this loss of control over my body when it comes to her. But it doesn't stop me from watching Calista or imagining it's her as I thrust hard against my palm. Her beneath me, her body pushing against mine with each stroke, her moans of pleasure driving me to the edge of ecstasy and insanity.

No matter how mad I am at myself, I can't help it when Calista begins to touch herself again. My body tightens, and my need for her becomes overwhelming. I can almost feel the warmth of her skin against mine as sweat beads on my forehead and heat engulfs every inch of me.

My hand moves faster, and my grip tightens, punishing as I think of her beautiful face and the curves of her body. I almost come twice, but I wait for her to finish.

For her to say my name.

She does like a good girl.

I spill onto my hand, gritting my teeth to keep from shouting in pleasure despite my internal frustration. Hoping this will be enough to satisfy me. At least for a little while.

That lie is greater than any other.

I take a few minutes to compose myself before cleaning my hand and buttoning up my pants, my sexual relief having no impact on the fury radiating through me. The one caused by my temporary insanity, driven by my need for Calista.

A need that not only lingers but is stronger now that she moaned my name.

"I refuse to be alone in my obsession," I grit out between clenched teeth. "You will suffer like me. I'll accept nothing less. Then, maybe we can ease the desperation in one another as I fuck you until there's nothing left of me, until I've lost myself in you so completely that I no longer recognize myself."

My anger undulates in my gut, churning with a force that has me gripping the steering wheel as though it were Calista's neck. Although if it were, she'd be dead. I draw in a deep breath, then another, needing some semblance of calm. In my need for her, I forgot about everything.

This complete loss of control fucks with my head.

So, I'll do the same with her.

I pull onto the road in the direction of Calista's residence. After parking further down the street and out of sight, I make my way inside the building, my lock picks in my hand. Within minutes, I'm inside her apartment.

The interior isn't as bad as the exterior, but that's not saying much. Even so, Calista has made this space her own. Pictures hang on the walls, and there are personal effects in every space, as well as a bottle of sanitizer. Strange but endearing.

All of her things are neatly arranged in straight lines, which doesn't surprise me considering how uptight she can be. Her scent, a combination of jasmine and something unique to her, fills the room. I take a deep breath, letting the fragrance envelop me.

Then I'm in her bedroom, looking down at her as she sleeps. My coat is still on her body, partially covering the perfection of it. Which is probably for the best.

I'm not sure I could see all of it and not touch her.

No more than a second passes before I'm trailing my fingers down her cheek, a sample I can't deny myself. She hums in her sleep and leans into my touch.

"Dreaming of me?" I whisper. "You better fucking be."

She came so hard thinking about me that she doesn't stir

as I continue to stroke her skin. It's softer, more supple than I thought. And I can't get enough.

"What the fuck are you doing to me?" I ask her. "Why can't I walk away from you? Or get you out of my fucking head?"

I run my gaze over Calista and force myself to withdraw my fingers, my hands fisting to keep from grabbing her. Instead, I reach for the comforter and pull it over her sleeping form. After I've tucked the blanket around her to combat the winter chill in the room, I search for a prize, a small consolation for not fucking her like I want.

Calista will come to me.

Even if it requires a little persuasion...

"Where are those pink underwear, hmm?"

Once I find them, I bring the fabric to my nose. The scent of her cunt instantly makes me hard. With a curse, I shove the pink material in my pocket.

Now, the only color in the dark room is the string of pearls around her neck. I carefully remove them and grip them in my fist, my thoughts becoming clearer the longer I stare at the necklace.

Calista forced me to fuck myself. She pulled my cum from my body with my name on her lips and her moan in my ears.

I snap the string holding the pearls together. Selecting a single orb, I place it on the nightstand, right where she'll see it when she opens her eyes.

One pearl for one bit of cum.

Until *I* give her a pearl necklace...all over her skin.

Marking her as mine.

CHAPTER 14

H ayden

I BLINK AGAINST THE AFTERNOON SUN STREAMING THROUGH the windshield of my car and sip my coffee.

Unfortunately, this caffeinated beverage didn't come from the Sugar Cube. It took all of my remaining self-control not to go in there. It's because of my fierce desire to see Calista that I avoided the coffee shop.

She's already fucked with my psyche more than I care to admit.

Besides, I've decided to give her time to see that she needs my help. She's an intelligent woman and will come to the same conclusion eventually, although it might take some more convincing from me.

In the form of nightly visits.

I scan the surrounding area, my vigilance high. Unfortunately, T&A is an establishment that's meant for night entertainment, which forces me to conduct this meeting with the manager during the daylight hours. I prefer the cloak of darkness, but I have no problem meting out justice whenever karma calls for it.

Jim unlocks the front door. From this distance I can make out the wrinkles in his shirt and the stains on his jeans. This man contributes nothing to society. It will not miss him.

After waiting several minutes, I exit my vehicle and make my way to the rear entrance. I quickly pick the lock, not wanting to be seen lingering outside this place, and turn the knob. Once indoors, I secure the lock once again. The room is nothing like it was the night before, now void of its degenerate customers, loud music, and bustling waitresses.

Technically, Calista would be considered one, even though she only worked there for a mere fifteen minutes. Maybe ten. It would've been less than five if my court case hadn't gone over the allotted time. Fucking day job.

It doesn't matter. She'll never step foot in this place again. If everything goes according to plan, no one will.

I walk up to the bar and retrieve a glass and a nearly empty bottle of cheap whiskey. It's not usually my drink of choice, but when digging in the garbage, one shouldn't be surprised to find trash. After pouring a decent amount on the countertop, I fill the tumbler and sip the contents, waiting for my target to come out of the back office.

Jim shows up and stops in his tracks the moment his eyes land on me. When I flick my gaze to his, he pales.

"Hey, you can't be here," he says. "How did you get inside?"

"Join me." I lift my now half-full glass. "Although you'll have to find yourself a different drink since I finished this one off."

He eyes me warily, unable to hide his suspicion from leaking onto his features. "Yeah, sure."

I finger my glass, tracing the rim, keeping my movements unhurried, restrained. He pours himself a shot of vodka and taps it on the counter before downing the contents. I salute him with my drink and take a long swallow.

"Ask me why I'm here," I say.

"Come on, man. I don't know what you're talking about."

I click my tongue in admonishment and he flinches at the staccato sound. "Jim," I say, drawing out the name. "Ask me why I'm here."

"Why are you here?" he asks, his voice thin. Like he's having a hard time breathing.

"You know why," I say. "Now tell me. I want to hear you say it."

"If I do, will you leave?"

I nod. "You have my word."

"Okay." He gulps, causing his Adam's apple to bob. "Well, the thing is, I didn't actually hire the girl. Once you left, I realized that I didn't have a phone number on file to reach her so I couldn't contact her and tell her not to show up for work. Mack didn't know about our...*agreement*," he says, stumbling over the word. "So he let her start her shift. It wasn't supposed to happen."

"I see."

He meets my gaze. The hope inside almost makes me smile. "I'm glad you get it," he says.

"First of all, it wasn't an agreement. That would've meant that I needed your cooperation. Which I certainly don't. Our prior conversation was an understanding between two parties with consequences attached. However, given your actions, I believe you think they weren't real."

I take a sip of my drink. "Even with your inferior intellect, I assumed you'd be smart enough to heed my warning. That was my mistake. Or perhaps I didn't make myself clear?"

"No, not at all." Jim holds out his hands, his shoulders lifting. "I got what you were saying. It's just that things got mixed up. Look at this."

He ducks behind the counter. Automatically, my hand grips my pistol, lifting it so the barrel is properly aimed. When he reappears with Calista's backpack in his arm, I quickly stow away the firearm.

"Here," Jim says, placing the item on the counter between us, careful to avoid the spilled alcohol. "She left this."

I dip my head in acknowledgment but leave the item untouched. If this idiot thought that returning Calista's backpack to me would lessen my wrath, he's dumber than I thought. Another mistake on my part.

I'm discovering that I tend to make a lot of errors where Calista is concerned. She warps my thinking until it's nothing except instinct, lacking the finesse and forethought I'm used to employing.

"Are we good?" Jim asks. He licks his lips and pours himself another shot, quickly downing the contents. "I spoke to the customer you...*handled* last night, and he agreed not to press charges, so everything is cool. No harm, no foul."

I tilt my head. "Are you done lying to me?"

"What?"

"Come now, Jim. We both know you not only hired Miss Green, but you also planned on fucking her."

The flush on his face disappears, regardless of the

alcohol trying to heat his skin. Pale, his eyes wide enough to see his dilated pupils, he takes a step back. A hum of satisfaction travels through me at witnessing his terror. It's why I'm still here and the reason he's not dead. Yet.

I guess you could say I like to play with my victims before their demise. Like smoke does with oxygen, I siphon their fear, letting it empower me. Some have even called me the Grim Reaper. It fits. If a person sees me in this capacity, it's definitely because I've come to take their life.

"That's not true," he says. "I have nothing but respect for women."

"I read your texts. The game is over. Apologize."

The man's brow furrows as he decides whether or not to tell me the truth. The outcome is irrelevant. I'll pull it from him, even if I have to rip his skin from his body. Perhaps he sees the dark intent in my eyes, the one I'm not bothering to conceal. It would explain his immediate acquiescence.

"I'm sorry, okay? She's so fucking hot I couldn't help myself."

My simmering anger boils over, barely restrained. The need to kill this motherfucker has my muscles vibrating with the desire to move. To mete out justice, yes. But more than that, I want him to suffer. *Greatly.*

"Are you telling me you didn't notice?" he asks. "I mean, that's why you're here, isn't it? Because you want her for yourself?"

I dip my head in acknowledgment. "Undoubtedly."

He clenches and unclenches his fists, his adrenaline getting the best of him. In the flight-or-fight response, he's obviously the former. Too bad for him, I excel at the latter.

"Look, man, I'm sorry about all of this." He walks up to the counter, beseeching me with his gaze while resting his palms on the flat surface. "Why don't you both come back tonight and have free drinks on me?"

I sip on the whiskey.

"So, what do you say?"

My gaze finds his over the rim of my glass. In a swift, downward arc I slam the tumbler against the edge of the bar. The remaining liquid splashes against the wood and drips onto the floor, immediately forgotten at the high pitch of glass breaking. Shards fall, scattering across the bar like diamond fragments, leaving behind a single jagged edge.

I ram it into his hand.

The glass slices through tendon and bone with the force of my strike, only stopping once it drives into the wood underneath his palm. Blood wells. His scream of agony echoes in the room, a delightful sound.

"What the fuck?!" he shouts.

He further showcases his stupidity by attempting to wrench back his hand, only to find it secured to the counter by the glass. More blood spills, coating his fingers and pooling on the wooden surface.

I reach into my pocket and retrieve my lighter. He goes still at the subtle click as a single flame appears, dancing when my breath stirs it.

"I warned you," I say. "I gave you a chance to walk away and you didn't take it. Instead, you thought you could touch what's mine. *Fuck* what's mine. For that, there's no devil in hell or god in heaven who can save you. Burn, motherfucker."

With a flick of the wrist, the flame meets the spilled alcohol and sweeps over the wooden surface. Fire licks at the bar and Jim's skin. Smoke fills the air along with his screams for help. He flings curses at me while attempting to dislodge the glass from the wood, keeping him pinned as the fire swells around him.

I stand there and watch, allowing myself a few seconds of gratification before I spin on my heel and leave.

With a smile on my face.

CHAPTER 15

C alista

I HAVE A STALKER.

The evidence is too strong to ignore. That's to say nothing of my intuition. Over the past weeks, I've felt a presence looming, watching.

At first, I chalked it up to nerves, or maybe even poor nutrition—but anxiety doesn't steal your necklace. Nor does it place pearls on your nightstand during the middle of the night.

I've woken up to eight of them in the last week.

After scanning the Sugar Cube to confirm there are no customers near the register, I look at Harper. She's cleaning the coffee machine with a rag. When she meets my gaze, she grips the metal spout and runs her hand up and down while waggling her brows.

"What?" she says, feigning innocence. "A girl's gotta practice."

"If that's the size you're working with, then you won't have to practice for long."

She squeals. "Where has this Calista been all my life? Dare I say that I've found a secret perverted side hiding underneath your prim and proper exterior?"

I shake my head with a grin. "You're rubbing off on me."

"I do have that effect on people."

"Harper, can I ask you a question?" When she nods, I take a preparatory breath, steeling myself for her response. "*Hypothetically*, if someone had a stalker, what necessary steps would that person need to take to remove said stalker from their life? Hypothetically."

"Wow. Politician's daughter much?" Her face loses all traces of mirth. "Seriously, Cal, what's going on?"

I bite my lip, working the tender skin between my teeth. "I'm not sure."

"But something's happening, or you wouldn't have asked me such a crazy, *hypothetical* question." She walks over to stand next to me and takes my hand, her gaze clouded with worry while avidly searching mine. "You can tell me."

"I think someone's been in my apartment," I whisper, all but forcing the words from my mouth. Hearing them out loud gives them life, makes this real. "I'm so scared."

"Holy fuck balls. Okay, I want to know everything, and don't leave out a single detail."

I launch into the story of how I went to bed wearing the pearl necklace my father gave me on my sixteenth birthday, only for a single pearl to be sitting on my nightstand when I woke the next morning. The necklace was missing, obviously, but nothing else was taken.

However, I don't tell her that I've received more individual pearls. Instead, I confess that my feelings of being watched intensified. I tell her I've felt this way since the day of my father's funeral but wrote it off as grief and due to the stress of finding myself penniless.

Harper lets me talk without interruption. She even shushes a customer who asks for a cake pop, then goes so far as to get me one while ignoring them.

I grip the stick tightly, hoping it'll stop my hands from shaking. It doesn't work. I'm afraid nothing will ease the fear and that it'll only continue to grow.

"Isn't that what happens to stalker's victims?" I ask. "Don't they end up dead?"

Harper grabs my shoulders. "First of all, we're not going to let that happen to you. Second, I need a moment to think." After ten seconds of silence, she nods. "Suspects. That's where we should start. Give me a list of potential stalkers. And go."

"I have no idea."

"Any past relationships that ended badly?"

I shake my head. "My ex-fiancé called off the engagement, so it's unlikely he wants me back. I haven't spoken to Adam since he took the ring back."

"Oof, that's cold. What about someone you rejected?"

"I haven't dated anyone else."

Her lips pull to the side. "This is beyond me. When in doubt, ask Google. Unfortunately, being stalked isn't on my list of personal experiences. Now, if you asked me how to Houdini yourself out of some Shibari knots, then I'm your girl."

"*Unfortunately*?"

She waves a hand in dismissal before retrieving her cell phone from her apron pocket. "What to do when you think you're being stalked," she mumbles to herself.

I peer over her shoulder. "'Avoid all contact.' That's going to be hard since I have no idea who it is."

"'Be alert and proactive to protect yourself,'" she reads. "Yeah, no shit. Don't fail me now, Google. I'm counting on you. 'Enhance security measures.'" She looks at me. "Do you have a gun?"

My eyes widen. "Do you?"

"Not yet."

"I have pepper spray."

"Put a knife under your pillow too," she says. "What about a security system?"

I blow out a breath, disturbing the tendrils of hair resting on my cheek. "You know how much I get paid. It's not like I can afford it, even with the extra hours I'm working."

"'Inform key people in your life,'" she continues. "Check. Once we tell Alex, that'll be another check." She jerks up her head to pierce me with a hard stare. "What about Mr. I-want-to-ride-your-dick-Bennett? He was super protective over you that one time."

"And?"

"And maybe he'll care this time."

I cross my arms. "No. I don't want to have anything to do with him."

"There's something you're not telling me." She sweeps her gaze over my face as I fight off a blush. "A *lot* of something."

I bow my head, unable to look at her. "If I tell you, will you promise not to tease me about it?"

She salutes me. "Cross my heart and hope to die while in the middle of an orgasm."

Despite my best efforts, a smile tugs at my lips. It fades when I think of Hayden. "So...I might've gotten a job at T&A. Just long enough to pay my bills," I say, holding out my hands in supplication. "However, Mr. Bennett made me quit."

"He what?"

I nod. "He marched me out of there like I was his unruly child and told me I could never go back. I think I worked there for a whopping three seconds before he showed up."

"Niiiice."

"No, not nice." I frown at her. "Are you not hearing me?"

"Kind of. I'm distracted by dick right now."

"Harper..." I say, my tone full of warning.

She rolls her eyes. "Fine. It doesn't matter anyway."

"Why not?"

"Because T&A was burned to a crisp last week. It's nothing but ash, so it's not like you'd still have a job anyway. The way I see it, Mr. Spank-me-harder Bennett did you a favor."

I press my lips together. Although I want to admit she's right, I can't. But only because I don't want to be indebted to a man like Hayden. The payments would be steep. Perhaps even devastating.

"So, back to your stalker problem," she says. "Have you received any messages or anything from this person?"

I shake my head. "I don't have a cell phone, and I haven't found any weird papers lying around. Actually, nothing except my necklace was taken. The rest of my apartment was untouched."

She gasps. "You don't have a cell phone? How do you even live? This is worse than I thought. You can't even fucking call 9-1-1. Unbelievable."

I smile at the customer who walks up to the counter, silently grateful for this small reprieve. The transaction is over too quickly, and I sigh. Although I'm glad to have confided in Harper, it's forced me to realize how dangerous my situation is. Not only that, it's bleak.

My shoulders slump as any remaining hope seeps from my body. "I need money. If I had some, I could move, or at the very least, I could buy a few security cameras and a cell phone."

"Well, you're not working at a place like T&A again. That's for sure."

"Then what can I do? I'm already working long shifts here. I don't have time for anything else really."

Harper grabs me for a hug and squeezes me tight. "Don't worry, we'll think of something."

"Thank you."

The rest of my shift goes by in a blur. My thoughts cycle around and around like a whirlpool until I feel like I'm drowning in the magnitude of my problem. In the end, I can't think of a single solution that doesn't involve me becoming a prostitute.

Or asking Hayden for help.

The real question is: do I want to face the lawyer or deal with my stalker?

I rush over to where Harper stands by the coffee machine. "I've got an idea, but it's crazy."

"I love crazy."

"I can get the money from Hayden."

She scrunches her forehead. "From who?"

"Mr. Bennett."

Her eyes widen while the green hue sparkles. "You're going to *Pretty Woman* his ass."

"I don't know what that means."

"Have you lived under a rock your entire life? Good grief. It's the story of a rich man who falls in love with a prostitute."

I frown. "In that case, I'm not going to do what you're thinking, but it does involve the lawyer. There's a piece of information he wants from me," I say, carefully choosing my words. "If I can offer to sell that to him for enough money, then I can move out of my apartment and buy a security system to keep me safe."

Harper nods slowly. "I think that could work. Are you going to tell me what that piece of information is?"

"It's...private."

"More private than you having a stalker?"

I nod. "It's something pertaining to my life before now. I don't like talking about it."

Her gaze softens, and her voice gentles. "Okay, honey. If you think that'll work, then go for it. I thought he would've come back to the Sugar Cube by now, but I haven't seen him."

"That's because I told him I didn't want to speak to him anymore."

"You what?" She slaps a hand to her chest. "You're going to be the death of me. How could you push away such a fine specimen of a man? I've failed to teach you. From now on, it's wax on, wax off. If you say you don't get that movie reference, I will literally shriek in outrage."

I put my fingertips to my temples and apply pressure to alleviate the headache that's forming. "You can be my sensei."

"Phew," she says, blowing out a breath. "That was a close one. As your karate master, I want you to contact Mr. I-want-to-sit-on-your-face Bennett. Like right freaking now."

CHAPTER 16

C alista

MY PALMS GROW SWEATY AT THE THOUGHT OF SEEING HAYDEN, and I rub them on my apron. Several times. After a moment's hesitation, I retrieve his business card, the one I didn't have the courage to throw away. It's been sitting in my pocket since he first offered it to me, and I'm grateful to my past self that I didn't get rid of it. Who knew I'd actually be in a position to not only need his help, but actively chase it?

Harper snatches the card from my hand. "'H. Bennett. Attorney-at-Law. 20010 Greystone Blvd. Suite 901.' Wow. He didn't put his first name on it. Talk about boundaries." She shifts her attention to me, a sly smile playing about her lips. "And yet, the elusive Mr. Bennett gave you his first name."

He didn't just give it to me.

He ordered me to use it.

I shrug, feeling the opposite of nonchalant. "I told you,

he and I knew each other because of my father's trial, but we're mere acquaintances."

She shoots me a dubious look. "Yeah, acquaintances, where one of you knows a deep secret that the other wants. One that's big enough that he'd be willing to pay you hundreds of dollars for it. Feed your lies to someone else."

"You really think he'll pay that much?"

"Why don't you tell me?" She shrugs. "You're the only one who knows the value of the information you're keeping from him."

"I need to think about this."

She waves the card in my face. "Well, don't take too long. Time, and stalkers, wait for no one."

"Thanks for that." I sigh and take the business card, running my thumb over the letters. "Do you mind if I make the phone call real quick? I need to do it before I chicken out."

"Go for it. You know the Sugar Cube isn't that busy at this time of day. I can handle the customers."

"Thanks."

I duck my head and walk over to the phone located on the back wall behind the counter. My fingers tremble when I dial the number listed on the card. Harper gives me a double thumbs up. I smile at her, but I'm sure it's more of a grimace.

After the first ring, a woman answers, her voice crisp and no-nonsense. "District Attorney's Office. How can I assist you?"

"Um, hi. I'd like to speak to Mr. Bennett please."

"He's not taking calls at this time. Would you like to leave a message and a callback number?"

I grind my molars. Harper's right; I really need a cell phone. It's not like I can live inside the Sugar Cube until

Hayden calls me back. The idea isn't unappealing. Unlike my apartment, the cafe has a security system, a telephone, and food.

"No, that's okay," I say. "I'll call back when he's available. Can you tell me when that'll be?"

The woman hums and the sound of her typing drifts through the phone. "It depends. Are you a family member of a victim?"

I was. "No."

"Listen," she says, her voice cutting, "if you're calling for personal reasons then you should try his cell. If you don't have that number, then it's because he doesn't want to speak to you. Got it?"

I nod, even though she can't see me. "Yes, I do. Thank you for your time."

"Have a good day."

The way she says it sounds like she's wishing for me to get run over by a car.

I hang up with a sigh. Harper races to my side, her gaze searching my face. "What happened?"

"The receptionist wouldn't let me speak to him. She made it sound like I was an ex-girlfriend desperately wanting to get back with him."

"I can't see Mr. Fuck-me-harder Bennett with a girl-friend. As a result, she's probably dealt with the one-night stands in his life who want a relationship. Or she's used to random women trying to hit on him all the time. I can understand. I'd be more than happy to call his office and offer him a blowjob."

"Harper!"

She shrugs. "Just telling you the truth. Anyway, don't worry about that phone call. It's time for phase two."

"Phase two?"

"Yup. You need to go to his office."

I shake my head emphatically. "I barely got up the courage to call him. How do you expect me to show up at his workplace?"

"He did it to you without any issues, so why not?"

"Because he came here for a coffee. I wouldn't have the same excuse."

Harper purses her lips. "You're doing this. It's either that or embrace your stalker. What's it going to be?"

"I think I hate you."

"Of course you do." She gives me an air kiss. "In order to make sure you don't turn into a pussy and bail on the plan, I'm going to cover the extended part of your shift. That should guilt you into doing this."

I throw up my hands. "I don't think I hate you. I actually do."

"Right back at you. Now go, before he leaves for the day. Alex should be here soon to start his shift, so I won't be alone for long. Off you go."

"Fine."

"You can thank me later."

~

I STARE UP AT THE BUILDING, WONDERING HOW IN THE HELL I'm going to march inside and convince Hayden to help me. Assuming his secretary lets me speak to him.

Surprisingly, the walk here was quick. His office is very close to the Sugar Cube, which explains why he was there a few times last week. Reasons that had nothing to do with me, I'm sure.

Taking a deep breath, I pull on the glass door and step into the foyer. The main lobby is large and open with a high ceiling and marble floors. Along one wall is a reception desk staffed by a handful of secretaries directing calls and helping visitors. Beyond that are hallways leading to conference rooms and numerous offices, Hayden's among them.

I make my way over to the front desk and approach a woman with jet-black hair and horn-rimmed glasses. Her entire focus locks on me. She sweeps her gaze over me from head to toe before dismissing me.

"How can I assist you?"

"Hello," I say, pasting a smile on my face. "I'd like to speak to Mr. Bennett please."

"What's your name please?"

"Calist—No, Callie."

Her brows lift. "Do you have a last name, *Callie*?"

"Green."

"One second."

"Thank you."

I fold my arms, creating a barrier between me and this woman. I'd rather hug a cactus than her, she's that prickly.

"Hello, Mr. Bennett," she says into the receiver. "I'm sorry to interrupt you, but there's a Callie Green here to see you." She frowns. "Yes, sir. No, sir. I understand."

After she hangs up the phone, the woman peers up at me as though I'm a freak. Or a unicorn. I hold her gaze, unsure what brought on this change in attitude from her. Whatever Hayden expressed during their exchange must've been interesting.

He appears a moment later and all of my thoughts concerning the secretary vanish. He's dressed in another expensive suit, tailored to fit nicely against every swell of muscle in the expanse of his chest. His black leather shoes are polished to a shine, and a burgundy tie adds a splash of color against his crisp, white shirt.

Hayden walks over to the secretary's desk, and I have to resist the urge to take a step back. The energy rolling off of him is full of anticipation, even eagerness. It'd be flattering if he didn't intimidate me so much.

"Josephine, this is Miss Green," he says, gesturing to me. "She is a person of great interest to me and should be shown the ultimate respect at all times. Whenever she requests to speak to me, you will contact me immediately and put all of my other plans on hold. There's nothing and no one more important than her. Understood?"

The woman looks from me to Hayden and back again. Three times. The shock on her face must be the same found on mine. When did I become so important to him?

And why?

CHAPTER 17

Hayden

SHE'S HERE.

I run my gaze over every inch of Calista, drinking in her presence like a man dying of thirst. It's been too long since I've had her look at me. Since I've heard her voice. If I could survive on those things alone, I'd never want for anything else.

When it comes to this woman, I'm fucked.

Beyond fucked.

Over the past week, I've kept my distance from her in the daylight hours to prove to myself that I could, that she doesn't have control over me. But I nearly failed. If not for my visiting her at night in her apartment, I wouldn't have been able to stay away from her.

Even then, I followed her into the coffee shop when I shouldn't have. Twice now. But after the night at T&A and witnessing her moaning my name, I decided to give in to my desires.

Both carnal and cerebral.

Having Calista in my life and in my bed will either rid me of my obsession or take me to the point of no return. Either way, I'll know what she is to me.

It's fortunate that she sought me out. I'm not sure how much longer I would've waited before kidnapping her.

Josephine looks at me with her brow furrowed. Like I'm insane. If she only knew the thoughts I've had when it comes to Calista, she'd think I was certifiable.

"Yes, sir," Josephine says. "I'll make sure you're promptly notified when Miss Green comes to the office." The woman looks at Calista, unable to hide the bewilderment in her gaze. "Miss Green, I apologize if I came off as rude."

Calista's cheeks bloom with a pink tinge. "Don't worry about it."

I tilt my head. "Miss Green, let's have our conversation in my office."

She nods, causing the loose strands of her hair to glide along her jawline. My fingers twitch with the need to touch the silky strands. To wrap them around my fist.

Calista walks beside me down the long hallway and into my office. I immediately shut the door behind her. The click of the door's mechanism fills me with satisfaction. I have her alone, without prying eyes.

While she's awake.

Seeing her when she's asleep in her apartment is not the same experience as watching her stand before me with her face flushed as her body reacts to me. Chest heaving, her breasts straining against the material of her shirt, squeezing her thighs together as she squirms under my gaze. I enjoy every second of it.

"Please have a seat." I extend a hand to the leather chair in front of my desk and settle in mine on the other side. After resting my forearms on the surface, I lean forward, unable to stifle my eagerness. "Why are you here, Callie?"

Her pupils contract when the term of endearment registers. "Mr. Bennett," she says, her voice coated with hesitation, "I need your hel—no." She shakes her head with an exhale. "I want to know: why did you intervene on my behalf at the Sugar Cube and then again at T&A?"

She runs her gaze over me, the hazel within churning like molten gold. I've never felt the need to be honest with anyone if it didn't suit my agenda, but with Callie, I want to be truthful.

And I will...to an extent.

She can't know the depth of my obsession until I understand it first and have everything under control. When I'm certain she won't run from me. Not that it would stop me from chasing her.

And keeping her.

"That's simple. I saw you needed help, and I provided it," I say.

"Yes, but T&A isn't a place you normally visit, so why were you there?"

I tilt my head, a smile playing about my lips. "Have you been stalking me?"

Her entire demeanor shifts. From the way her skin pales to the alarmed look on her face, the mere mention of a stalker, even in the form of a joke, is devastating to Callie.

She lifts her hand to her throat and quickly drops it. A spark of satisfaction ignites my blood. Her necklace is currently in my pocket, albeit not all in one piece. I've been carrying around the pearls since that first night.

She'll get all of them back eventually.

Given the number of times I've fucked myself because of her, it'll be sooner rather than later.

"No, I haven't been following you," she says. "I'm trying to figure out how you always seem to be around when I need you."

That's right. You're finally getting that you need me. And only me.

"Coincidence, I'm sure. Why are you here, Callie?"

Although her gaze remains doubtful, she waves a hand in dismissal. "I need to know how important it is that you finish the investigation of my father's murder, Mr. Bennett."

"It's Hayden. And the answer is *very*."

Even more so since Zack said that there was no record of anyone matching her description being treated at a hospital on June 24th. If I didn't know for certain that he was the best, I would've fired him. The hacker promised he'd continue looking into the matter, probably to appease me since I lost my shit. But I can't wait for him.

Not when the source of the answers sits directly across from me.

Calista presses her lips together. I can almost hear the cogs turning in her mind. "Hayden," she says, her voice lowering in volume. Almost as if she's scared to say my name. "Why do you care so much about my father's case?"

I almost groan at the sound of my name on her lips and tongue. "I already told you. It was one of the few high-profile cases in my career that I lost. Even with the senator acquitted, he still ended up dead. Whatever the reason, I want to know why. Don't you?"

"Obviously," she says. "That's why I hired the P.I. in the first place."

"Then we are agreed."

Her luscious mouth pulls down into a frown. "Not quite.

I'm willing to assist you in the investigation by filling in the gaps of missing information, but it'll cost you."

"Indeed?" I lean back in my chair, fighting a smile. My little Calista has grown a set of claws. I flick my gaze to her perfectly manicured nails, imagining them digging into my back as I fuck her. "This is very close to bribery, Callie."

"I prefer to think of it as quid pro quo."

A smile takes over my mouth before I can stop it. One that's both rare and genuine. This woman seduces me at night and amuses me in the day. So unique.

So mine.

"A favor for a favor..." I tap my chin in thought although I made my decision to give her whatever she wanted when I first heard her say my name. "I can work with that. What's your price?"

She blows out a stream of air and then says, "Okay. One piece of information for five hundred dollars."

"Is that all?"

Calista winces before she smoothes her features. "Make it one thousand dollars."

She has no idea that I would give her the millions of dollars I own if it meant getting to know everything about her. Very few people know about the wealth I amassed after investing the money I made from my career as an attorney. The only reason I continue to do this job is because it provides me satisfaction when meting out justice.

Not as much as killing the guilty with my bare hands. But we all have to make sacrifices for the greater good.

"You drive a hard bargain, Callie, but I'm willing to pay."

"Great."

Relief sweeps across her face, loosening the tightness pinching her cheeks and the corners of her mouth. She looks at me and smiles. For the first time.

I clear my throat, composing myself before I reach across this desk and haul her to me. So I can bend her over it. Or kiss her. Which would be a first for me.

I don't kiss women.

I'm happy to lick their cunts and suck their tits, but kissing someone is intimate. It's an emotional connection I've never cared for. Or wanted to encourage.

Until Calista Green.

"I have some conditions that must be met," I say.

She nods and the hazel of her eyes grows clouded with suspicion.

"I don't like to be kept waiting. Therefore, you will always answer my phone calls and promptly respond to my texts upon receiving them."

She averts her gaze, a flush staining her neck. "I don't have a cell phone."

"That'll need to be rectified immediately." When she opens her mouth to speak, I lift a hand, and she presses her lips together. "We're doing this my way, Callie. You might have the information I require, but I'm the one who will control every aspect of this agreement."

Control...that's laughable. I have none when it comes to her. But that won't stop me from trying to regain some semblance of authority in this situation. It's an illusion. Much like my ability to leave her alone.

"Okay," she whispers. "I just don't want to be your charity case."

"I respect your pride, but this isn't meant to demean you. It's simply to ensure I get what I want."

She looks up at me from beneath her lashes. "What happens if you *don't* get what you want?"

"I'd rather not say."

"Is that a challenge?"

My lips twitch at her sharp wit and the way she's blatantly thrown my words in my face. "Perhaps. Anyway, you'll have a cell phone within the next twenty-four hours. Now I need your bank information to pay you."

After grabbing a piece of paper and a pen, I slide the items in Calista's direction. Then I pick up the phone on my desk and dial the number to my financial institution. My personal banker answers, his voice cheerful.

"Hello, Mr. Bennett. How are you?"

"I'm fine, Ronald."

"How can I assist you today, sir?"

"I need to make a wire transfer." I look at Calista and she pushes the information toward me. "The information is as follows."

Ronald sets up everything on his end, his fingers clicking hard enough on the keyboard that it reaches my ears. "All set, sir. What is the amount you wish to transfer?"

"Ten thousand dollars."

I would've given her ten times that amount right off the bat, except I don't want to give her the choice to be rid of me. With enough money, she'd certainly walk away.

She shoots from her chair, almost knocking over the piece of furniture. "Hayden!"

Hearing her say my name with such passion has my cock pressing against the seam of my pants. Then, there's the thought of her screaming my name...

I hold up my hand, and she crosses her arms, her expression morphing from shock to unsettled. "Sit down," I say, my tone leaving no room for argument.

"Is everything all right, sir?"

"Yes," I say to Ronald on the phone. "Finish the transaction."

"You're all set, sir. Anything else I can do for you?"

"No."

"Thank you for your business, Mr. Bennett. Have a great day."

I hang up the phone.

Calista leans forward, placing her fisted hands on my desk. "Why did you do that?"

"I already told you. I'm going to get what I want, one way or another. With that money in your account, I'm well on my way. Now, let's discuss the events of June 24th."

CHAPTER 18

C alista

My heart pounds so furiously within my rib cage that I wonder if I'm about to have a panic attack. It wouldn't be the first time. I came here to obtain enough money to buy a phone, and I ended up with enough financial security to last me for the next couple of months.

Now, it's time for me to pay the devil with information I don't wish to think about, let alone discuss.

"I was at the children's shelter off of Montlake Drive that night," I say. "There was a charity event the following morning, so I was there baking goods in preparation for that."

The man in front of me has the best poker face. Hayden's features remain stoic, his expression one of mild interest. If not for the glint in his blue eyes, I'd think we were discussing the weather.

Not one of the darkest times in my life.

"What happened?" he asks.

"I felt sick, and I passed out."

Hayden's gaze narrows slightly, creating lines at the corners of his eyes. That minor change is the extent of his reaction. For someone who wants information, he certainly doesn't show his eagerness.

Or perhaps, the information I have isn't good enough. The idea of returning his money to him has my mind spinning.

He tilts his head. "Why do you think that happened?"

I drop my gaze to my lap, wiping my sweaty palms over my jeans. "I forgot to eat, and my blood sugar dropped. When I regained consciousness, I called my father."

"Were you drinking? Did you take something?" he asks. His voice holds a note of curiosity but without any judgment. It gives me the wherewithal to continue.

"No. The only medication I took was something to get rid of a headache. You know, generic and over the counter."

Technically, that's true. But that wasn't the real drug. Or at least, the effects were not that of a simple pain reliever.

They were much worse.

I sneak a glance at Hayden. "Most people think it was an attempt to get my father's attention, but I swear it wasn't. Even when Kristen came into our lives, he never made me feel left out. I would've liked to have her as a stepmother, and the baby would've made us a family."

He slowly nods. "I'm sorry for your loss, Callie. Not just your father, but for everything that could've been."

"Thank you."

His unexpected but genuine sympathy causes a small burst of warmth in my chest. Why am I affected by the words of a man I'm actively trying to dislike? My body's reaction to him would say otherwise; it more than likes him. I throw up mental shields when my mind begins to conjure the image of me touching myself with his name on my lips.

It was the best orgasm of my life.

I swore I'd only do it that one time. My first reason was that I was certain I'd never see Hayden again. Since he discovered how poor I am, I assumed he'd be disgusted and we'd never cross paths again. Maybe at the Sugar Cube, but that wouldn't surprise me, given how close his office is.

The second reason I promised myself that I'd only fantasize about him was due to the fact that he's treated me like his little sister. I'm certain he's not more than ten years older than me, but I have yet to see him look at me with desire like he did when we first met. There are times when I wonder if I made up the entire thing and projected my attraction onto him.

Regardless of my confusion concerning Hayden, I find myself torn between wanting him and giving in to the urge to run away. Especially from this conversation.

"Given your physical state," he says, "I assume your father took you to a hospital?"

I release a breath, which does nothing to calm my racing pulse. My moral compass won't allow me to lie to Hayden, but I'm ashamed to admit that I'm not above concealing certain details. Lies by omission.

The deadliest kind. They don't need to be believable.

Just silent.

"I was looked over by a medical professional," I say.

"I see," he says. "What hospital was it?"

"Do you really need to know? The details are irrelevant. The exam consisted of nothing except routine care and my discharge the same night."

His lips thin with displeasure. "I want to know everything about you, Callie. No matter how insignificant you think something is, chances are it's meaningful to me."

"Why? This is supposed to be about my father, not me."

"It's all connected."

I frown, unable to conceal my skepticism. This man is digging into every aspect of my life, and I don't believe all of it will help him understand my father's case. There's a hunger in Hayden's eyes that is deeper, fiercer than what he gives voice to.

Unfortunately, so is my need to keep this information secret.

"If I give you the name of the location, can I leave with the money and your promise to move on from this topic?" I ask.

Hayden watches me, remaining perfectly still. In those seconds, I nearly fracture under his intense stare. My pulse ratchets up, the speed so swift that I place a hand on my breast to keep my heart from escaping my rib cage.

His gaze zips to my chest. And lingers. It sweeps over me like a phantom caress.

Despite the ugliness of the topic, my skin breaks into a flush with his eyes on me. How can I be aroused and on the cusp of a panic attack simultaneously? Hayden not only perplexes me, but he's confused my body as well.

"I can't agree to that," he says. "I need to know everything."

If it were any other subject, I wouldn't hesitate to tell him. However, revealing this secret won't just hurt me and force me to relive the horrific event again. It could unlock the things in my mind that I've repressed.

I can't risk it.

"There's nothing else to discuss," I say, my words thin and airy, a struggle to get out.

Hayden narrows his gaze, and I flinch. "Tell me about the bruises," he says. "I'm assuming your father took the picture as evidence, then covered up the details of your attack for political reasons, but that doesn't tell me what I want to know." He leans forward, and his gaze narrows. "Who hurt you?"

The idea of Hayden discovering the sordid details of that night has my body taking over. Adrenaline surges, igniting a panic that has me feeling like my chest is in a vise, each breath causing the pressure to increase until I'm panting. I squeeze my eyes shut and take deep breaths to keep from hyperventilating, but it's no use.

"I can't do this."

"I have to know," Hayden says, his tone more forceful. "Who put their fucking hands on you? I want a name."

My eyes fly open at the unadulterated anger in his voice. For the first time in this interrogation, Hayden's showing emotion. And it's strong. His gaze bores into mine, the blue glittering with malice and his body taut with tension lining every muscle.

I get to my feet despite my shaking legs. Shame heats my skin and pricks my eyes with tears, and I blink furiously to keep them from falling. "Take your money and leave me alone."

"Who are you trying to protect?" he asks. He stands and plants his hands on the desk, leaning toward me. "Is it your father or yourself?"

My need to escape takes over, and I spin around, bolting for the door. I'm an idiot for thinking I could negotiate with someone like Hayden. His intention to uncover the events in my past is like a disease, and he won't stop until he's infected the healthy parts of me.

And worsened the parts that are still sick.

"Calista, wait."

His voice and the use of my name have me walking faster. I grip the doorknob and wrench my arm back, only to jump at the loud noise reverberating in my ears. Hayden's palms slam against the door, his hands flat on either side of my head. I freeze, my entire body stiffening with fear. And awareness.

The scent of him fills my nose.

The warmth of him seeps into my skin.

The feel of him pressed against my back has me longing for more.

This man is dangerous. For so many reasons.

I close my eyes and rest my forehead against the wood. The world falls away until it's only me and Hayden. My panic and his presence.

My breaths are loud in my ears, and my lungs work hard to keep the air flowing despite my inability to pull in much oxygen. At the feel of Hayden gripping my shoulders, I finally suck in a much-needed breath. It clears the haze clouding my vision, and I blink up at the man after he spins me to face him. His lips are moving, but his words fail to register in my mind. I stand there as his voice drifts over me like a melody, a baritone sound fighting the darkness that's ready to swallow me whole.

Hayden wraps one arm around my back and bends his legs in order to hook his other arm underneath my knees. From one second to the next, I'm in his arms. I stare up at him as he walks across the room to his desk and settles us in the chair with me on his lap. This proximity makes my fight to breathe that much harder.

He cups my cheek, placing his thumb under my jaw to hold up my head. "Look at me, Callie."

I flick my gaze to his. The blue is like shards of ice, chilled with his worry for me.

"That's it. Concentrate on me," he says. "You are safe. Nothing will hurt you."

His voice carries a confidence that rings true within me. It battles my need to hide from him. To conceal the filthy and damaged parts of me.

"I've got you, Callie. You're safe with me. I'll never let anything hurt you. Anyone who tries will suffer. Now, breathe in and out slowly through your mouth."

When he runs his thumb over the seam of my lips, I inhale. The breath sweeps past his finger and into my lungs. Into my soul.

Time holds no meaning as Hayden reassures me again and again, guiding my breathing with words and gentle touches. Our surroundings slowly take shape and cement within my psyche. But his office is nothing more than a fleeting thought compared to the man holding me to his chest.

He is the only thing in my world right now.

Hayden's heartbeats pound furiously against my ear, a stark contrast to the calm tone he uses to speak to me. I swallow to alleviate my dry throat and stare up at him, my vision clearer than a moment ago. His dark beauty stares back at me like Lucifer before he fell from grace.

"You're safe," Hayden says, sweeping his thumb over my cheek. "I've got you."

I lift my arm to brush his jaw with my fingertips, ignoring their trembling. Is it with trepidation...or from the pleasure of touching him? "You don't need to worry about me, Hayden. I'm fine."

I force a smile. It wobbles on my face when he frowns at me, but I keep it there while continuing to caress him. My need to soothe him is almost as strong as my need to touch him. I bite the inside of my cheek to repress a sigh as I trail my fingers along the curve of his cheek, the length of his jaw, and the arch of his brows. One, then the other.

Hayden turns to ice, hard and unmoving against me. Yet he doesn't stop me from exploring him. I bring my index finger to his chin, following the minor cleft there, then drag my fingertip along his nose and his bottom lip. It's just as soft as I thought. Maybe even more so.

With regret, I let my hand fall away.

Only for Hayden to snatch it in his and bring it to his mouth.

"Don't stop," he whispers, his lips brushing my skin. "I need more."

CHAPTER 19

H ayden

C<small>ALISTA HAS AWAKENED SOMETHING IN ME</small>.

Something I thought dead and buried.

Fragments of my childhood rise like ghosts from their tombs, their ominous presence chilling my skin. I concentrate on Calista's face when another tries to take its place. That of another woman.

The only one I've ever loved.

My mother's features briefly take over in the form of blonde hair and light blue eyes the same shade as mine. Her voice drifts past my ears, the words full of hopes and dreams that never come to fruition. But I hold her in my arms regardless, determined to fight the demons ravaging her body. How can someone fight an enemy they can't see?

Addiction is the strongest adversary I've ever encountered.

The depression.

The panic attacks.

The delusions of a better future.

I clench my teeth and hold my mother closer as if to shield her from the battle within, knowing the poison is already coursing through her bloodstream. My focus narrows until the only thing I can see is her glazed expression; pale blue eyes dull from the drugs, becoming more lifeless as each second passes. A moment of time I'll never recover. Because deep down, I know how this all ends. It doesn't stop me from saying what she needs to hear.

"You're safe," I tell her, my thumb tracing the curve of her cheek. "I've got you."

A hint of jasmine.

A warm touch.

A soft voice.

The gentle caress along my jaw, accompanied by my name being spoken, pulls me from the dark recesses of my mind.

"You don't need to worry about me, Hayden. I'm fine."

I look down at Calista as if seeing her for the first time. In return, she smiles up at me. To reassure me.

To comfort me.

Even in the midst of anxiety ravaging her mind and body, this woman's only concern at this moment is me. I frown at this selfless act. It takes me back to that day at the funeral where Calista consoled everyone else instead of receiving support like she should've.

Despite my churning thoughts, she continues to explore my face, slowly and deliberately, as if wanting to commit it to memory. All the while, Calista's body quakes in my arms. In contrast, I've become immobile, a living statue.

Until she touches my lips.

Something about that shatters the remaining vestiges of

my childhood memories. Despite my lingering affection for my mother, I'll never confuse the feel of Calista's touch with another's. Each stroke of her fingers brands me, the heat of her skin on mine is a fire that burns deeper and hotter than a supernova.

Calista drops her hand, tucking it close to her chest. My brows snap together at the loss. Craving the feel of her touch, I take her hand and bring it to my mouth, my lips brushing her fingers.

Her tremors increase in strength. Is she afraid of me?

"Don't stop," I whisper. Even with me speaking at a low volume, it doesn't disguise the vehemence coating my tone. I am desperate for Calista. In ways I didn't realize until now. "I need more."

I flatten her palm against my cheek and briefly close my eyes, siphoning the tenderness from this woman. She stares up at me, her gaze wide, the hazel within molten gold. What does she see when she looks at me?

"I'm here," she whispers back. "Whatever you need."

Calista Green has given me permission to take.

To consume.

To own.

How can I resist?

I. Can't.

CHAPTER 20

C alista

SOMETHING'S HAPPENING.

I can feel the shift in Hayden. In our dynamic. It's like a living thing, breathing in and out, giving and taking.

Me submitting and him claiming.

His yearning for connection isn't lost on me. In fact, it causes a deep stirring within, pulling it from the depths of my soul. I've always wanted to bond with another person, and I thought I'd have it with Adam, but I was mistaken.

Can I have it with Hayden?

As if privy to my thoughts, he draws back. Only a little, but enough for me to see his gaze and the turbulence within.

Confusion wars with logic.

Desire battles with skepticism.

Vulnerability fights with the need for connection.

What will win in the end?

I press my hand against his cheek, anchoring myself to him before whatever storm is brewing inside him is released; a tempest that will wreck me. Completely.

"Are you all right?" I ask. However soft, my voice is an intruder during this emotional conflict.

Hayden's brow furrows. "I believe I should ask you that question since you were the one experiencing a panic attack."

"How'd you know?"

"My mother used to have them."

Any embarrassment I had at being seen in such a vulnerable state evaporates like a puff of smoke. The stench of it all lingers. It permeates the room, causing my stomach to roil, my muscles clenching.

All on Hayden's behalf.

Maybe he didn't have an easy childhood like I'd assumed. My heart aches for him.

"I used to help her through them as best I could," he says. "But there's only so much you can do when a person's under the influence of drugs."

I sweep my thumb over the angles of his cheek, wanting to comfort him in any way I can. I told Hayden he could take whatever he needed from me, and I meant it. If he only knew the things I'd be willing to give him...

All because of this intimate moment.

I finally see Hayden as a human being with both flaws and feelings. It makes me want to curl inside his arms and never leave. From what I've gathered, we've both lost a loved one and are in need of someone who understands.

And I do. Deeply.

He closes his eyes, leaning into my touch. "No one should have to suffer through that alone."

"Thank you." I blink back tears when my vision blurs. "I

don't usually have an audience during my episodes. I haven't had one since my father died."

"I'm so sorry for that, Callie."

"Hayden." I pull him to me until our foreheads touch. "I can tell you really mean that, and if you want to help me, please find his killer."

He stiffens under my fingertips. "I'm not sure redemption can be found for that person."

"I'm not after redemption, or even revenge. I want understanding more than anything."

"Understanding." His breath whispers over my lips. "You never cease to amaze me. After everything, you should want blood...yet your heart remains pure."

I shrug. "I'm still grieving and angry about his death. I'm not perfect."

"I disagree."

His hand slides to my nape, fingers massaging away my turmoil even as he holds me captive. His touch sends shivers through me, adding to the minuscule trembling still skating through my body. Concealing the way he affects me.

"You can trust me to find the person responsible and make them pay." His gaze bores into mine. "Just tell me the name of the hospital."

As much as I want to give Hayden the answers he's seeking, the cost of him knowing is too high. It's a debt I never asked for and something I can't get rid of, no matter how hard I try.

I smile up at him, but it's full of sadness and remorse. "I can't."

CHAPTER 21

C alista

"YOU REALLY NEED TO GET A PHONE," HARPER SAYS, HAND ON her hip.

"Good morning to you too."

She waves a hand. "It's too early for pleasantries."

"But not for criticism?" I close and lock the door of the Sugar Cube, unsuccessfully stifling a yawn. "You're right, though."

"I know I am. Stop it," she says, covering her mouth with her hand. "That yawning shit is contagious, and we just got here. So, how'd it go?"

I reach for my apron, tying the ends. "How'd what go?"

"Oh my fuck." Harper squints at me. "You know exactly what I'm talking about which means you have stuff to tell. Spill."

"Fine. Once I got to his office, the receptionist was a little challenging, but then Hayden showed up and invited me to his office."

Harper's eyes widen and her jaw goes slack. "And?"

"And I asked him if the information was worth anything to him. Turns out it was."

"How much?"

I bite my bottom lip, unsure about how much I should reveal. My friend has been nothing but supportive; however, she's convinced things between Hayden and me are more than they actually are. Telling her that he gave me thousands of dollars would only reinforce her opinion. But telling her he held me in his arms and soothed me like an upset child? I'd never hear the end of it.

"A few months' worth of pay," I say.

Harper lets out a whoop. The sound echoes in the empty coffee shop, and I grin, shaking my head. "This is the most energetic I've ever seen you."

"Considering it's nearly six in the morning, it'll probably be a one-time event. Oh my goodness! That information must be really important if he's willing to pay so much. We have to celebrate."

I walk over and set Mr. Bailey's newspaper on his designated table. "I just got the money, and you already want me to spend it?"

She folds her arms and sets her chin. "Yes, I do. First, on a cell phone."

"Agreed. And the second thing?" I ask, making my way back to her side.

"A night out with me."

I shake my head. A little too emphatically, if the pain in Harper's gaze is any indication. Guilt lances me, making my heart bleed, and I inwardly reprimand myself.

"I would love to go out with you, but this money is to

help me get rid of a stalker." I slap my forehead. "I can't believe I've gotten to this point in my life."

My friend takes my shoulders and smiles at me. It's meant to be encouraging, but there's a tightness around her mouth that I can't dismiss. "Calista, you work harder than anyone I know. All I'm asking is that you enjoy life instead of merely survive it. Okay? Besides, you didn't follow through with your end of our deal. Mr. I'll-suck-your-dick-please Bennett came to see you again, and you didn't flirt with him, so you owe me a night out."

I drop my head, avoiding her gaze. "I don't have anything to wear."

"I have plenty. We're about the same size so we'll make it work. Say you'll go."

"Okay." The simple acquiescence has my stress easing. "It would be nice to enjoy myself for once."

"That's what I'm saying."

I glance at the clock and note the time. "Time to unlock the doors."

"Might as well get this day started. Then we can go out tonight."

"Tonight?" I repeat, my voice high-pitched. "That fast?"

She winks at me. "Of course. If I don't get you out now, you'll think too much and come up with a million reasons not to go. We're doing this."

She marches over to the door and inserts her key. Once the lock clicks open, she pushes the glass door open and sticks her head outside.

"All right, you caffeine-dependent losers, get in here and get your fix."

I position myself behind the register, rearranging the bills inside to hide my amusement. Sometimes I wonder why Alex hasn't fired Harper. She's like a loaded gun that could go off at any moment. It's what makes her exciting and me cautious.

My shift begins and continues in the same manner as it always does. The customers are in a hurry, and I do my best to accommodate them but with a smile. The world is full of darkness, so why not try to be the light in someone's day?

As usual, my thoughts drift to Hayden whenever I'm not ringing up a transaction or chatting with Harper. No matter how much I go over the event in his office, I can't make sense of it all. The only thing I know for certain is that I saw a side of him that I didn't know existed.

His reassurance might've been firm, but he was gentle. Tender in a way that I would've never imagined him capable of. Now that I've experienced it, I want more.

Why?

Am I so blinded by his looks that I can't think beyond my attraction to him? Or did he tattoo himself on a piece of me that I shared unwillingly? Vulnerability is hard to deal with, let alone exposing it to another.

Hayden shared his with me as well.

In my gut, I know it's not a normal occurrence for him to talk about his mother. Especially not when she has issues with drugs. And addiction. He didn't say it specifically, but there was a lot he didn't say out loud that I still picked up on.

Even so, he reverted to a boy caring for his mother at the onset of my panic attack. My heart expands in my chest, making it ache on his behalf. Hayden might be confident and strong-willed, but at the end of the day, he's a human, with human experiences and emotions.

Like pain.

And need.

"Don't stop," he whispers. "I need more."

I grip the edge of the counter to steady myself as Hayden's command replays itself in my mind, the desperation behind his words warming me all over. Even in places it shouldn't.

The door opens, and I jerk up my head, pasting a smile on my face to hide the inappropriate thoughts in my mind. A delivery guy strides up to me with a package in his hands. It's a small white box, no more than twelve inches in length, without any logos to give me an idea of what's inside.

"Calista Green?"

I frown. "That's me, but I didn't order anything."

The guy shrugs his massive shoulders, no doubt acquired by his physically demanding job. "This has your name on it, so it's yours. Please, sign here."

Harper sidles up to me, her greedy fingers snatching up the package. "Discreet packaging...What could this be?" She shakes it and grins at me. "Please tell me it's a dildo."

Both the delivery guy and I swing our gazes to her. He grins at her and Harper waggles her brows at him. Meanwhile, I close my eyes and take a deep breath to get my blush under control.

"Here you go," I say, returning his pen to him. "Thank you."

Harper waves. "Have a good day, handsome."

The guy dips his head in our direction. "See you next time."

Before the man passes through the door frame, Harper is tearing into the package like a child on Christmas morning. Or a demon opening Pandora's box.

"A cell phone!" She sets down the now-opened package and turns to face me. "Damn, that was fast."

I shake my head, confusion etching itself into my

features. "But I didn't order one." It only takes me a moment for realization to dawn. "Hayden."

"He did this?"

"Yes. He said that he..."

Harper waves her hand in front of my face. "What did he say?"

"I don't know how to say this without it sounding weird."

"Oh, honey, I live for weird."

Regardless of whatever situation I find myself in, my friend never fails to make me feel better. My love for her swells until I feel like it'll pour out of me. I throw my arms around her in an uncharacteristic show of affection. She's quick to return my hug.

"Thank you," I say.

"For what?"

"Everything. Not judging me. Supporting me. Being an amazing friend."

We separate, and she smiles at me. "Anytime, babe. I know you'd do the same for me." Harper makes a circling motion with her hand. "Now give me the weirdness."

I take a fortifying breath and dive in. "When I spoke to Hayden yesterday, he said that he wanted my phone number so that I would be accessible to him at all times because he doesn't like to be kept waiting. When I told him that I didn't have a phone, he said it would be rectified immediately."

I point at the box. "He followed through."

"Why is that weird?"

"He said I had to 'answer his calls and promptly respond to his texts upon receiving them,'" I say, making air quotes while rolling my eyes. "It feels like he's my older brother and I'm his kid sister. Like I'm someone he resents for having to look after."

Harper's brows rise, nearly disappearing into her hairline. "Honey, if the way that man looks at you is brotherly, then he's seriously into incest because there's nothing about the way he watches you that says 'blood relation.'"

My mouth falls open, and I stand there, blinking over and over.

"You heard me," she says. My friend lifts her hands to make air quotes, her stance mocking. "That man wants to show you some 'brotherly love' like no one's business."

I snatch up the cell phone as an excuse to avoid looking at her. As soon as it's powered on, the device chimes, indicating a text. I quickly go through the settings, finding that everything has already been programmed.

Including Hayden Bennett's number in the contacts.

> Hayden: As soon as you get this, text me back so I know you received the phone and everything is in working order.

My fingers immediately begin typing out a text, as if Hayden's voice is in my ear and he's standing right next to me. I hate how my body obeys him before my mind has had a chance to think it over.

> Calista: I did. Thank you for the phone.

> Hayden: You're welcome. Keep it on you at all times and always answer me.

> Calista: 🙄

When he doesn't immediately respond, I sigh. Did I really think the brief tenderness I experienced from him would continue? I suppose I did since disappointment is washing over me. But I was wrong. If anything, he's more standoffish. It pricks my temper, and heat blooms on my cheeks.

> Calista: The emoji was a joke.

> Hayden: When you say something funny, I'll be sure to laugh.

> Calista: I doubt you know how.

> Hayden: Are you done?

I glare at the phone. Ending this conversation is the only sensible thing to do. It's either that or show my ass by antagonizing him some more, which would amount to nothing. However tempting.

> Calista: I'll make sure to bring the phone with me to work.

> Hayden: Keep it on your person and be sure to answer me.

I frown at his brusque manner. No matter how grateful I am that Hayden paid for this phone and gave me money, it still came at a cost. One I wish I didn't have to pay.

> Calista: K.

> Hayden: That type of response is beneath your intelligence, Miss Green.

> Calista: 😊

> Hayden: Is this a pathetic attempt to flirt with me, or are you deliberately provoking me?

I grit my teeth and turn the phone off before I throw the damn thing across the room. After shoving the device in my pocket, I blow out a breath, determined to keep my thoughts away from the infuriating man.

Someone walks up to the counter, and I lift my head, a greeting forming on my lips. "Welcome to the..."

The words die on my tongue, their flavor something bitter and rancid as my brain registers the person on the other side of the counter. The last person I ever expected to see.

CHAPTER 22

C alista

My ex-fiancé.

At my job.

Where I'm dressed in torn jeans and an overly worn t-shirt with my hair in a ponytail. It's so far removed from the put-together, posh appearance I'm used to presenting. Without my pearl necklace, I'm even more removed from my old self, but I can't hide behind my casual attire.

Adam will definitely recognize me.

His charcoal overcoat and olive-colored scarf are achingly familiar. Not because I miss him, but his presence reminds me of another lifetime, the one before my family fell from grace in so many ways. Looking at my ex threatens to unlock a chest of memories filled with tender moments, companionable silences, and laughter.

Not just with him, but with my father.

My breath catches in my throat, and I force myself to

exhale, to release the remnants of my past. There's nothing to be gained from lamenting over what I've lost. Even if my heart still aches.

Adam's gaze locks on me, and surprise registers on his handsome face, but it's quickly hidden by a mask of indifference. The chill of his response slices into me, cutting me open and allowing my insecurities to bleed from me. They cover me now, and tears prick my eyes. I fist my hand, stabbing my palm with my nails to keep from falling apart.

I won't give him the satisfaction.

"Hello, Calista," Adam says. His voice is just as I remember it, smooth and compelling, instantly able to put someone at ease. Too bad I'm desensitized to that. And to *him*. "It's been a long time."

"Yes, it has."

He nods, his brown eyes clear, instead of clouded with warmth. Or regret. I'll never understand how I thought I loved him, how I gazed into those eyes with affection and thoughts of a future together. Not when the man I was supposed to marry dumped me because of my father's indictment.

Adam didn't even wait for the final verdict.

"How are you?" he asks.

I want to spew my troubles at him, to lay them at his feet, but I refrain. I don't want him to know the part he played in my struggle to survive. The one I battle daily.

"I'm fine. What can I get you?"

"A chai latte."

I grab a cup and the permanent marker and write his order on there. After walking over and handing it to Harper, who's eyeing me like a hawk, I return to the register and give Adam his total. He pulls out a hundred-dollar bill.

"Keep the change."

Anger, hot and burning, swells in my chest and heats my face. I glare at him and count his change back to him, slapping the bills on the counter. As well as the coins.

"I don't need your pity."

Harper comes to stand beside me and juts her chin at Adam. "Who's this idiot?"

Between my fury and my nerves zipping along my skin, I nearly burst out laughing at her crass behavior. I should have expected it, but somehow my friend always surprises me. And I love her for it.

"Harper, meet Adam Thompson, my ex-fiancé. Adam, this is Harper, my best friend."

She nods once and picks up the Sharpie to scribble something on his cup. Then she gives him a saccharine smile. "Here's your order. I hope you get run over by a bus on your way out."

My eyes widen, enabling me to clearly see the strikethrough on Adam's name, as well as the new word added. *Dickhead.*

I burst out laughing. The insult registers, and Adam glares at Harper, his facade cracking enough for us to see his irritation. She makes a kissing noise at him and gives him the finger, which only has me laughing harder. When tears spring to my eyes, they're not from sadness, which is a relief.

My ex is quick to save face. He snatches up his money and tosses his coffee in the trash on his way out. My amusement continues even though I think that's a wise decision. I wouldn't put it past Harper to have some laxatives nearby, reserved for "special customers."

"I can't believe you wanted to marry that asshat," she says.

I wipe the tears from my eyes and nod. "It's true. But in my defense, I didn't know that he was a shallow jerk."

"I forgive you."

"Thank you." I grab her hand and squeeze it gently. "I feel like I should hug you again."

She winks at me. "Only one hug per shift. I will say, today has been crazy. It's probably good we're going out tonight. You really need it."

I'm not sure I agree, but one thing's for sure: the men I've been attracted to suck. With Adam gone, that just leaves Hayden.

And I'm not certain I'll ever be rid of him.

CHAPTER 23

C alista

I'M IN HELL.

The dance music thrums through the club, each pulsing beat vibrating through my chest. Flashing neon lights illuminate the darkness, just enough to reveal the large open space where people are dancing, their bodies moving in time with the song blasting all around us. A bar stretches along the right wall, and the colorful LED panels behind it enable me to make out the wide array of bottles and glasses.

The air is warm and thick, filled with scents of perfume, cologne, sweat, and alcohol. I fist my hands when my fingers twitch, my brain screaming at me to grab the miniature sanitizer out of my purse. If it wouldn't hurt Harper's feelings, I'd douse myself in it right now.

"Do you want to dance or drink first?" she asks, her voice loud in my ear.

"Whatever you want."

"Drinks!"

She grabs my hand, and I trail behind her, taking in the VIP section at the back of the club to the left of the bar. While the exclusive space doesn't have any physical barriers keeping the rest of the patrons from entering, there are two security guards just outside the entrance. Within the area are plush couches and private tables, and well-dressed individuals sipping their beverages while taking in the scene before them. Or ignoring the rest of us.

"What's your drink of choice?" Harper asks me. She pulls me to her side in front of the bar and throws an arm around my shoulder. Her secure hold makes me feel less vulnerable to the countless eyes that could be watching us.

"Cherry vodka sour," I say.

"Cherry vodka sour for her." She points to me and then herself, shooting a wink at the bartender. The tall blonde man returns the gesture, and Harper's smile widens. "And I'll take an apple martini," she says. "Might as well keep the fruity theme going."

I nod at her in thanks while keeping my eye on the bartender. I watch his every move, every twitch of his fingers, never letting the glass out of my sight. Not even to blink.

Because that's all it takes for someone to drug you.

When he delivers the beverages without any signs of foul play, I relax and take a sip. The alcohol slides into my belly, immediately heating me from the inside. Harper takes a large gulp from hers and grins at me.

"To the dance floor with your sexy ass!"

The flashing lights overhead reveal Harper's features. Her face is alight with excitement, the dramatic smoky look of her makeup emphasizing the shape and color of her green eyes. Her wild red tresses are pinned up in a messy topknot on her head, and her lips are stained red, pairing nicely with the shimmering gold minidress that clings to her body. She's so lovely it's hard to look anywhere except at her.

In contrast to Harper's bright and shiny appearance, my outfit is a simple, form-fitting black halter dress. The plunging neckline was an issue when my friend suggested I wear it, but then she challenged me not to be a pussy. So here I am, wearing something that makes me feel both sexy and exposed.

It's similar to the way I feel whenever I'm around Hayden.

"Come on, beautiful," Harper says, pulling me away from my thoughts about a certain attorney. "Let's see what you've got."

I shake my head with a small laugh. "I'm not very coordinated."

"I'm sure that's a lie. Just do what I do."

Drink in hand, my friend morphs into a goddess right before my eyes. Harper sways to the music as though every beat and every note controls her. Eyes closed and arms raised, she moves with a sensual grace that commands attention, and the people around us watch her with unconcealed interest. She's beautiful to look at.

Some of the men draw near to her, but she simply smiles at them while getting closer to me. "Come on, Calista. Let's do this shit."

I down half the contents in my glass, needing all the liquid courage I can get. Then I let the energy of the crowd and the rhythm of the music take me away. Other than the fact that I promised Harper I'd come, forgetting everything in my life for a few hours of peace is why I'm here.

No murdered father.

No creepy stalker.

No Hayden.

We dance to several songs as one bleeds into the next. My leg muscles throb, and my forehead is damp with sweat due to my exertion, but the happiness streaming through me—thank you, vodka—is something I don't want to end. If this is what it's like to be young and carefree, then I owe Harper my gratitude for persuading me to go beyond my comfort zone. It helps that she continues to turn down male dance partners in favor of staying with me.

"This is amazing," I say to her, shouting to be heard above the music.

She nods. "I know, right? Let's take a break and get another drink."

"Okay."

Harper takes my hand. Once our glasses are full, she leads me to a tiny booth near the VIP section. A man dressed in an expensive-looking shirt and black slacks raises his hand and tilts his drink in our direction. I avert my gaze, knowing he's not trying to get my attention.

"Hottie, nine o'clock," Harper says, leaning close. "He has brown hair and a nice smile, and he won't stop looking at you."

"The one in the VIP section?"

She grins at me. "Ah, so you did notice him. Yes, that one."

"I thought he was looking at you. Not that I'd blame him. You're gorgeous."

"Thank you, but don't deflect. I know you're hung up on Mr. Choke-me-big-daddy Bennett, and I get it. He's possibly the hottest guy I've ever seen. However," she says, drawing out the word, "he hasn't made a move."

She's right.

Even if I was the type of woman who could have sex

without letting my feelings get involved, I can't imagine someone like Hayden mixing business with pleasure. And I'm certainly in the former category after he wired ten thousand dollars to my account. It makes me wonder if he'd be interested in me if I didn't have the answers he's looking for...

"Excuse me?"

Harper and I turn our heads toward the voice and find a waitress standing in front of our table. Her spiky dark hair and black eyeliner draw my gaze and she smiles at me.

"The gentleman over there," she says, pointing to the man we were just discussing, "wants to buy you ladies a drink."

I cover the opening of my glass with my palm. Harper's brows snap together at my reaction and I inwardly cringe. One day I'll explain my behavior to her, but not tonight.

"I'm good."

The waitress slides her gaze to Harper. "And you?"

My friend looks at me, and I stiffen under her scrutiny, but then she grins. "We're good, but please tell him 'thanks.'"

The woman nods. "Have a good night and let me know if you need anything. I'm Kat."

As soon as we're alone, Harper shifts in her seat to face me. "What's going on with you?"

"I don't want to owe anyone or give him the impression that I'm interested."

"But you *are* interested." My friend rolls her eyes, staring at the ceiling briefly. "You need to get your mind off of that lawyer and your ex. Try other flavors. Most men are stupid, but not all of them are idiots. At least, that's what I keep telling myself."

I bite the inside of my cheek, mulling over her words. "I

could give him a shot, but I'm really having a good time with you. This is the best girls' night I've ever had. I don't want to ruin it with some guy who might turn out to be an asshole."

"Fine, but we're not leaving without his number. Okay?"

A sly smile works its way onto my mouth. "I'm not sure Mr. Bennett would appreciate me using the phone he gave me to hook up with some random guy in a club, but who cares? He shouldn't have given it to me if he didn't want me to use it."

"That's right." When Harper raises her drink, I do the same. "To cell phones and booty calls," she says.

I tap my glass to hers and take a long swallow. The vodka hits me again, making my veins feel like they're filled with sugar and mischief. "Do you want to know something?" I ask.

"What?"

"I turned the phone off earlier because I was mad at Hayden for ordering me around like a fucking soldier in his army. But I forgot to turn it back on since Adam came in and threw me for a loop. A big fucking loop-de-loop."

I giggle and Harper grins while shaking her head. "You're feeling pretty good right now. Cursing like a sailor and everything. It's nice to see you enjoy yourself and let loose. I should get you drunk more often."

"I'm not drunk, but I am happy." I give her a big smile, as if I have something to prove. But with Harper I don't. She accepts me as is. "And I think you're the best friend I've ever had."

"Ah, babe, right back at you."

I'm in heaven. This night has turned out better than I imagined when I first walked in. Now, all I want to do is dance some more and forget about Hayden for as long as I can.

"Don't look," Harper says, "but the guy from the VIP is walking this way. And he's bringing his hot friend." When I swing my gaze to the left, my friend hisses at me. "God, you're so obvious! At least get your cell phone out so you can get his number."

"Okay."

I swallow the nerves gathering in my throat and unzip my purse. After powering on the device, I stare at it to keep from looking at the mysterious guy heading in our direction. I still think he's interested in Harper, but holding my phone gives me something to do.

The screen flares to life, illuminating the horror that has to be covering my face.

There are eighteen notifications.

Thirteen unread texts.

Five missed calls.

CHAPTER 24

C alista

I'm back in hell.

Because Hayden is the devil.

I read the messages from him, and my gaze gets wider and wider with each one until I'm sure my eyes are going to fall right out of my head.

> Hayden: I'm going to assume by your lack of response that you're provoking me.

> Hayden: It needs to stop.

> Hayden: Still no confirmation? Tsk. Tsk. Maybe you were flirting with me.

Was I? With the alcohol warming my blood, it's hard to recall my intentions from earlier today, but I can't deny that I wouldn't have minded if Hayden had flirted back. Obviously, that was too much to hope for. Given his high-handed manner, provoking him was my main goal when I turned off the phone.

And boy, did it work.

> Hayden: Either way, our relationship is strictly business and it needs to stay that way.

> Hayden: I want your agreement on this, Miss Green.

missed phone call from Hayden Bennett.

> Hayden: You didn't answer my texts and now my call is going straight to voicemail...

> Hayden: I am not a patient man. Don't test me.

> Hayden: You're definitely testing me.

> Hayden: Trust me when I say you won't like the results.

> Hayden: Callie, are you hurt?

missed phone call from Hayden Bennett.
missed phone call from Hayden Bennett.
missed phone call from Hayden Bennett.

> Hayden: I received confirmation that you are at work, Miss Green.

> Hayden: Now that I know you're safe, my temper is rising.

missed phone call from Hayden Bennett.

> Hayden: Your shift at the coffee shop has ended, so you don't have any excuses for not returning my calls or texts. At this point, an electronic affirmation will not be enough to satisfy me. I'll receive it in person.

My hands start shaking so badly that I almost drop the cell phone. Then I do when another text comes through. The device clatters on the table, and I snatch it up, ignoring Harper's stare drilling into the side of my head.

> Hayden: Enjoying your night out, Miss Green?

> Calista: Yup. TTYL.

"Good evening, ladies."

My head snaps up, and I close my mouth so quickly that my teeth click together. I lock the screen on my phone and shove it into my purse, pasting a smile on my face. The two men from the VIP section standing at our table are more good-looking up close than they were before.

And that's saying something.

The first is rakishly handsome with artfully tousled brown hair and a roguish grin that has my stomach filling with butterflies. His athletic physique is displayed in an open-collared shirt and tailored trousers, the careless grace with which he moves a testament to pursuits, both leisurely and pleasurable. If this was the first time I'd met such a man, I'd be impressed. However, I encountered people like him from the day I could talk.

His companion possesses a polish and refinement that hints at moneyed lineage and education. His golden hair is swept back from an aristocratic brow, and piercing blue eyes survey the room as if searching for a diversion to escape boredom. Broad shoulders fill out an immaculate button-down, paired with trousers that hang just right on a narrowed waist and cling to his muscled thighs. A tennis player for sure.

Again, this type of man is nothing new to me. Especially when visiting a country club, as my father was often doing. With me in tow.

"Hello there," Harper says.

I wave, unable to form coherent words just yet. It's difficult to do so while scanning the place for any sign of a deranged attorney lurking in the shadows. Finding nothing, I shift my attention to the pair staring down at me with unconcealed interest.

"I'm Darren," the blonde says. "And this is Levi."

"I'm Harper and this is Calista," my friend says.

"It's great to finally meet you two." Levi gestures to the VIP section. "We wanted to invite you to join us, but when you refused our gift, I couldn't leave without trying again." He looks at me, his grin widening when a flush works its way onto my cheeks. "Can we join you?"

Harper nods. "Sure!"

Levi takes the empty spot beside me, trapping me between his body and Harper's. I grab my drink and empty the glass, giving myself a moment to gather my composure.

"Do you want another?" Levi asks me, dipping his head in the direction of my empty tumbler. "I'm happy to buy you anything you want."

I clear my throat. "I'm fine, but thank you."

"Are you having a good time?"

"Yes. And you?"

Levi leans closer to me. His cologne fills my senses, and I almost sigh. It's a clean scent with hints of lemon that remind me of my hand sanitizer. Not exactly sexy to a normal girl, but I find cleanliness appealing.

"I'm good now that I'm getting a chance to talk to you," he says.

"Thank you."

Harper takes a swallow of her drink, using it to shoot me a pointed look, equal parts exasperation and encouragement. I don't know how to break it to her that I'm not a sultry femme fatale. If anything, I can barely flirt and not all that well. Obviously.

"So, what do you do for a living?" I ask.

My friend's mouth thins, and she rolls her eyes before turning her attention to Darren. I've been dismissed and left to my own devices. Speaking of which...

I retrieve the buzzing phone from my purse and find a notification on the screen.

> Hayden: This conversation is not over, Miss Green. Who are you with?

Oblivious to my pulse racing and my hands growing sweaty, Levi answers me. "I own a tech company. It's boring really. I want to know about you."

"There's not much to tell," I say. "I'm just normal."

"Your beauty is anything but normal."

"Thank you."

"Do you want to dance, Calista? I saw you dancing earlier, and I have to admit that I couldn't stop watching."

I part my lips to respond, but my cell phone buzzes in my lap. Again. "Shit."

> Hayden: I'm coming to get you.

"Shit." I scan the text again, just to make sure I'm

reading it correctly. Maybe I *am* drunk. "I'm sorry," I say to Levi. "My older brother is very protective. And very annoying. He won't stop texting me until he hears from me. Just give me a second."

"Take your time."

> Calista: First of all, Mr. Bennett, you shouldn't know where I am. And if you do, we need to talk about fucking boundaries. Second, I'm busy, so this conversation can wait until toomorrrow.

> Calista: tomorrow* whoops.

> Hayden: First of all, language. Second, boundaries don't exist between us. Third, stop drinking.

> Calista: *orders another motherfucking drink* 🥂

> Hayden: That better be a glass of motherfucking water. I don't want you throwing up in my car when I take you home.

> Calista: I'm not going anywhere, so leave me alone. Unlike you, there's a man here who's actually interested in me.

> Hayden: If he touches you, what I did last time will seem like a joke in comparison.

> Calista: 🙄 I'm not answering you anymore tonight. Kindly fuck off, Mr. Bennett.

> Hayden: I'm definitely fucking something, Miss Green.

I toss the phone in my purse and turn to look at Levi, praying the arousal streaking through me isn't plain to see.

Verbally sparring with Hayden might be the hottest, most thrilling thing I've ever done. I'm more turned on than I've ever been in my entire life. All from his texts. Freaking ridiculous.

"Did you convince your brother that you're in good hands?" Levi smiles broadly, and the lights above showcase his perfectly straight teeth. "I would hate for him to worry about you."

I huff. "I don't want to talk about my brother. Didn't you mention dancing?"

"Absolutely."

Levi takes my hand and leads me from the booth and onto the dance floor. Harper and Darren are quick to follow, but I immediately forget about my friend when Levi takes my hips and pulls me flush to him. His muscled chest and rock hard thighs press against my spine and legs, making me all too aware of how sexual dancing can be.

I sway to the music and Levi is there, his breath skimming my neck and his fingers gripping me tight. Only, in my mind it's Hayden. My body's reaction to that imagery is strong. My panties, already wet from our texting, become drenched at the idea of him holding me like this, with his cock brushing my ass and his lips trailing down the side of my neck.

"You're so fucking hot," Levi says in my ear.

I turn to look at him over my shoulder, still moving in time with the thumping bass. "Thank you."

He grinds into me, his fingers digging into my dress to keep me close. To control me. I let him, wanting to be relieved of the burden that comes with choice. Since my new life began, I've done nothing except make hard decisions, but tonight I'm letting someone else lead me. There's a freedom in this that I never appreciated until now.

However fleeting and insignificant, I'm going to soak it in.

Levi spins me to face him, and I nearly stumble. He holds me securely, smiling down at me while guiding my arms around his neck. Then his chest is pressed to mine, and his cock is nestled between my thighs.

Dancing is definitely sexual.

Not that I mind. It's nice to be seen and appreciated as a woman. That's something I wish Hayden would do.

"Can I kiss you, Calista?" Levi asks, his breath skimming my mouth.

I stare up at him, looking into his brown eyes while wishing they were blue. Has Hayden ruined me for other men? I don't have the answer to that, but on the off chance it could be true, I need to get over him. And remove this strange hold he has on me.

When I nod, giving Levi my permission, I'm doing it without thinking of Hayden.

Only for him to appear just behind Levi as he lowers his head to kiss me.

Hayden's gaze meets mine, the blue within no longer ice. His eyes are a pair of blue flames, the hottest temperature, burning with an unholy wrath that feels like a wave of heat sweeping over my flushed skin. It sears me, rendering me ash that's helpless against any type of force.

Right now, that's Hayden.

He slaps a hand on Levi's shoulder and yanks him away from me. My mouth drops open, and my arms fall to my sides as I watch Hayden confront Levi like an enraged husband. Even though he's never even kissed me—and certainly never asked to.

Harper is by my side in an instant. She's obviously in full control of her faculties while I continue to absorb the violent storm in front of me: Hayden, a tempest hell-bent on destroying anything in his path.

Does that include me?

"What's going on?" she asks.

I don't have the slightest idea. But even if I did, I can't look away from the scene unfolding on the dance floor. Several people have backed up, creating an open space for Hayden and Levi. Smart move.

"What the fuck, man?" Levi shouts.

Hayden doesn't answer him. No, he looks directly at me. "Would you like to explain it to him, Miss Green?"

His voice, calm and even, is easily heard above the loud music. Or maybe that's just the effect he has on me. I shake my head. Emphatically.

"Is this the brother you were talking about?" Levi asks me. "I can see why you think he's an overbearing prick."

Hayden quirks a brow while looking at me and I flinch. "Brother?" he repeats. The attorney clicks his tongue in admonishment. "Miss Green, I thought you were above lying." Then he turns to Levi. "If I'm her brother, then the things I want to do to her are beyond incestuous."

"I told you!" Harper hisses in my ear, clutching my arm.

When Hayden reaches for his right cuff link, both Harper and I stiffen.

"Oh, fuck," she says.

I repeat the sentiment under my breath. The last time Hayden acted this way, he was more than ready to beat the shit out of someone for harassing me. Does it matter that I encouraged Levi in this situation? If the fury etched into Hayden's features is any indication, then he doesn't give a damn.

"I warned you," he says to me.

If he touches you, what I did last time will seem like a joke in comparison.

The warning rings loud and clear like a gong being struck, reverberating in my head. My fear, on behalf of Levi and myself, propels me forward. I rip my arm from Harper's grasp and race to stand in front of Hayden, positioning myself between him and Levi.

"Please," I say, holding out my hands. "Don't do this."

Hayden drops the serpent-shaped cuff link in my upturned palm. The ruby eye of the snake winks at me as the overhead lights shine on it. I fist my hand around the piece of metal and step closer to the man in front of me.

The one ready to defend me once again.

Whether or not I want him to.

"You're so beautiful when you beg," Hayden says. He reaches for the other cuff link, and I swallow the ball of nerves gathered in my throat. "As much as I enjoy witnessing that, I need you to understand that I mean what I say."

He hands me the other cuff link and begins to roll up his sleeve. Panic like I've never known zips along my arms and legs like an electrical current, giving me a jolt. With one hand gripping his jewelry, I use the other to grab his dress shirt. My fingers curl around the expensive material, and I get on my tiptoes, still not close to his height, even with heels on.

Then I kiss him.

CHAPTER 25

H ayden

EARLIER THAT DAY...

CALISTA GREEN HAS GOTTEN THROUGH.

Every barrier.

Every strategically placed defense.

Every part of me that I've kept hidden.

She's seen me. Open and emotionally vulnerable, a place of weakness I loathe, yet she stayed. Not ridiculing me, or worse, pitying me. Instead, she showed compassion.

Something I lack.

Something I want more of.

Only from her.

Although she is the most beautiful woman I've ever met, Calista's nurturing, caring side is what I find most attractive. It's what has drawn me to her since the beginning even though I've tried again and again to dismiss her. Despite my efforts, I yearn for what she gives with a hunger that ravages me daily.

Hourly.

Every fucking second.

It's what propelled me to comfort her in this office. During work hours, no less. And she's the first.

I thought her panic attack triggered my automatic response, the one rooted in me due to my past. Except it wasn't. I *wanted* to help her.

As perplexed as I was by my behavior, the pleasure I received from it confounded me even more. There was no disgust. Not only that, but I enjoyed holding and consoling Calista.

It soothed me in a way I've never felt.

And I never would've stopped if she hadn't left.

I've become addicted to her. I know this and won't deny it any longer. But what I can't come to terms with is my need for her. How strong it is.

How all-encompassing.

She has obliterated my control. Like a vortex, she pulls me to her, leaving behind my goals and desires—even my need for justice—until nothing exists except her.

I haven't killed anyone since the day she buried her father.

Well, except Jim. But that was for Calista, not me.

Rules bring about law and order, a peace to chaos, and a punishment to crime. The justice system isn't always just, which is why I don't feel the need to operate within it. My motivations are my own.

Just like my code of ethics. These maintain my sanity, provide stability, and give me purpose. They're also a warning, an echo of my past. The events of my childhood sliced into me like a knife, cutting away weakness with every stabbing of the blade and every drop of blood spilled.

Even so, my need to right the wrongs of society doesn't drive me, doesn't ignite me the way Calista does with a mere glance. And when she smiles?

Fuck. Me.

I would do anything to have her look at me that way.

ANYTHING.

I drop my head and massage my temples, squeezing the hell out of my skull as if that'll relieve my mind from these tumultuous thoughts.

It doesn't help. Nothing does.

Except being with her.

Even knowing this, I want to push Calista away. I have many secrets, but I revealed the one that means the most. The one that weighs heaviest on me.

My mother, the drug addict.

My reason for getting justice.

My reason for killing.

I reach into my desk drawer and retrieve the tiny object inside, setting it in front of me. It's round and white, an ordinary medicine tablet that's supposed to treat headaches and minor aches and pains. Except it's a depressant with an unknown compound that results in behavior similar to a "date-rape" drug.

The symbol on it is a starburst, which could've been chosen to represent euphoria or instant relief. But to me, it's an explosion. Like a bomb, this little pill took my mother's life.

And the party responsible hasn't been found.

Every year, finding the manufacturer of this drug becomes more hopeless. Regardless, I won't give up because my mother deserves to be avenged. Just like Calista.

Someone fucked with her, and I won't stop hunting them.

How can I fully immerse myself in my obsession with her and make her mine while not knowing what memories torment her? I suppose I could fuck Calista's secrets out of her, but that doesn't sit well with me. I prefer to execute a well-thought-out strategy as opposed to using brute force. In my experience, manipulating people to give me what I want goes further than violence.

Although with Calista in my life, I'm more volatile than ever.

Just another way she's ruined me.

A quick glance at the clock on my office wall has antici- pation running through me. After putting away the pill, I retrieve my phone from my pocket and send her a message before placing it on my desk, waiting for Calista to text me back. The cell phone I bought her should've arrived by now.

Will she follow my instructions?

> **Hayden:** As soon as you get this, text me back so I know you received the phone and everything is in working order.

My phone dings, and I snatch it up, a smile working its way onto my face when I see Calista's name appear on the screen. Such a good girl.

> **Calista:** I did. Thank you for the phone.

> **Hayden:** You're welcome. Keep it on you at all times and always answer me.

I've always prided myself in how effectively I communi- cate. I explain everything in detail so that any message I send can't be misconstrued. No, I make sure people understand exactly what I'm saying, so I can get exactly what I want.

> Calista: 🥺

My brows gather at her response as I try to make sense of it. Is this her way of telling me I'm being overbearing? Or is she flirting with me? I sit there, mulling over this for several minutes, still unable to come up with an answer.

I know for certain that Calista's attracted to me. Or else she wouldn't have come while saying my name. However, I want to know what happened on June 24th. Every fucking detail. The fact that this unknown sits between me and her pisses me off.

She will surrender to me.

In all ways and in all things.

Or I will control her through her secrets. Once I learn them.

> Calista: The emoji was a joke.

> Hayden: When you say something funny, I'll be sure to laugh.

> Calista: I doubt you know how.

She's not wrong. I barely smile, let alone laugh. Although I did when I killed her father. I doubt she'd appreciate that.

The joke's on me. He was innocent.

My mood immediately plummets, despite conversing with Calista.

> Hayden: Are you done?

Calista: I'll make sure to bring the phone with me to work.

Hayden: Keep it on your person and be sure to answer me.

Calista: K.

Hayden: That type of response is beneath your intelligence, Miss Green.

Calista:

If she were here with me, I'd redden her ass for that. Even so, I find myself reaching into my pocket as arousal replaces my anger. A soft material brushes my fingers, and I bring the pink underwear to my nose, inhaling. My cock gets hard.

It always does when she challenges me.

Hayden: Is this a pathetic attempt to flirt with me, or are you deliberately provoking me?

Hayden: I'm going to assume by your lack of response that you're provoking me.

I unzip my pants and free my cock, gripping it hard enough to force a grunt from my lips. The soft material of her underwear is still nestled in my palm, and I bring it up just enough to stroke my length with it.

I close my eyes and imagine her here with me, standing before me and blushing with embarrassment. I can almost feel the warmth of her skin under my hands as I spank her ass red, the same shade as her face. She'd squirm against me, pushing back against me despite her shyness at being exposed in such a way.

Shifting slightly in my chair, I can't help but groan softly into the quiet room as I increase the pace of sliding her underwear up and down my cock. I feel them wrapping around me like the soft palm of her hand, pressing into my skin with each stroke. Her delicate scent still clings to the fabric, and I can almost taste her sweetness on my tongue.

My breathing grows more ragged, and it's not long before I'm jerking on my cock more forcefully, faster and harder than ever before, the rough movements causing my biceps to ache. Fantasizing about her presence intensifies the sensations to an unbearable level.

Grunting her name, I'm undone.

I come hard against her underwear, imagining the relief that'd come from being inside her body. Inside her pretty pussy, which haunts me. The warmth of her skin against mine, my hips pushing against hers as I thrust into her. Again and again. I can almost hear her breathy moans in my ear as I collapse in the chair, fully exhausted.

Her underwear stained with my cum—like I want her skin to be—goes back into my pocket where they belong for now. Until the next time, at least.

Now I owe her another pearl...

This is what she does to me. I forget myself and everything else except her. Calista is the one thing that makes me vulnerable.

And I hate it.

I'd hate her too if I didn't want her so much.

CHAPTER 26

Calista
The present...

I DON'T KNOW WHAT POSSESSED ME TO KISS HAYDEN.

Maybe I thought to distract him. Maybe it's something I've wanted to do since the day I met him. Either way, Hayden Bennett is mine for this brief moment.

I wish it could be longer.

He goes perfectly still, the length of his body like granite against mine, cold and hard. However, his lips are warm and soft. I let instinct take over and continue sweeping my mouth over his, light and coaxing. Silently begging him to kiss me back. Even going as far as teasing him with little flicks of my tongue along the seam of his lips.

For a breathless moment, he remains motionless. Then a low groan rumbles at the back of his throat, and his arms encircle me, crushing me against his chest. He immediately takes control of the kiss.

And me.

His mouth ravages mine, our lips and tongues colliding in a battle for dominance. He's already won, but this is a show of strength. And of need. Every breath, every touch heightens the denied and reckless longing I've been fighting.

He deepens the kiss, and his fingers dig into my skin, branding me inch by inch. Second by second. His hands trace my curves through my dress before finding bare skin along my back, leaving a scorching path that continues down the backs of my thighs.

I'm lost in him.

Sensation bombards me from all over. My skin sighs with pleasure wherever he caresses me, and the places he doesn't cry out for him. A moan builds in my throat, half encouragement, half desperation. I want more.

I want *all* of him.

The music pounds, the resounding beat an echo of my heart as it pulses wildly. I slide my fingers into Hayden's hair, gripping the silky strands and anchoring myself to him before I lose myself completely. Arching into his hold, I'm thrilled by the feel of his hard body pressing mine, the length of his cock pulsing against my belly.

I release the moan gathered on my tongue, offering it to him, telling him without words how much I need him; in ways I can't describe and certainly don't understand. He absorbs the sound, answering with a low growl that only heightens my arousal to an unhealthy level.

He must sense the dangerous territory we're in because he breaks the kiss. My hands fall to his shoulders, and I cling to him, not only dazed, but unwilling to let go just yet. Breathless and disheveled, our gazes collide, mine bright with passion and his dark with lust. I stare up at him, still burning wherever he touched me, unable to put out the fires traveling along my skin, heating me to the point of combustion.

At that moment, an eternity passes as desire continues to rush through our veins. Then sanity returns, and Hayden's gaze shutters, becoming glacial once more. If not for his lips reddened by our kiss and his hair sticking up in places from me gripping the strands, I'd never know this man just fucked me with his mouth.

"You're full of surprises," he says, his voice full of awe. And something else I can't identify. Something that makes my heart stutter in my chest.

Before I can respond, Levi interjects. "He's definitely not your brother."

The sound of his voice yanks me fully into reality. I begin to turn to look at him, only for Hayden to grip me so forcefully that I can't do anything except twist my head. The other man glares at me and I inwardly wince.

"I'm sorry," I whisper.

"Save your apologies for me, Miss Green," Hayden says. "I've already made it clear that I don't share." When I swing back to look at him, his gaze is locked on Levi. "She's mine."

"Yeah, whatever."

I stiffen at Levi's retort because Hayden's eyes narrow to little more than slits. "Hey." I grab a fistful of Hayden's shirt and pull on it until his focus shifts to me. "You said you were going to take me home. Let's go."

Hayden flicks his gaze from me to Levi and back, with a muscle throbbing along his jaw. I reach up and run my fingertips over the area, hoping that a simple touch will soothe the beast in front of me. The one holding me tenderly. Possessively.

"Please, Hayden."

My plea is what causes the change in his demeanor. If I

thought I knew the power of words, the power of petition behind them is stronger.

"We're leaving," he says.

I turn to locate Harper, finding her staring at us with unabashed delight and amusement. "I need to make sure my friend is okay first."

"She's the reason you're in this predicament," he says, his tone sharp.

"I don't care." I hand him the cuff link, my gaze stern. "I won't leave without knowing she's all right."

Hayden blows out a breath. Then his hands fall away from me, but he secures an arm around my waist, hauling me to his side. "Be quick."

Without any hope of getting free from his hold, I motion Harper over. Leaving Darren behind, she walks up to us, her gaze searching Hayden's.

"Bennett," she greets.

He dips his head in acknowledgment. "Flynn."

"How'd you know my last name?" She rolls her eyes. "Never mind. What are your intentions with Calista? I want to know *before* you kidnap her."

I massage the spot between my eyebrows. "Harper..."

"What?" she asks, her lips pursed. "Do you think I'm going to just let you leave with him and not know what he's up to?"

"You didn't seem to have this issue when she was with someone other than me," Hayden says.

"That's only because Levi and Calista hadn't gotten to the mouth-fucking yet. If they had—"

"He'd be dead," Hayden says flatly.

"Okay, that's enough." I give my friend a smile that starts to falter under Hayden's stare. "I really appreciate you looking after me," I tell her. When he scoffs, I shoot him a dirty look. "Everything's fine, and I'm choosing to leave with him, but I don't want you to be alone."

Harper's brows gather. "Me? I'm fine. It's you that should be worried...well, about *you*." Her gaze briefly darts to Hayden. "You don't have to go with him if you don't want to. We can leave right now."

Darren, still standing fairly close to her, frowns, but she waves a hand in dismissal. "It's always 'girl-bros before man-hoes.' Sorry, dude."

Like Levi, Darren slinks off into the crowd. The people in the club haven't dared to venture closer, but they have gone back to dancing. It helps dispel some of the tension now that the other men have left. It's almost back to being a girls' night out.

As much as it can with Hayden filling the space with his brooding energy.

"If you hurt her," Harper says, poking his chest, "I'll kill you."

He gives her a curt nod. "Understood."

"Harper, don't say things you don't mean," I say, my gaze darting back and forth to confirm no one overheard her.

"She meant it." When I blink up at Hayden, he stares back, certainty etched into his features. "I've seen the eyes of a killer, and she is very serious."

Harper grins maniacally. "Yes, I do. Remember that, Bennett."

HAYDEN GUIDES ME THROUGH THE CLUB WITH HIS HAND ON MY hip, keeping me flush to his body the entire time. The further we get, the more the crowd becomes scarce, until we're outside and completely alone. My nervousness builds with every step I take, like a snowball that eventually becomes an avalanche.

Except I'll be the one buried alive because of Hayden.

Maybe that's why I set my foot down at a wrong angle. The heel of my shoe snaps off, throwing me off-balance. I don't have time to cry out for help before I'm quickly falling to the ground. Hayden's arm tightens around my waist and he keeps me upright by crushing me to his side while using his free hand to grab my arm.

"Are you all right?"

I nod, still breathless from my near accident. "I think so. My heel broke." I laugh, but it's hollow and mocking. "Of course it would break today of all days."

"Why is that?"

"My ex-fiancé bought me these shoes and I saw him today. It's the universe trying to tell me something."

Hayden's mouth thins. "Take them off."

Before I can offer a retort, he snatches me up into his arms, holding me tight. I grip his shirt, the sudden movement making my heart race. Though, not more than the man holding me.

I stare up at him, stunned to find myself in his embrace. His eyes blaze into mine, intense and searching. For a moment, the sounds of the city around us fade away, my entire world wrapped up in the man dominating my senses.

He carries me effortlessly across the sidewalk and stops in front of a trash can. "Take them off and throw them away."

"I'm sure they can be repaired." When he shakes his head, I bite my bottom lip. "They're the only pair I own. I can't just get rid of them."

"I'll replace them ten times over. Throw those shoes away before I lose what little patience I have left. If I would've known another man bought them for you, I would've burned them long before now."

I stretch my arm to awkwardly reach for my shoe, followed by the other, and toss them in the trash. As soon as it's done, some of the tension lining Hayden's body dissipates. Not enough for me to completely relax, but I'll take anything I can get. It's hard for me to anticipate the right moves with him.

Especially when everything I do seems to piss him off.

Except the kiss.

That might be the one thing he hasn't gotten mad about. Which makes me wonder why he's always showing up when all I do is frustrate him. The alcohol in my system encourages me to give voice to the question, but my heart begs me to wait. What if the answer crushes me? I can't hear his response yet.

Not when he's cradling me to his chest like I'm precious to him.

CHAPTER 27

C alista

THE SPORTS CAR IS JUST LIKE I REMEMBER IT, LUXURIOUS AND
sleek.

I really hope I don't puke.

Hayden settles me in the passenger's seat and secures
my seat belt while I watch him, not bothering to conceal the
fact. I've given up trying to hide my attraction to him. If he
doesn't know I want him after that kiss, then nothing I do
will get the message across.

He walks to the other side and fills the driver's seat with
his body, and the interior of the vehicle with dark energy. It
washes over me, shrinking the space around us until all I
can see and feel is him.

Hayden turns the car on and grips the steering wheel,
then freezes. Except for his eyes; they find me.

"Why did you kiss me?" he asks. His voice is quiet but

demanding. However, his need for my response is loud. "I want the truth, Callie."

"Because I wanted to."

His gaze narrows infinitesimally. "Are you sure it wasn't to save that man's life?"

"Partially, but that wasn't my main motivation. If anything, he was an excuse." I bow my head and fiddle with my purse, unable to meet his eyes. They've always seen through me, forcing my secrets to the surface where they're visible. But I want to know his, what lurks behind those blue depths. "Why did you kiss me back?"

"Because I wanted to."

My lips twitch with repressed exasperation. "You can't use my answer."

"Why not if it's the truth?"

My skin breaks into a flush at hearing that, but I'm also relieved. For a long time, I thought I'd fantasized about a man who wasn't attracted to me. Now I know better. He kissed me like he wanted to fuck me right on the dance floor.

I might've let him.

"Speaking of the truth...why were you here, Hayden?"

His gaze drills into mine, making me squirm under the intense perusal. "I think the real question is: Why were you here? To provoke me?"

I sigh, the noise full of frustration. "This might come as a shock, but not everything in my life is about you."

"I wish I could say the same." He closes his eyes briefly and lets his head fall back against the headrest. "You have no idea how much."

I part my lips to ask him to explain that cryptic remark, but my tender heart revolts out of fear. What if he's toying with me? I'd bet all of the money in my bank account—

which is larger thanks to Hayden—that he's never gone without a woman's company, if desired. I'd also wager he's never been in a serious relationship. Not just because Harper made the comment, but due to the fact that this man is unattainable.

Because he chooses to be this way.

I wouldn't go so far as to say I've caught him, but for some reason I've snared his attention. Even now when he opens his eyes and looks at me, I know he's mine. The only problem is I'm not sure for how long...

A night?

A week?

How long does it take to break someone's heart?

I've lost my former life, my fiancé, and my father. I'm not strong enough to be with Hayden, only to lose him when he decides he's through with me. I don't know much about men, but I'm positive that he can't give me the commitment I'd eventually want.

He pulls the car onto the street, and our silence accompanies us through the city. I gaze out the window, taking in the beauty of my surroundings while continuously drawn to the beauty of the man beside me. The one time I sneak a glance at Hayden, his eyes are already on me.

"This isn't the way to my apartment," I say. "Where are you taking me?"

"Home."

"*Your* home?" I clarify.

He nods, eyes locked on the road ahead. This time, when I turn to stare out of the window, it's with my head pounding. He's taking me to his residence, the place he lets his guard down, even if it's only in sleep. After getting a glimpse of this vulnerability in his office when he spoke of his childhood, I want to see that part of him again. It makes him feel human to me, instead of this gigantic imposing force that could destroy me at any moment.

The threat of destruction that constantly surrounds Hayden is the very reason I need to stay away from him.

"I appreciate the fact that you want to look out for me," I say, still staring out of the window. "But you can't interfere in my life anymore."

He scoffs. "You have no idea what type of danger you're in."

I swing my gaze to him, giving him a pointed look. "I think I do."

"No, you don't."

"Then tell me."

Tell me the reasons why I should run from you, the reasons I should hide my heart.

"I want to possess more than your secrets, Callie. I want to possess *you*."

My lips part on a gasp while my heart ricochets within my rib cage, making my chest ache. "What does that even mean? You can't just own someone."

"I beg to differ."

I stiffen in the seat as my brain floods my body with adrenaline and the need to escape. Hayden may not hurt me physically, but he's more than capable of shredding my sanity. I haven't survived everything in my life only to fall apart now.

My pulse thrums underneath my skin so loudly I worry he'll hear it.

Run.

Run.

RUN.

I bite down on the inside of my cheek until blood spills across my tongue. The coppery tang invigorates me, reminds me that I'm alive and more than ready to preserve that life. I'm not ready to embrace my stalker, but at least whoever that is hasn't expressed their desire to own me.

Unlike the man beside me.

The minute the streetlight turns red and the vehicle comes to a stop, I unbuckle my seat belt and throw open the door. My fear catapults me out of the car, and I race down the busy sidewalk with Hayden's voice ringing in my ears. The sound of him calling my name dissipates, but my fear intensifies with every step I take.

My feet slap against the pavement, instantly covered in grime and filth. I don't let myself think about that or what Hayden will do if he catches me. Maybe it's a matter of *when* he catches me, but that only makes me run faster.

"I will always *chase you."*

His words from before are an unsettling cadence in my mind, pounding like a drum. I can't hear anything except his voice in my head and everywhere I turn I see his face covering those of random people. I shake my head and the visions of him clear, giving me a brief moment of lucidity. With my lungs burning, I turn down an empty street and conceal myself in the shadows.

The brick wall claws at the skin of my back and the soles of my feet throb as I suck in oxygen, willing my heart rate to slow down. It's futile when thoughts of Hayden envelop me. His insane declaration echoes in my mind.

Why does he want to possess me?

A chill wracks my body, and I tremble, causing the abrasive wall to dig into my back. Is his idea of ownership completely centered around sex? Does he think to own my body and use it for his pleasure?

My body quakes again, but this time it's with arousal. The memory of Hayden's kisses sweeps through me, and I wrap my arms around my middle as if to fend off the effects of it. I can't let him kiss me, let alone touch me. It would only take one time, one moment of being completely under his control, and I'd never be free of him.

The sound of squealing tires nearby has me glancing over my shoulder in panic. My breath gets caught in my throat as I catch a glimpse of a black sports vehicle that could be Hayden's.

"No," I whisper, my denial as feeble as my voice.

I force myself into motion, letting my apprehension propel me forward. I run until I'm close to passing out and round the corner at the end of the block, seeking another alleyway to hide in. After having witnessed Hayden in court, I know he's relentless when in pursuit. My chances of escaping his clutches are minuscule now that he's revealed his intent to have me.

But if he wants to possess me, he'll have to catch me first.

I may not be able to escape his obsession, but I'm damn sure going to try. I won't make this easy for him.

My strength begins to flag, and my inability to draw breath forces me to stop. I lean heavily against the wall of a pawn shop, the store closed and the area deserted. I'm not familiar with this part of the city, but once I get enough oxygen into my body, I'll make my way home.

I briefly close my eyes and focus on pulling air into my lungs, again and again. My heart rate still pulses wildly, but not as erratically as before, and soon my breathing evens out. I push away from the building and take a step forward, only to immediately halt.

Hayden stands at the mouth of the alleyway, his gaze dark and sinister.

CHAPTER 28

C alista

THERE'S NO ESCAPE FOR ME NOW.

The idea of freedom from this man is an illusion.

I can only watch as he leans against the wall with his arms crossed, his lips twisted in anger.

"What did I tell you, Miss Green?"

I wince at the name, the one he only uses when he's upset with me. "I'm not playing this game with you, Hayden. Leave me alone."

"Did you really think I wouldn't come after you?"

"The thought crossed my mind," I deadpan.

He lifts a brow. "I can see the alcohol is still running through your system."

"I'm pretty sure your statement to possess me sobered me up really fucking fast."

"Language, Miss Green."

"Fuck you, Mr. Bennett."

Regret fills me, and I wilt under his glare. Maybe I *am* still drunk. If so, it's not doing me any favors.

Hayden pushes away from the wall and slowly stalks toward me, closing the distance between us with measured and purposeful steps. His gaze holds mine captive, his blue eyes bright with anticipation.

What is he going to do to me?

I press my back into the wall as if I can disappear within it, my heart beating so fast that I worry I might be having a heart attack. He reaches out to cage me in, planting a hand on either side of my head before leaning in.

"You're only delaying the inevitable," he says, his voice a low rumble.

My chest heaves as my breathing becomes jagged, due to his nearness affecting me so deeply. "I have to try."

The side of his mouth lifts in a smirk. "I admire your spirit, but you want this as much as I do. Your body knows it, even if your mind refuses to accept it." He leans in closer, his breath fanning across my lips. "You belong to me, Callie. You have since the first time I saw you. I knew it then, and I'm telling you now, you're mine."

I shake my head. Or maybe that happens because I'm trembling so violently that it causes my head to move. Either way, Hayden's eyes widen, glittering with emotion that causes my thighs to clench.

He grabs my wrists and pins them to the wall above my head, immobilizing me with his hands. And his body, as he presses it against mine. "Keep fighting me," he says, his voice becoming guttural. "It only makes me want you more."

"And if I give in? Will you throw me away like every other woman?"

"There's no escaping this. I know. I've tried." He inhales deeply, pressing his body into me so forcefully that I can feel his heart beat. It's racing just as much as mine, if not more. "Once you accept this thing between us, you'll never leave."

I inwardly shrink as defeat washes over me like a cold wind. He's right. I knew this when I ran. If I ever take the chance and explore this attraction with Hayden, I know deep down that it'd be the death of me. I'd lose myself in him to the point that I'd no longer exist. That is what truly scares me.

Not Hayden, but my feelings *for* him.

He remains silent, his gaze boring into me, daring me to continue denying everything: this connection, this yearning I've tried so hard to fight while simultaneously embracing it during every moment I'm with him. I close my eyes and search for the remaining threads of my resolve.

Only to have them shredded at the feel of Hayden's lips on mine.

He claims my mouth in a kiss that's gentle. It's completely opposite to the dark violence rolling off of him. It stuns me, and I stand there, eyes closed and unmoving.

But not unwilling.

His lips move over mine with such tenderness that I melt into him within seconds. Despite his hold on my wrists, he uses his other hand to caress my face while his tongue moves over my lips, coaxing rather than demanding a response from me.

"Open for me, Callie. I'm dying to taste you again. I need to know if you're as sweet as I remember, or if I imagined everything because I'm so obsessed with you."

A moan gathers in my throat, and I force it down, unable to surrender just yet. Even so, Hayden's kiss awakens my body and leaves me breathless. My inhibitions crumble with every sweep of his lips across mine.

"Please, baby," he whispers, his voice dripping with raw desire.

The words hang in the air like a living entity, sending a surge of electricity through my veins, leaving my skin prickling. My lips part, a soft gasp escaping me as his plea wraps around me and causes my heart to expand. I understand now why Hayden likes to hear me beg. There's something powerful in it.

Before I can process anything else, Hayden takes advantage of my acquiescence, flicking the tip of my tongue with his. The feel of him ignites a wildfire of desire that threatens to consume me. The same inferno that's burning inside him.

His cock is hard against me, clear evidence of his arousal, yet his movements are slow and deliberate, his hand gripping my hip as if to keep me still. He claims dominion over my mouth, slowly seeking and tasting every part of me until I'm desperate for him.

His grip on me tightens, his fingers digging into my skin, a gentle urge for me to surrender completely. And with each stroke of his tongue, I feel myself losing control, willingly succumbing to the depths of desire he stirs within me. I finally give in to the hunger that we share and yield to the intoxicating power he holds over me.

I part my legs in invitation, wanting to feel every inch of him, to feel the length of him against the part of me that aches. He hooks my panties with his index finger and twists his arm to rip them from my body. The material flutters to the ground, immediately forgotten when he leans into me, filling the space between my thighs, his cock pressing into my clit. A whimper leaves my lips, the noise wanton and desperate.

The sound is the catalyst that causes Hayden to finally touch me.

He breaks the kiss to look at me. In response, I lean into his fingers as he trails them down my hip and then dips them between my thighs, stroking the soft skin there. I'm already wet, and his fingertips glide over the area, spreading the effects of my arousal all over. When I thrust my hips into his hand, he stops to grip my thigh, the tension in his fingers showing me he's barely hanging on.

I want him to lose control. Just like I have.

"Please, baby," I say with a voice I don't recognize. It's sultry yet aching. For him.

Hayden's lips crash against mine with a ferocity that steals my breath. There's no doubt or hesitation now. I kiss him back with everything that I have, telling him that I want him just as badly, giving him permission to lead me wherever he wants.

And he takes it.

His fingers find my clit, and he rubs me with finesse, an expert touch. Pleasure slams into me, and I choke on a breath, my lashes fluttering. He teases me mercilessly until I'm mewling against his lips, the sound gliding against his tongue. The noise morphs into a gasp when he eases his finger inside me. I rise to my tiptoes at the pressure, coming back down when he begins to stroke me. Then I'm grinding onto his hand with wild abandon.

He thrusts two fingers inside me, sucking in a breath, the hissing sound full of anguish. "You're so fucking tight. I'm going to wreck this pretty pussy."

I moan at the dark intent in his voice. The sensations he creates with his skilled fingers are almost too much as he drives them into me, hitting deeper each time until I'm so full I begin to imagine what it'd be like to take his cock. That only has me drenching his hand.

My entire body trembles with anticipation as my orgasm

looms. He uses his thumb to circle my clit in time with his thrusting fingers, bringing me closer and closer to the edge of ecstasy. His lips are still on mine while his hand works me between my legs.

"Come for me," he says against my mouth, nipping at my bottom lip.

I convulse around Hayden's fingers as a sob leaves me. I strain against his grip on my wrists when I arch my back, but he keeps me upright as I lose control over my body. He continues to fuck me with his hand, drawing out my orgasm until I'm thrashing my head, unable to take it anymore.

"I can't."

"You can, but not right now."

Even though he stops moving, he keeps his fingers inside me. As if trying to stay connected to me a little bit longer. To possess me a little more.

I open my eyes to find him watching me. His gaze is illuminated with triumph, but also with a gentler emotion... something dangerously close to affection. He releases my wrists to brush the backs of his fingers along my cheek, and I resist the urge to lean into his touch, to soak in the rare show of tenderness from him.

"Now that I've caught you, I intend to keep you, Callie."

A shiver passes through me at the possessiveness in his voice. In his vow.

I can't help but feel a mixture of excitement and uncertainty as his words sink in. The intensity of his gaze and the sincerity in his voice leave no room for doubt about his intentions. My heart races in my chest, and I find myself captivated by the depth of emotion swirling in his eyes. It's dark and potent, like him.

His fingers continue their gentle exploration along my cheek, tracing a path that ignites a trail of warmth in its wake. While his other fingers remain deep inside me. I lean slightly into his touch on my face, unable to completely suppress the longing that blossoms within me. Even so, I fight it.

Too much is at stake. My heart, for one thing.

"You can't keep me, Hayden." My protest sounds weak to my own ears, but I keep my expression firm. "I don't belong to anyone. Not even you."

His hand leaves my cheek as he slides it into my hair, grasping the nape of my neck to tilt my head back. Unable to look anywhere else, my gaze collides with his. Icy blue meets a warm amber.

Determination meets rebellion.

"You belong with me. *To* me." He brings his face so close to mine that the tips of our noses brush one another. "You can fight it all you want, but we both know it's pointless. What's happening between us is inevitable, and I'll do everything within my power to get you to accept it."

CHAPTER 29

C alista

THERE WILL BE NO MORE RUNNING OR ESCAPING. AT LEAST, not tonight.

Hayden made sure of that by carrying me to and from the car, as well as securing the child lock feature. I sit with my head leaning against the headrest and my eyes closed. Right now, I can't bear to look at him, at the devastatingly gorgeous man who swept into my life like a hurricane. He's pulverized the emotional barriers I built when my father died, and my heart sits at the center of everything, like a trophy waiting to be claimed.

Or crushed.

Is it possible that he used the word "possess" because he means to keep me close in a way that he doesn't understand just yet? Knowing bits of his childhood, it's possible Hayden isn't familiar with how to function in a healthy relationship.

Especially one that involves heightened emotions such as desire, jealousy, and uncertainty.

I may not have much experience, but I'm certain I'm further along in that regard. Even so, I recognize this for what it is: he's desperate to have me.

Is this some impulsive decision that he'll regret in the morning? Or is this something that'll last more than a few hours? Perhaps a few weeks? At the cost of my body and my secrets.

Hayden's made it clear he wants both.

The constant push–pull, hot–cold from him frays my nerves. I never know which version of himself he'll choose to show me. The tender lover? Or the violent, overprotective man who thinks to keep me safe through controlling me?

Even so, I enjoy both sides of him.

Just as the Earth needs both the day and the night, the light and dark, so do I.

We pull up to a high-rise tower, steel and glass gleaming under a full moon. In minutes, we're inside the elegant lobby, with me in Hayden's arms. Again.

"I can walk," I mumble, not wanting the man at the front desk to hear me. He's already looking at me with keen interest. Is it because I'm barefoot and disheveled? Or due to some other reason?

"Your feet are bleeding, Callie."

I look at Hayden, soaking in his profile while he strides toward the elevator. "They are?"

He nods, his jaw clenched. The tension in his body spreads, and his arms grip me tightly. I frown, unable to guess why he's irritated with me.

"I didn't mean to stain anything. I hope you're not upset about something I wasn't even aware of."

He stops in the middle of the grand room to look down at me. I nearly shrink back at the fury etched into his features. "You think I'm angry about the interior of my car?" he asks.

I shrug. "It's the only reason I can come up with."

"What about the fact that I don't want you to experience pain in any capacity unless it's the pain of my cock driving into your cunt? What about the idea that you're hurt because you're so fucking scared of me that you don't realize I would kill someone to keep you safe? Fuck my car. I want your blood on it, my cock, and anywhere else that'd mark me as yours."

"Jesus." My voice is breathy, almost nonexistent. "Hayden, don't."

His gaze hardens. "Don't what? Tell the truth? There are too many lies between us for me to continue adding to them. I'm done with that."

He stalks toward the elevators with me in his arms, my mouth hanging open and my lungs squeezing as I gasp for breath. How can one man affect me so profoundly that I can't control my own body's response to him?

"My feet don't hurt, Hayden," I whisper against the side of his neck. He swallows, and his Adam's apple bobs within his throat. I watch it in fascination, drinking in his masculinity. "You don't need to worry about me."

"I don't know how to stop myself."

My heart lurches in my chest. I rest my forehead in the crook of his neck and sigh, needing a moment to compose myself before I say something irrevocable. Something that has to do with the feelings swirling inside me and gaining momentum with every confession that comes out of his mouth.

We reach the elevator, and the doors glide open with a soft chime, revealing an interior paneled entirely in mirrors. My reflection is duplicated into infinity, surrounded by endless replicas that stare back at me. Hayden steps inside, and nerves zip along my spine at the idea of being in an enclosed space with him. Overhead, the soft lights cast a flattering glow, enhancing each reflection and revealing truth. The effect is both dizzying and disorienting, seeing myself as I am in this moment.

A woman who wants everything Hayden will give me.

Good or bad.

Pleasure or pain.

Joy or heartache.

I can't leave without knowing how this is going to end.

THE PENTHOUSE IS A STUDY IN CONTRASTS, MIRRORING THE man who owns it. One minute Hayden is comforting me on his lap, and the next he's filled to the brim with rage, the violence within him leaking out for all to see. The light and the dark, the two distinct entities inside him.

The place is similar, filled with stark blacks that are offset by pristine whites. In the living room are floor-to-ceiling windows that offer a view of the glittering city skyline, but inside is a smooth minimalism. A white marble floor stretches the length of the open concept, reflecting the bright colors just outside. The walls meet the windows in clean lines, painted a deep charcoal, and the furnishings are sparse, each snowy-white piece angled in front of a jet black fireplace.

Like Hayden, this place is perfection, but lacking in

warmth. In the things that make it welcoming and inviting. A home.

"This is beautiful," I say, more to myself than him. I highly doubt he's concerned with my opinion, but being here resurrects memories from my old life, one full of luxury. I don't miss the money as much as I miss the security it brought. Living in a place like this ensures I'd never lose a moment of sleep worrying about someone breaking in.

Like a stalker.

The thought dampens my enthusiasm for the opulence surrounding me. Not only that, but it brings about a worry I hadn't considered before. Am I putting Hayden in danger by being here?

When he heads further inside, I tap his chest, bracing myself against the subject matter. And his reaction.

"Wait," I say.

Hayden stops and looks at me, brows snapping together in displeasure and confusion. "What is it?"

"I don't think it's a good idea for me to be here."

"Because you're scared to be here with me?"

I nod and his body stiffens against mine. "But not in the way you're thinking. I'm scared for you."

"Why?" he asks.

I bite my bottom lip and worry it between my teeth, unsure of how to communicate my concerns in a way that'll get him to take me seriously. Or not too seriously that he explodes. There's a fine line I'm walking when it comes to Hayden. He's like a bomb, ready to detonate with a single spark.

"Stop that," he says, his voice sharp. When I scrunch my face at him, he blows out a breath. "When you do that to your lip, all I can think about is fucking your mouth."

"Holy shit."

"Language, Miss Green. Why are you worried about me? And don't give me some watered-down version. I want the absolute truth."

I open my mouth, close it, and open it again. "I think I have a stalker."

CHAPTER 30

C alista

WHEN HAYDEN CONTINUES TO STARE AT ME, WORDS POUR from my mouth like a faucet, spilling everywhere. "I have no idea who this person is or what they want, but they stole my necklace and have been leaving individual pearls on my nightstand every day for a week. At night. I could've written everything off as me losing my necklace and that would've made sense, until a single pearl appeared. I would never willingly break that necklace. My father gave it to me, and it's one of the few things I have left from him."

Hayden says nothing. In the seconds that follow, the silence creeps along my skin like a swarm of bugs, making me antsy. When I think he's about to acknowledge what I've said, he surprises me by walking further into the penthouse.

"Did you hear what I said?" When he nods, I grit my teeth, praying for patience. "And?"

"And I don't give a fuck."

For a couple of seconds, I stare at him. Then I struggle in his hold. "This isn't something you can brush off. Put me down so we can talk about this like adults."

Ignoring my protests, he stays in motion. The only change is he tightens his grip on me to the point it forces a wheeze from me. I glare up at him although he can't see it. However, I'm immediately distracted from my irritation when he steps inside a large room.

The master bedroom is a chilly sanctuary of dark opulence, the strict decor continuing in dramatic fashion. More floor-to-ceiling windows overlook the city, but thick blackout curtains remain drawn to cocoon the room in somber shadows. The focal point is a massive platform bed, a black wooden frame with padded leather in matching charcoal gray. Not a crease disturbs the smooth surface of the duvet and sheets, and the dark floor planks are bare, the ebony wood continuing underfoot.

In place of art, a massive black-and-white photograph dominates the wall opposite the bed. It depicts a lone figure standing before a dilapidated building under ominous gray skies. The subject stares away from the camera, the person's face obscured by shadow. It's a portrait of shrouded anonymity, the lone splash of grim color reinforcing the room's bleak palette.

I suspect it's a woman from the shape of the body, but I can't be certain. Even so, jealousy flares in my gut and spreads, making my stomach churn. For a moment, I forget about my stalker, wanting to know who the hell that person is.

And if she means anything.

"That's a beautiful picture," I say, meaning it despite my sudden insecurity. I shift my gaze to Hayden's face, ready to decipher every blink and shape of his lips as he responds to the question I need an answer to. "Is it someone you know or a random photograph you purchased?"

"I know her personally."

Ouch. "The woman in the picture or the artist?"

"The woman."

Sonofabitch. "Who is she?" I try to keep my tone light and slightly disinterested, but when Hayden turns to look at me, I feel exposed by the way his gaze pierces me.

"The woman is someone who changed my life."

"For good or bad?"

"Both," he says.

I hate her. Whoever she is.

He doesn't speak again until we're inside his spacious bathroom that looks more like a spa than a place to shower. I briefly admire the luxury surrounding me, but my thoughts are centered on Hayden when he sets me on the edge of the counter, keeping his hands on my waist as though afraid I might try to run again.

I won't. But if I do, it'll be to steal that portrait and light it on fire.

I glare up at him, wishing I was upset that he manhandled me as opposed to being jealous over a still image of a woman who may or may not be important to him. That logic doesn't translate, not when he placed her in the most intimate room in his house.

"I need to clean your feet so I can assess the depth of the lacerations," he says. "Hold still."

His gaze softens as it drifts down to my battered and bloody feet. My anger fizzles out, replaced with a ball of warmth in my chest at his blatant concern for me. He finally removes his hands from me and I sag, getting a moment to breathe properly without his touch sending me into cardiac arrest.

Hayden turns on the sink, grabs a washcloth and soap, and then checks the water's temperature. His long fingers encircle my ankle and my hip as he helps me shift my position. "This is going to sting."

"I'll be fine."

He guides my foot underneath the warm water, and I bite my lip to get from making a sound. But God, how it hurts.

Hayden keeps my leg suspended, his gaze on the blood and dirt swirling down the drain. His face morphs into a frown at the damage revealed and he begins bathing my foot with a soapy washcloth, his ministrations methodical but gentle.

I run my gaze over him, drinking in the way he switches from one sole to the other, his head bowed and his eyes focused. With him this close and his hands on my skin, this position feels too intimate, too vulnerable, yet I remain still, not wanting to miss a moment.

Hayden rinses and bandages the numerous cuts and abrasions, and when he's finished, he releases my bandaged feet. Then he reaches for me, his long fingers encircling my hips, and leans close. The air between us is charged with unspoken words as his gaze finds mine.

"Better?" he asks.

"Yes."

"Are you going to stop running, Callie?"

I stare up at him, lost as to how we've come to this place, but finding myself unable and unwilling to refuse. I give the barest of nods, accepting the sanctuary offered in his embrace. At least for now.

"Good," he says. "You don't need to worry about a stalker finding you here. The security is second to none. You'll be safe until I take care of it."

"Thank you." I drop my gaze to his hands and then look at his face. "Can you help me get down?"

With concern swirling in his gaze, Hayden assists me into a standing position. He keeps a tight hold on me, steadying me throughout the transition. The padding on my feet cushions them enough to prevent any major discomfort, and I sigh with relief.

"That mouth." He reaches out to brush his thumb along my lower lip. "The things I want to do to it..."

Before I can come up with a response, he lets his hands fall to his sides. "Do you need anything?" he asks.

That simple inquiry is like a loaded gun, able to take me down and make my heart bleed. What I *need* is emotional distance from Hayden before I fall in love with him. Every gentle touch and protective action entwines me with him. Soon I'll be so wrapped up in him that I won't be able to leave him without hurting myself.

"I'd love a glass of water."

He lifts a sardonic brow. "Dehydrated from your night out?"

"No. I'm parched from all the running I did earlier."

His mouth twitches with suppressed amusement, but then it overtakes him, and he smiles at me. A genuine smile. It lights up the room and blinds me to anything except Hayden and how devastatingly handsome he is. But it's more than that.

Seeing him happy, even if it's for a second, moves me in a way that's profound. It does something to my soul, a place he shouldn't have any access to.

"Can you walk?" he asks, the joy on his face disappearing at the mention of my injuries. "Maybe I should just carry you to the kitchen."

His obvious concern for me has my heart squeezing in

my chest. Even though I love being in his arms, I want to reassure Hayden that I'm fine. I hate seeing him upset. Especially because of me.

"The bandages provide enough padding so that I barely feel the cuts," I say, waving a hand in dismissal when his frown deepens. "Lead the way."

With a look of skepticism, he places his hand at the small of my back, his palm warm against my body. The familiar scent of his cologne lingers in the air, soothing and comforting, and I inhale, soaking it in. Like I have every time I've been in his embrace.

My first few steps are awkward as I adjust to the padding on my feet while hiding my discomfort from Hayden, but once we reach the kitchen I'm confident that my wounds are minor and of no concern. At least, not as bad as he's been treating them. It's endearing. You'd think I stepped on the blade of a machete from the way he's taken care of me.

I've never had anyone do that. Not in the way Hayden has.

He's quick to retrieve a bottle of water from the refrigerator, unscrew the cap, and offer it to me. I take it from him, careful not to touch him. Having Hayden's fingers on my skin makes it impossible for me to think coherently. Or at all.

"Thank you," I say. I take a long drink and he watches me, making a normal activity challenging. While trying not to choke, I empty the bottle, feeling like I deserve a gold medal for completing such a feat. "I appreciate what you did tonight, but I think we need to have a conversation about boundaries."

He folds his arms, causing the material to strain against the contours of his chest, which distracts the shit out of me. "Is that so?" he asks, his voice dangerously soft.

The warning underlying his words has me refocusing my thoughts. "Yes. I'm assuming you tracked me through my cell phone, and that's not okay."

"I don't see the problem."

"It's an invasion of privacy," I say, throwing up my hands. "I'm not your pet who ran away and needs you to rescue them." When he lifts a mocking brow, I take a deep breath to ease the frustration unfurling in my gut. I squeeze the water bottle pretending it's Hayden's neck. "Do you understand what I'm saying?"

"I need to know every second of every day that you're safe." He shrugs. "If that means planting a chip in you or tracking your cell phone, I'll do it."

My mouth falls open before I snap my jaw shut. "Do you hear yourself? You sound insane."

"If I'm crazy, it's because of you."

As if he slapped me, I jerk back. "Me?"

"Yes, you."

His arms fall to his sides and he takes a step toward me. I take one back in response because his nearness overwhelms me and destroys my defenses. He walks up to me, trapping me between the counter and his body as he looms over me, his blue eyes coated in frost.

I repress a shiver and avert my gaze, watching him grip the counter's edge on either side of my hips. He leans into me, pressing the length of his body to mine, and that delicious contact has my blood singing.

"What did I ever do to you?" I ask, staring at his forearm and the veins visible just underneath his skin. "You're the one who won't leave me alone."

At the feel of his fingers taking hold of my chin, I press my lips together. He lifts my head until our eyes meet. It's nearly unbearable to look at him. Not when he stares at me like I'm his reason for living.

"Because you're in my blood, Callie. Underneath my skin. No matter how hard I try, I can't cut you out without killing myself in the process."

CHAPTER 31

C alista

"HAYDEN," I BREATHE, HIS NAME A GASP AND A SIGH ALL in one.

"It's never been this way for me. I don't know how to deal with it except to make sure that you're safe and cared for at all times. That's the only thing keeping me from going completely insane and kidnapping you. Although I've thought about it. *A lot.*"

His words steal the air from my lungs. Taking a deep breath, I curl my fingers into his shirt, clinging with a desperation that frightens me as much as his confession. "This isn't healthy. For either of us."

His gaze holds mine, stripping away layers of armor and defiance to expose the lonely woman beneath the exterior I present to the world. The one who craves his affection with a thirst that could drown her. Am I in this thing as deep as he is? Not yet. Only because he's accepted it and I haven't.

"It might not be healthy or what's considered normal." He releases my chin to slide his hand in my hair, tangling his fingers in the strands to hold me immobile. "But I don't want normal if it means I can't have you."

A choked sound escapes my throat as his words pierce the last of my defenses. No one has ever looked at me the way Hayden does. And they certainly have never gone through the lengths he has to keep me safe. Not even my father cared this much, and he loved me.

Whatever Hayden feels for me, it might be stronger than love.

But it's more dangerous as well.

"Elite Health Care," I whisper. Hayden's brow furrows, and I close my eyes, unable to repeat myself while looking at him. "Elite Health Care is the name."

Still gripping the back of my head, he uses his other hand to trace my eyelids, his touch lighter than the stroke of a butterfly's wing. "Look at me." When I do, I find confusion warring with the dawning comprehension that travels over his features. "The clinic," he rasps. "That's where you were that night."

Witnessing the understanding blooming within his mind is swiftly followed by feelings of shame so raw my chest burns. Tears prick my eyes as I nod in confirmation. Keeping this piece of information from him is only delaying the inevitable. Similar to my relationship with him.

Hayden will ultimately get what he wants from me, and I'm powerless to stop it.

"Why are you telling me now, after refusing me for days?" he asks.

That's the real question, the one that has my mind spinning and my heart pumping crazily. All night I've wrestled with the notion that Hayden is only pursuing me because he

203

wants the details of my past, and that once he has them, he'll be done with me. All of this passion and intensity from him will fade, and I'll be left behind with my secrets exposed and only my loneliness to comfort me. By telling him the things he wants, I'm expediting the end of whatever this is between us.

Because I can't imagine him keeping me when he knows everything.

I take a shuddering breath, willing the rapid beat of my heart to slow. "I'm telling you because I'm tired of running from you, Hayden. I'm tired of pretending this thing between us will somehow fade if I avoid it long enough."

His eyes narrow, searching mine. "And knowing the truth will make me run *from* you instead?"

A humorless laugh escapes my lips. "I doubt there's anything that would make you run away in fear. But to answer your question, I think it's more likely that knowing the truth will make you realize I'm not..." I pause, choosing my words carefully. "I'm not what you really want. And that's okay, but I'd rather you know that sooner rather than later before I—"

Fall in love with you.

I worry my lower lip between my teeth to stop myself from talking. For fuck's sake, admitting that would've been disastrous. I wish I could blame the alcohol, but I doubt its effects on me are stronger than Hayden's presence. With the two combined, I'm liable to say something stupid.

"What did I say about biting your lip?" He places his thumb on my bottom lip, gently prying it from my teeth. "I want to have this conversation with you, but you're making it difficult. Now all I want to do is fuck this pretty mouth."

He swipes his thumb over the seam of my lips, and I immediately part them. Inviting him. He dips his finger inside and sweeps the pad over my tongue before dragging it across my teeth. His body trembles, and he closes his eyes as though battling to stay in control of himself. When he looks at me again, the blue of his gaze has darkened with hunger.

"You make me ache, Callie. In ways I didn't know I could."

"You've done the same thing to me."

I flatten my hands against his chest, unsure if I have the emotional fortitude to push this man away. The raw longing etched across his beautiful face has me shaking with desire. And fear.

"I think it's best that we don't kiss or do anything else until you've solved my father's murder and reviewed all of the information that I'm going to give you." A shadow crosses his features, and I rush to explain. "If this thing between us is inevitable, then putting it on pause won't matter in the long run."

"Perhaps, not, but that doesn't mean I want to suffer in the interim," Hayden says. He releases me completely and takes a step back. The hunger in his eyes doesn't fade, but his face takes on a cool expression. "I'll agree to that, but I have conditions that must be met."

"What are they?"

I hate the distance between us, but it's something I desperately need if I'm to negotiate with Hayden. Without the warmth of his body seeping into mine, I find myself chilled and wrap my arms around my waist. Or maybe I'm fortifying myself for what he's going to say.

"First, you'll move in with me." When I sputter, he holds up a hand. "You said you have a stalker, which means you're in danger. I can't do whatever's necessary to solve your father's murder if I'm spending all of my time worrying about you. With you living here, I'll know you're safe."

"Are you serious right now? I've known you for all of what? A fucking minute? And what about my job?" I extend my arms, nearly flapping them in agitation. "Stalker or no, I can't just stay here all day and do nothing."

"Language," he says, his tone laced with warning. "If you want to dirty your mouth, I know plenty of ways to do that without the use of words. As for your job, I will escort you to and from work, as well as assign you a personal bodyguard during the time we're apart."

"Hayden, this is crazy. I can't agree to this."

"You can and you will." When I glare at him, he continues as if my anger is a mere annoyance. "Secondly, you will give me your word that you'll notify me immediately if anyone threatens you in any capacity. Whether that's a random stranger or your ex-fiancé stopping by the Sugar Cube. And lastly, once I find your father's killer, you will give yourself to me. Completely, without restriction."

I gape at him. Because there's nothing else for me to do except scream in frustration or pass out from shock. I'd love to say that Hayden is just messing with me in some wild attempt to get me in his bed, but the look of certainty on his face says this goes beyond sexual gratification.

Hayden Bennett wants to fucking own me.

I drop my gaze, unable to bear the intensity of his. Because when I look in his eyes, all I can see is the determination written in their depths. As well as his need for me.

I start to bite my lip and quickly release it at the growl that leaves Hayden's throat. Ignoring the flash of lust that streaks through his gaze, I cross my arms and consider his conditions. As much as I chafe at the restrictions, the safety he's offering, both physically and financially, is too enticing for me to turn down. If I didn't have a stalker prowling about in my apartment, violating my private spaces, I'd have more courage to tell Hayden to kiss my ass. But with my life on the line, I'm less resistant to his demands if they'll keep me breathing.

"If I agree to this," I say, "then you have to promise to respect my decisions and not try to dictate everything I do or where I go. I need to be free to spend time with Harper, go to work, and just live my freaking life without your interference. I'm sure you can understand that?"

He gives me a blank stare, and heat rises to my cheeks. How can he unravel me with a single glance? It's baffling.

"I'm fine with that as long as none of it involves another man," he says. "Unless you want me to threaten his life. I might not have claimed your body, but I'll be fucked before I let someone else touch you."

My gasp is nothing more than a puff of air, and not enough to satiate my lungs' need for oxygen. I drop my gaze and suck in several deep breaths, having given up on trying to calm my fluttering pulse. If the things Hayden says gives me a heart attack, then that's how I'm meant to go.

He places his index finger under my chin and lifts my head. "Once this case is solved, you won't have any excuses left and no places to run. Right now, you're the only obstacle in my way, but you're also the only woman I want. Despite what you believe, that's never going to change."

"I don't believe you, but even if I did, what do you want from me? Sex? A relationship? Love?" I jerk my chin away and scoff. "I doubt you can answer that. I know I can't."

At least I can't without sounding as deranged as he does. It's not that I'd marry Hayden tomorrow, even if he asked me. What I want is for us to be together with the end goal of figuring out what we mean to each other. And that takes time.

But with time can come disinterest. Have I bought myself enough time to test Hayden's infatuation? And my own?

"I do know what I want, Callie. You. *All* of you." He takes my face between his large hands, the tips of his fingers digging into my head. Not enough to hurt, but enough to keep me still. "Agree to my terms. I won't take no for an answer."

"Give me seventy-two hours."

He nods slowly and then drops his head to rest it against mine. "Until then, I intend to convince you."

"Until then, I intend to resist you."

CHAPTER 32

C alista

I CAN SENSE HAYDEN'S RELUCTANCE TO LET GO OF ME, BUT HE does and steps back. The imprint of his hands burns still against my skin, his final words echoing through the restless chambers of my heart. I stare at him, torn between relief for the delay and regret for a reckoning I'm still not ready to face.

How could any reprieve be long enough to prepare me for a man hell-bent on possession of my body, my secrets, and my very soul?

This man offers sanctuary and solace with one breath, command and conquest with the next. Safety and stability in exchange for absolute surrender on his merciless terms. However, I have no one to blame but myself.

I knew what I was getting into the moment I sought out his help.

It begs the question: Am I really upset? Or am I pretending to be because I'm not and I know I should be?

"Are you ready for bed?" he asks me.

It's a simple question, but I can't stop the nervousness that flows over my skin. After this lengthy conversation, I'm confident that Hayden won't try to have sex with me. So why don't I feel at ease?

"Yes."

He tilts his head. "This way."

Once again he places his hand at the small of my back and guides me down the hallway. To his room. When I stop, he does the same, turning to look down at me with confusion written on his face.

"That's your room," I say, by way of explanation.

"I know that."

"Don't you have a guest room?"

He nods. "I do, but you won't be sleeping anywhere unless it's with me."

"Hayden..."

His eyes soften as he takes in my obvious distress. "I gave you my word, Callie. My only objective tonight is to keep you safe. Nothing more, no matter how much I want to."

My stomach dips at the hunger in his voice. I might be fighting my attraction to him, but Hayden is fighting more than that. He's battling his primal instincts. That's what drives him to delve into the baser wants, the ones that seek out satisfaction at any cost.

He presses his hand against my spine, and I allow him to lead me inside. I walk over to the bed and sit on the plush mattress, more than ready to sleep in my dress. Not that it covers much, but it's better than sleeping naked. I'm not brave enough to test Hayden's limits, even if he did make me a promise to keep his hands to himself.

He makes his way over to a dresser and removes a plain, white t-shirt before offering it to me. "Here. Change and then come to bed." At my hesitation, he exhales, the sound full of frustration. "What did I say? You know, you're going to have to trust me at some point."

"I know, and I do to a certain extent. But asking me to undress in front of you and share your bed is pushing the limits of that trust." I cross my arms, distress giving way to irritation at him. "A guest room and t-shirt seem perfectly adequate for ensuring my safety tonight."

"You don't have to change in front of me." He juts his chin in the direction of the bathroom. "Change in there, but you will sleep in my bed."

Lifting my chin, I take the offered shirt and head into the en-suite bathroom, changing and washing up for bed. By the time I emerge, Hayden has dimmed the lights and lies atop the covers with his hands folded behind his head. I run my gaze over him, taking in the relaxed position, finding it at odds with the tension lining his body.

He sits up as I approach the empty side of the bed and pulls the covers back in invitation. I take a deep breath and slide beneath them, my movements stilted due to my uncertainty. He settles against the pillows once more and we lie in strained silence for several moments.

Until Hayden releases an exasperated sound and rolls to face me. "For fuck's sake, relax. I'm not going to kill you."

"There are things worse than death. In fact, sometimes killing is a mercy."

"You believe that?"

I nod. "It depends on the situation, but yes, I do."

"I've always seen death as a solution."

"It can be that as well."

He studies me. I can feel his gaze traveling along my

profile, down my throat, and across my chest. It's a phantom caress, one that still ignites my blood. I turn my head to meet his gaze.

Instantly falling under his spell.

"Hayden?"

"Yes?"

"I already lost my father to death," I whisper, unable to speak at a normal volume with tears scratching my throat. "Please don't let it take you too. I don't want this stalker to hurt you."

Hayden stares at me, his eyes widening, allowing me to see the emotion swirling inside. It pulses like a living thing, growing stronger until the blue becomes all I can see.

In one swift motion, he shifts positions, eradicating the distance between us. Hovering over me with his hips pressed against mine and his fisted hands on either side of my head, he stares down at me with raw intensity. The air thickens with a mixture of desire and vulnerability, as if the weight of our connection hangs in the balance. Then he lifts a hand and captures my face, running his thumb along my lower lip.

"Never," he says, the sound guttural and deep, as if summoned from the depths of his soul. "Do you hear me, Callie? I'll never leave you. Not in this life or whatever comes after. You are mine. And I will burn this world to fucking ashes before I let anything take you from me. Or me from you."

His passionate declaration wrecks me in the best possible way.

I fist the material of his shirt and yank him to me, molding my mouth to his. I part my lips, opening eagerly to welcome him, to invite him to take what belongs to him. He groans into the kiss, making me clench my thighs, my body yearning for his touch.

The heat and feel of him lying on top of me seeps into my bones, leaving an imprint on my DNA as well as my heart. He delves his tongue into my mouth with a fierce hunger that slowly chases away the tendrils of doubt and fear, replacing them with desire and longing.

When I moan into his mouth, he tears his from mine, easing back to let his gaze roam where I want his hands to explore. After the thorough perusal, his eyes find mine, and he shakes his head.

"I thought you said 'no kissing'?"

I shrug. "I said you couldn't kiss me, but that doesn't mean I can't do what I want."

"That's unfair, but I'll never deny you." He grinds his cock into me, causing my breath to hitch. "I'd give you anything if it meant I'd get to keep you."

"Keeping me means surviving you."

His brows snap together. "Explain."

"If I give myself to you—"

"*When*," he interjects.

I glare up at him, but it lacks any real heat. "If I give myself to you, you'll break me into pieces so small I won't be able to put myself back together or make myself whole."

"I'll fuse your broken pieces with mine. Together, we'll be whole, Callie."

Hayden's eyes blaze, the blue within the hottest flames as he gazes down at me, his promise floating in the atmosphere. I tremble at the savage beauty etched into his face. It tells of a longing so acute it leaves him raw and me in danger. Not of my heart being broken, but of it being stolen completely.

This man could reach inside my rib cage, claim my

heart, and leave me empty where it once beat for him. An echoing in my chest that'll last for the rest of my life. I'd rather be a part of him than separate and hollow.

His pupils contract at the acceptance that's sure to be on my face, a direct reflection of my thoughts. He lowers his head, claiming my lips in a kiss, and I gasp against his mouth, tightening my grip on his shirt to anchor myself as the world threatens to disappear. It always does when I'm with him.

He groans and slides a hand behind my neck, angling my head as he deepens the kiss. He drinks from me, devours me, as his tongue strokes and flicks, igniting flames that dance along my senses. Only when my lungs burn for air does he lift his head. Our ragged breaths mingle, both of our chests heaving.

"Sleep now," he says.

"What about you?"

He squeezes his eyes shut as though in pain. "I need to leave you alone right now, or I'll break my promise to you."

"Will you come back?"

His eyelids lift and he gazes at me with such tenderness that I nearly sigh. "I will always come back to you, Callie."

CHAPTER 33

H ayden

I NEED A FUCKING MIRACLE.

Living with Callie under my roof and in my bed *without* touching her is going to require supernatural assistance.

I stalk toward my home office with the feel of her body lingering on my hands. Hunger like I've never known wars with my sanity, trying to push me over the edge, to give in to the darker emotions.

The ones that'll have Callie running from me. Again.

My office comes into view, and I step inside while shutting the door behind me. I don't want Callie to see me while I get my shit together. That might require me fucking myself.

So that I don't fuck her.

I settle into the leather seat and grip the edge of the desk while I compose myself. Now that I know the name of the clinic Callie visited that night, I'm going to discover her

215

secrets. Nothing I learn about her will change the way I see her.

Calista Green may bear the flaws all humans possess, but to me, she's perfect.

I retrieve my cell phone and dial Zack's number. He answers on the first ring, easing some of the tension in my body. It would've been bad for him if he made me wait tonight, not when the knowledge I've been seeking is finally within reach.

"Hey, *capo*," he greets. "What can I do for you at this late hour?"

"I need you to comb through every file that appears on June 24th at a private clinic called Elite Health Care. Calista's is one of them."

"Do you want me to call you back or do you want to wait while I search? It won't take long now that you've given me the exact location."

"I'll hold."

The sound of his fingers striking the keys is the only noise that penetrates my mind. Unless you count the air flowing to and from my lungs by way of my ragged breathing.

The unsolved mystery of Callie's past haunted me from the moment I wanted to possess her. I've lost sleep from thinking about what happened to her. Whatever it was had to be harrowing if it triggered a panic attack.

"Green is a female in her early 20s," Zack mumbles to himself. "How much do you think she weighs, and what's her height?" After I answer him, he continues. "Whoever worked with this file wasn't very smart," Zack says. "I doubt she's a forty-year old male of the same height and weight that came into the place with a handprint on her neck."

"Are you sure it's her file?" When Zack remains silent, I

clear my throat. Usually that's enough to prompt him, but this time it doesn't. "Zack?"

"Mr. Bennett, you're not going to like this."

I clench my teeth at his formal use of my name. If I wasn't apprehensive before, I sure as fuck am now. "Just tell me."

"I'm pretty certain this is her medical file," he says slowly. "And it says she had high levels of GHB in her system."

"Are you sure?" Because if Zack confirms what I just heard, I'm going to fucking murder someone. After torturing them to the highest extent. "Your answer is putting someone's life at risk, just to be clear."

Zack blows out a breath. "I'm 99 percent sure Calista Green was given a large dose of the date rape drug."

"Send me the file," I say, each word clipped.

"Sent. And Mr. Bennett? I'm sorry."

Zack ends the call. It's uncharacteristic of him to hang up on me, but he must've sensed my all-consuming horror. My phone chimes with a notification, and I quickly open the attachment. I need to see with my own eyes the things my mind wants to deny.

The medical record, a mere composition of black characters on a white background, stare back at me, fucking with my sanity. My heart pounds with a jagged cadence, heralding dread and something darker as page by page, her past unfolds before me. Calista drugged, bruised, and lying on the kitchen floor...

Was she sexually assaulted?

The blood drains from my face at the trajectory of my thoughts, causing bile to rise in my throat. I swallow it down and take deep breaths, forcing myself to continue. By the time I have finished reading the entire file, I am drenched in sweat, my breaths coming hard and fast.

Until I double over with the force of a pain that's not mine.

Callie, a woman whose only desire in life is to help others, has been brutally violated. The chances she wasn't raped are too minuscule to offer comfort.

Rage unlike anything I have ever known surges through me and colors my vision red. I grip the edge of the desk, every muscle drawn tight by the urge to commit violence. With a growl, I erupt from my seat, sending the chair crashing into the wall behind me. Loose sheets of paper flutter in the air like leaves adrift on the wind, and the legs of the desk screech against the floor as I shove it aside, causing my arms to burn from the exertion.

But it's not enough. Not when the fury within me is a pressure that's increasing every second, seeking an outlet only destruction will satisfy.

I whip around and seize the chair to send it flying. The piece of furniture hits the fireplace with a resounding crash, the impact creating cracks in the marble. I grab the nearest books from their shelves and hurl them into the wall. They land with a thud that barely registers as I reach for another. And another.

The wreckage continues until the room mirrors the chaos within me. Chest heaving and sweat gathering along my spine, I stand amidst the ruin, my gaze darting wildly for something else to destroy. A gentle knock on the door is followed by Calista's voice. It's that of an angel whereas I'm the devil personified in this moment.

"Hayden? Are you okay?"

CHAPTER 34

H ayden

I LEAN AGAINST THE WALL AND PINCH THE BRIDGE OF MY NOSE, struggling to calm my breathing enough to answer Calista while searching for a response that won't give away the depths of rage I've yet to ascend from. My delayed response only prompts her to open the door.

She steps inside, her gaze immediately finding mine. Her hazel eyes are bright with uncertainty, and her bottom lip trembles with worry, but she still makes her way toward me.

"Don't," I say, holding up a hand, palm facing her.

Calista flinches and comes to an abrupt stop. The hurt look on her face has a pang streaking through my chest. What if she knew about the shit I wanted to do to whoever hurt her?

If she were smart, she'd run faster and farther than she did earlier.

After folding her hands in front, Calista twists her fingers in the material of my t-shirt, unable to contain her nervousness. "You know."

I nod, not trusting myself to speak. My gut is still churning, and my fists are so tight by my sides that my arms shake with the strain. If I could touch her without being a danger to her, I would. But right now, I'm not...stable.

Calista bows her head and her hair glides along the sides of her face, a curtain of silk to caress her pale cheeks. "I knew you'd look at me differently." Her whisper, filled with pain and disappointment, is loud in the silence. I stiffen with alarm at the dejection in her voice, having never heard it before.

When she lifts her head, her gaze has hardened into crystallized amber, fractured with agony. After turning on her heel, she leaves the office, briefly pausing to glance at me over her shoulder. "I was hoping you'd still want me once you knew, but I was wrong."

She disappears from sight before I'm freed from the trance she put me in with her confession. I take off after her, my strides eating up the distance between us. She quickens her steps at my arrival, which only has my blood pumping that much faster.

I catch up to her in the hallway and grab her arm, spinning her around to face me. Then I invade her space, wanting nothing between us, and press her spine to the wall. She blinks up at me, her eyes glistening with unshed tears, gutting me where I stand.

"I still want you," I say. "So fucking much."

"Then why..." She flicks her gaze in the direction of my office, her message clear.

"I'm enraged that this happened to you. And because I can't do a fucking thing to take the pain away."

She stills, eyes widening at my tone. I curse under my breath and force myself to relax my grip on her arm, though I don't release her. I need the contact with her, the reassurance that she's here with me.

"I need you to tell me everything you remember, so I can find who did this to you," I say.

"And then what?" She fists her trembling hands in my shirt, her eyes blazing with emotion. "What are you going to do?"

"I'll make them suffer in ways no one has ever suffered. Before I fucking kill them."

She shakes her head. "Please, don't do that."

"Why?!" I yell the question, unable to understand why she doesn't want revenge. It's something I've searched for all my life since my mother's death, and I can't imagine anyone else forgoing the satisfaction that comes from destroying the person who stole something from you.

My thoughts reignite the fury within me that craves release. My chest tightens until I can barely breathe while tension thrums through every inch of my body. I let go of her arm to slam my fist in the wall. She cries out in fright while I embrace the pain that shoots through my knuckles.

When I retract my hand from the drywall to examine the injury, Calista gasps. "You're bleeding!"

Before I can punch the wall again, she reaches for me. With her brow creased, she gently takes my hand, her touch having an immediate effect. The tenderness acts as a balm, easing the blaze of my darker emotions, the ones that threaten to burn me alive as they torment me.

It's confounding that this woman can tame the violence in me with the mere brush of her skin against mine or with a kind word.

Calista tugs on my hand, urging me to follow her into

my bathroom. I lean against the counter as she gathers the medical supplies I used earlier on her feet. Without hesitation, she cleans and bandages my hand.

I watch her.

The way her fingers caress me.

The way her gaze drifts over my face.

The way her body gravitates toward mine.

Every bit of contact with her douses the heat of my rage until something else stirs within me, awakening at her nearness. Desire. How could she ever think I wouldn't want her? It's unfathomable to me.

And the reason I'll never let her go.

Even now, after witnessing the destruction and violence I unleashed, her face holds no traces of judgment. Apprehension, yes. But that's going to take time to erase. Despite this, her only thought is to soothe and to comfort, as if my suffering were her own.

This humbles me.

When she finishes binding my hand, she looks up at me, her eyes shadowed with concern. "Do you want to talk about it?"

I shake my head. "It'll only make things worse. The thought of someone hurting you...I've never felt so out of control."

Calista drops her gaze, releasing me. I take her face between my hands, willing her to look at me once more. She does and it gives me the wherewithal to tell her the truth.

"You need to know that I won't change my mind about getting revenge," I say. "You deserve it, and I need it. Do you understand what I'm telling you?"

She slowly nods.

"Good." I bring our foreheads together, soaking in her presence. It washes over me like a cool mist, putting out the remaining embers heating my fury. At least for tonight. "When it comes to your well-being, there are no limits on what I'd do to keep you safe."

"I know," she says, her breath a whisper that grazes my mouth. "I haven't felt safe since my father died. Thank you for protecting me. I just hope it doesn't..."

"Tell me, Callie."

"I don't want you to get hurt. I couldn't handle it if something happened to you because of me or my past."

"Everything will be fine."

I pull her into my arms and guide her head to my chest, needing her close with her body pressed to mine. Hearing her admit she cares for me only makes me want her all the more. But it's not just that.

It makes me want her affection.

Perhaps, even her love.

I'm not sure I know how to encourage or nurture this feeling, but if it gives me more of her, the parts no one else has access to...? I'm going to pursue it until I get what I want. Like a trophy, I'll display her love for all to see while knowing she's mine.

"Let's get you to bed," I say into the strands of her hair. "You need to sleep."

She curls her fingers into my shirt. "Stay with me?"

"Of course."

I step back and take her hand in mine, leading her into the bedroom. The space is dark and quiet, lending itself to intimacy. Not only of the sexual variety, but the emotional as well. At this moment, I want to be close to Calista in every way possible, even if it requires me to be vulnerable in a way I find uncomfortable.

I'd do anything to be whatever she needs me to be.

She climbs into the bed and turns to look at me, her gaze

full of invitation. And longing. If there's a possibility that she could feel the same way about me like I do her, I'll die satisfied.

Calista pats the comforter with a shy expression. "You coming?"

I nod before stripping down to my boxers. Her gaze widens with every article of clothing that hits the floor. The appreciative gleam that lights up the hazel of her eyes instantly makes me hard. When she takes in the length of my cock, it has the fucker jerking and releasing pre-cum.

Before I lose control—for the second fucking time within an hour—I climb into the bed. Her focus never wavers. It stays on me like a shadow, only making it that much harder not to fuck her.

"Come here," I say, my voice gruff because of the sexual frustration pricking at me.

Calista slides over and presses her body to my side. I nearly fucking sigh because of how much I love the feel of her. Instead, I snake my arm around her back and place my hand on her hip, my grip secure.

We lie in silence and with each passing minute, my body relaxes, the muscles slowly uncoiling. And then molding to her. Calista fits against me like she was made for me. There's a rightness that settles along my body, allowing me to be at peace in a way that's unusual.

Funerals are the one of the few places I experience serenity, but that's changed.

Not only does Calista soothe me, she makes me feel like I'm home.

CHAPTER 35

C alista

I DRIFT IN THAT HAZY PLACE BETWEEN SLEEP AND WAKING, surrounded by the warmth of Hayden's bed and his comforting presence beside me. His arm rests lightly over my waist, his touch possessive even in rest. A whisper in the dark draws me from slumber as his voice floats over me, stirring my senses.

And burrowing into my heart.

"You've been a mystery to me from the moment I first saw you. I've spent weeks trying to understand why you're different than the rest and why you matter when I don't give a fuck about anyone else."

Hayden's admission is soft, meant for only me to hear. I remain still, keeping my breathing even as he continues. I don't want to do anything that'll stop him from telling me the things inside his mind, the things I'm desperate to know.

"I've never felt this loss of control, this all-consuming need for someone." His hand flexes against my hip, a sense of urgency in his fingertips. "I can't let you go now that you're here. If I did, it'd be like removing my lungs. I wouldn't fucking survive it."

My chest tightens at his poetic confession, my heart fluttering in response as if trying to escape and fly to him. His need matches my own, the connection between us refusing to be severed, no matter how much I fight it. But surrender means embracing the darkness that is in him.

A darkness that could eclipse my light.

I draw in a shaky breath as his lips graze my forehead in a kiss that's full of tenderness despite being incredibly soft and brief. "I know you think I only wish to possess you," he whispers against my hair, "but I want to protect you. To avenge you. And I will, even if it takes the rest of my life. I won't stop until justice has been served by my hands."

His arm tightens around me and my body tingles at our closeness, yearning stirring to life once more. I want nothing more than to open my eyes and meet his fervent gaze, to taste the sincerity in his kiss. But I remain unmoving, my pulse racing in time with his. As of now, I'm not ready yet to embrace the truth, even if it's been spoken in the dark in the barest of whispers.

His confession leaves me in turmoil, torn between fear and desire. The only thing I know for sure is that leaving him is impossible. Not because of him making me stay.

Because of me not wanting to leave.

~

I WAKE THE NEXT MORNING IN A NEW PLACE, DISORIENTED AND alone.

It takes several blinks to get my eyes to make sense of my surroundings, and the second my brain makes the connection that I'm in Hayden's bed, everything from the night before bombards me. My mind spins, and I remain still, unable to sit up just yet.

He found out my dark secret.

He destroyed his office.

He held me all night.

I sweep the room with my gaze, already knowing he's not here because I can't feel his energy nearby. It's a living entity, a force field that surrounds me. And now protects me.

After gathering my bearings, I slide from the bed, my gaze landing on the neatly folded clothing sitting on the nightstand. Alongside it is a handwritten note from Hayden.

I wish I could've been here to see how you look with the morning sun kissing your face, but I had a court case that I can't ignore. These clothes are the first sample of your new wardrobe. If they are satisfactory, then I'll continue filling the closet. If not, then I'll see to the changes this evening. As for today, I want you to stay home and rest. I already notified your boss at the Sugar Cube that you're taking the day off. Lastly, text me once you finish reading this. ~Hayden

I frown at the note as irritation surfaces, my cheeks burning. Although I don't mind him taking the initiative to provide clothing for me—considering my only other options are his t-shirt or my dress from last night—I wish he wasn't insistent on buying me an entire wardrobe. A hard lesson I learned from my father's death is that you can't depend on a man to provide everything in your life. Because if they're suddenly gone, you're screwed.

The thought of never seeing Hayden again softens my agitation, and I turn to examine the clothes he picked out, in need of a distraction. It consists of a black pencil skirt and a plum-colored silk blouse, along with a charcoal gray wool coat to shield me from the cold. Each item is stylish and made from luxurious material that'll be heaven against my skin. Then there are the delicate ruffles and strategically placed pleats that add a feminine touch. And if they weren't enough, the black knee-high suede boots do the trick.

After holding the different articles of clothing against my frame, I'm certain they'll fit. As annoyed as I was initially, I have to admit that Hayden has excellent taste. This outfit reminds me of my past life where I had a walk-in closet full of clothes similar to this in price and quality. I also had a fiancé who never came close to making me feel the things Hayden does.

Maybe not all change is bad.

I reach for my purse and retrieve my cell phone, amazed that the battery hasn't died. I suppose it wouldn't since Hayden is the only person—besides Harper—to contact me yesterday, and he stopped as soon as he walked into the club.

> Calista: Good morning. Thank you for the clothes. They're really nice.

> Hayden: Good morning, Callie. You're welcome. Did you sleep well?

His response is immediate. It's so fast I wonder if he had his phone out and was waiting for my text. I smile to myself, enjoying this attentive and caring side of him.

> Calista: Yes, and you?

> Hayden: It was the best sleep of my life.

> Calista: I'm glad. ☺

I bite my lip, unsure of what to say next. Should I tell him that there's no way I'm going to sit in his penthouse all day and do nothing? There are several unread text messages from Harper that I need to address, and I'd prefer to do it in person. Maybe she can help me make sense of the crazy going on in my life right now. If not, at least she'll give me a chance to get it off my chest.

> Hayden: Get some rest today.

> Calista: Lol. I just woke up. I'm definitely not sleepy.

> Hayden: Even so, don't leave the house. I'll see you tonight.

My frown returns full force, and I glare at the phone. If Hayden plans on hiring a private bodyguard then I don't see why I can't visit Harper. If he has a problem with it, then I might need to add that to our pending agreement. I know it's very likely that I'll give in to his demands, but I want to hold on to my delusions for a bit longer.

At least for the next sixty-three hours.

Maybe what really upsets me isn't Hayden's high-handedness, but my desire to fall into old habits and let him take care of me. It'd be so nice to rely on someone else and stop struggling alone, but it's too risky. I'll take the money, gifts, and protection Hayden offers while remembering it's most likely temporary.

My phone chimes, and I look down.

> Hayden: Is there a problem with my last message?

Calista: Nope. I'll see you tonight.

I swipe my finger over the screen and proceed to scan Harper's texts. Each one is more outrageous than the last, and by the time I'm finished I'm more than determined to go see her at work.

Harper: Did you survive the night? Is your hooha wrecked? Pretty sure whatever the lawyer did to you falls under "cruel and unusual punishment." I'm super jealous.

Harper: Seriously, please tell me you're okay. I'm pretty sure you are since Mr. I'm-going-to-fuck-up-Levi was determined to have you to himself.

Harper: Don't worry about Levi. I made him and his friend Darren happy by the end of the night. We're totally swapping sex stories when I see you at work.

Harper: Note to self: never party the night before a 5 a.m. shift. It looks like three hours of sleep and six espresso shots. I may or may not have started hallucinating about dicks floating through the coffee shop.

Harper: There's a guy in the coffee shop using a typewriter. Like, an actual vintage typewriter, the kind that makes a fuckton of noise. Pretty sure he's a time traveler. Should I offer to buy him an iPad or something?

Harper: Girl, this day is dragging without you. Rescue me before I gnaw off my own arm and use it to beat the shit out of a customer.

Harper: I swear, if I hear the phrase "you should smile more" one more time, I'm going to start throwing things. Just letting you know that the tip jar is going to be empty cause I'll need it to make bail.

Calista: I'm stopping by to see you 😐

Harper: THANK. FUCK.

I may or may not grin all the way to the Sugar Cube.

CHAPTER 36

C alista

"You bitch!"

Everyone in the Sugar Cube, including my boss Alex and me, turns to stare at Harper. I know I'm not the only person with my mouth hanging open.

"What?" She flips her hair over her shoulder. "I was worried about my bestie boo, okay?"

I give my co-worker a tiny wave and walk up to the counter, my face hot with embarrassment. "Hey, Harper. Hey, Alex. Sorry about not coming into work today. I accidentally slept in."

He waves a hand in dismissal. "When your boyfriend called me this morning to tell me you were exhausted and needed a day to rest, I was glad to hear it. Today is the first shift you asked to have off, and frankly, it's about time." He lifts a brow. "Which also makes me wonder why you're here."

"I need to talk to Harper. Don't worry, I won't interfere."

Before Alex can respond, my best friend beckons me. "Come on, Calista. Get back here before I die from curiosity."

I make my way behind the counter, put on my apron—earning a frown from Alex—and go to stand beside Harper at the coffee machine. "Why don't you teach me how to make a couple things while we chat between customers?"

"Deal. So..." she says, drawing out the word. "What ended up happening last night with your *boyfriend*?"

Her emphasis on the word makes me cringe. "It's not like that."

"Then what's it like?"

"Well, for starters, Hayden and I aren't official. At least, not that I'm aware of."

Unless you count him wanting to kill someone because of me.

Harper runs her gaze up and down my body. "Well, something's official. I know that outfit didn't come from you."

"You're right. Hayden picked it out for me."

"Damn. Is there anything that man can't do? I bet he's amazing in the sack." She sighs, her lashes fluttering. "I'm going to need details. Inches, girth, etc..."

"Harper! At least lower your damn voice."

She grins at me. "I was wondering if caliente Calista was gone now that the alcohol is out of your system. Glad to see her again."

"I mean it," I say between clenched teeth. "I'll leave if you don't attempt to keep this private."

"Fine." She lowers her voice to a whisper. "Tell me about the sex."

I inhale a preparatory breath, knowing she's not going to readily accept my answer. "We didn't have sex."

"This is a crime against humanity. Okay, so maybe you didn't do everything, but did you do *something*?"

My mind conjures images of Hayden and the feel of his hands on my skin...his fingers inside me. Instantly, my sex clenches, wanting fulfillment. My breathing thins and my blush returns.

"I knew it!" When I frown at Harper's loud response, she brings her voice back down to a whisper. "I knew it! What did he do exactly?"

"Perv much?"

"Perv a lot. Why are you surprised by this?"

I lean close, unwilling to let anyone overhear what I'm about to say. "He fingered me, and I came so hard that I nearly collapsed."

"Oh shit."

I nod. "But that's all that happened. I swear."

"Why didn't you do more?"

Because Hayden found out I was drugged and possibly raped, and lost his fucking mind.

"Because he didn't want to take advantage of me while I was drunk," I say.

"A lawyer with morals. That's hot in a way I didn't realize until now."

"So, tell me about you."

Harper launches into her story, which features a lot of sex and things I didn't even consider or know were possible. By the end I am blushing furiously and nearly run into the kitchen to put my head in the freezer. I don't have to because my friend has pity on me and changes the subject.

"Even though we both had a lot of fun last night, some-thing's weighing on you," she says. "I can see it in your face.

Did the stalker bother you again?" When I shake my head, she purses her lips. "Then what?"

"Hayden wants me to move in with him."

I lean back and wait for the fireworks show that is Harper Flynn.

"Interesting," she says slowly.

"That's it? Someone I barely know asks me to move in with him, and that's all you have to say?"

"Give me a minute. I'm thinking."

I smooth the material of my blouse, needing an outlet for the bristling energy coursing through me. "He said it was to protect me from my stalker, which is really nice, but I hardly know Hayden."

"You've known him longer than you think."

When I frown at her, she winks at me and walks over to Alex to hand him a freshly made cappuccino. By the time she returns to my side, I'm tapping my fingers on my thigh with impatience.

"You told me he was an attorney when he first walked in here," she explains. "How else would you know that if you hadn't met him? We haven't talked about the things that went on with your dad, and I'm cool with that, but I have a feeling you and Mr. finger-me-like-a-god Bennett had a moment at some point. Or else he wouldn't act the way he does around you. That might not be enough of a reason to move in with the guy, but having a stalker changes everything. The devil you know type of thing."

My forehead scrunches with the churning of my thoughts. "I think I need a cake pop."

Harper takes one from the display case and shoves the chocolate cake pop into my hands. "Here, you look like you need this. Sugar helps the brain, right?"

I nod. My mind drifts back to the day Hayden first

walked into the coffee shop, returning like a familiar stranger from the shadows of my past. I had known him, but he treated me very differently back then. Especially when I testified at court.

That didn't stop me from being attracted to him.

And it didn't stop him from wanting to protect me.

He's a monster and a savior, all in one.

My skin prickles at the memory of his threat: "I'll make them suffer in ways no one has ever suffered. Before I fucking kill them." There's no doubt in my mind that he meant every word. To a degree I don't want to clarify. He'll use his hands to enact vengeance.

And use those same hands to extract pleasure from me.

My thighs clench at the memory of his touch, the way his fingers whispered across my skin. "You're right," I murmur, my words more for me than Harper. "There's... something between us that I can't wrap my head around. He's acknowledged it as well and told me that we're inevitable."

"Wow, that's fucking romantic." She tilts her head. "Or psychotic. Take your pick."

A reluctant smile works its way onto my mouth. Only to disappear at my next thought. "That's true, but he's intense. It's one of the reasons that makes me hesitate when it comes to him."

I swallow hard and glance at Harper, who's watching me with a mix of concern and curiosity. There's no way I can tell her everything, but she's smart enough to read between the lines.

"So, he's a real bad boy, not some jackass pretending to be tough, huh?" When I nod, she arches her brow. "And not just the garden-variety kind. Interesting."

I groan. "I know how it sounds. But when I'm with him he's the only one who makes me feel safe."

"Considering you have a stalker, that's not exactly a bad thing."

"I know." I groan again, louder this time, and cover my face with my hands. "I feel like no matter what I do, it'll be a mistake."

"Look at me." When I let my arms fall to my sides, she pins me with a look. It's caring but stern and I stand a little straighter. "You're one of the strongest, most hard-working women I know," she says. "If being with Hayden felt wrong, you'd already be out the door. But you're still here and talking it over with me, aren't you?"

Her words resonate with unexpected truth, loosening the knots of tension along my shoulders. She's right. I wouldn't stay if I really thought Hayden would hurt me. Even when I provoked him last night, he always remained in control of his actions and his temper. The only time he didn't was because he was enraged on my behalf. Not *at* me.

"No one can take away your strength," she says. "Not even Mr. Tall-dark-and-dangerous-dick-size Bennett. But if he does step out of line, I've got a bat with his name on it. And it's not just any bat, but a 'Lucille.'"

I blink at her. "A what?"

"Zombie show reference. Don't worry about it. I'm just saying I'll fuck him up bad. Regardless of what you decide, please be careful."

"I think I'll stay with him and take it one day at a time. Worst-case scenario, I can sleep on the floor in your dorm, right?"

Harper chuckles. "Yep!"

I throw my arms around her and squeeze my friend tightly, beyond grateful for her support. And perspective.

Although my connection with Hayden is intense and complicated, I'm going into it with my eyes open to the risks. His protectiveness is seductive and giving up some of my independence won't be easy, but at the end of the day, I have a stalker.

Hayden is the perfect person to deal with that.

CHAPTER 37

H ayden

CALISTA ISN'T WHERE SHE'S SUPPOSED TO BE.

I glance down at my phone, noting her position on the map displayed on my screen. The Sugar Cube. Of course. After everything that happened last night, it makes sense she'd run to her friend. I'm not exactly sure how much she's going to reveal to her co-worker, but I'm not concerned.

I won't allow anything or anyone to get in between me and Calista.

Not even herself.

Ironically, she's the one putting up the biggest obstacle. Although some of her barriers dropped last night. Or she wouldn't have told me the name of the private clinic.

Every time I think about it, I almost lose my shit all over again.

I glance at the defense table, taking in the creases and stress lines on the attorney's face. She doesn't like losing a case—no one in our profession does—but she hates it when she loses to me. Maybe I shouldn't have fucked and discarded her.

The defense counsel meets my gaze and glares at me. I don't bother with a response. Instead, I dismiss her by averting my attention to the files and notes spread out before me. The murderer on trial is going away for a long time.

Pity.

I would've liked to kill this one for hurting his wife.

Despite the attention to detail and focus this job requires, my mind wanders. Always to Calista. She fills my thoughts, an obsession I'm powerless to shake free from.

She's testing me now by going against my instructions and leaving my home. I'm sure of it. Is she wondering whether or not I'll chase her? A frown tugs at my lips. After I caught her in the alley last night, she should know better.

I sit in my chair, resisting the urge to get up and leave. To reclaim my little bird that's flown the coop. The judge drones on, but I ignore his nasally voice. Instead, the sounds that fill my head are Calista's soft cries as she fell apart with my fingers inside her soft cunt. There was a sweet torment of knowing she'd be mine completely someday while I brought her pleasure that overwhelmed her body and mind.

My cock stiffens at the memory.

I retrieve my phone and type out a quick text to her.

> Hayden: Just thinking of you makes my cock hard. That's going to get the judge's attention in a way that doesn't help my case.

> Calista: If she's a woman, I'd argue that point.

I almost smile like an idiot. For some reason, I enjoy Calista's fiery nature. It started off as a tiny flame, but with time she's become an inferno. I can't help but stoke the blaze.

> **Hayden:** He's not female, but the jury does have a few women.

> **Calista:** There you go. See? I'm helping you.

> **Hayden:** I'm about to give my closing statement to a jury who won't give me a verdict on anything except my cock. Which is guilty when it comes to you.

> **Calista:** If this is your version of flirting, I'm going to need it to be PG from now on.

> **Hayden:** Say yes to moving in with me and I'll stop.

> **Calista:** My answer is still undecided, and no you won't.

> **Hayden:** Probably true. Don't leave the Sugar Cube. I'll pick you up once I'm done here.

> **Calista:** Yup.

I turn my phone off and set it aside. She always gives me short answers whenever she has no intention of obeying me. It happened last night and again this morning. I'd have to be stupid to think this latest text from her is something else than a subtle "go fuck yourself."

The problem is, I want to fuck her.

But I can't yet. Not until she's ready. With everything that happened to her on June 24th, I won't be another man who becomes her worst nightmare.

Rage surges hot and vicious at the thought of her traumatic experience, and I clench my fists beneath the table. Whoever was involved won't escape the plans I have for them. By the time I'm done, there won't be a part of them that'll be identifiable.

Let the hunting begin.

But I'm not only chasing them. I'll be wearing Calista down until she accepts my protection. However, a softer touch is needed with her. I'll worship her body and give her the world until she gives me her surrender.

And her heart.

That's the ultimate prize.

It'll have to be earned slowly. Step by step. One wall at a time. Eventually, they'll fall, and she'll be mine. Not only my lover, but my salvation.

My one chance at redemption.

Since I haven't been able to avenge my mother.

CHAPTER 38

C alista

HAYDEN'S TEXTS ARE GOING TO GIVE ME A HEART ATTACK.

Or an orgasm.

I'm not sure which.

This sexy, flirty side of him is...hot. That's all there is to it.

"Your face is bright red, girl." Harper holds out her hand. "Let me see the texts."

"Promise me you won't tease me about them."

"I cross my heart and hope to get laid."

I hand her the phone and watch as her green eyes widen before she bursts out with laughter. "Holy hot damn, girl. I can see why your face is on fire." She waggles her brows at me. "This man certainly has a way with words."

My sigh is long and loud. "I'm never showing you texts from him again."

"No, don't do that. I need this sexy shit in my life. It's gold."

"Harper, I swear..."

She's never going to let me forget these texts. And knowing Hayden, this is just the beginning. The flirting, the teasing, and the intensity—it's thrilling and terrifying all at once. Part of me wonders if I'm in over my head.

The other part of me wants more.

Harper cackles, her grin getting bigger by the second. "I wish I was on that jury."

"Okay, but seriously, don't you find his bossiness a little much?"

Her face loses all traces of amusement. She nods slowly. "It's definitely a lot, but he's very...single-minded when it comes to you."

"True."

"Hey," she says, squeezing my shoulder. "Don't over-think this. I know he's complicated, but this man is into you. And you deserve someone who knows what he wants and is willing to wait. If that wasn't the case, you would've had sex last night. Case in point, he's a gentleman. Kind of."

She smiles at me. "Not every relationship is meant to last, so don't take it so seriously. Now, your stalker? Take that shit seriously, and if you need Hayden to help you, I don't see the problem. Two birds, one cock."

My lips twitch. "That's not how the saying goes."

"Sometimes you just click with someone in a way that sets your soul on fire, and that's okay. It'll be fine as long as you listen to your instincts and make sure you get what you need too."

The door to the coffee shop opens, and I spin around, feeling a shift in the atmosphere. Hayden walks in with his gaze already on me. It crackles with the potency of his thoughts.

My heart leaps into my throat when he walks up to the counter. "Hey," I say, trying to sound casual, while ignoring my racing pulse. "What brings you here?"

"You." He folds his arms. "Are you ready to leave?"

I nod. "Just give me a second to say bye to Alex."

After running into the kitchen and telling my boss good-bye, I return to the front and smile at Harper. "I'll see you in the morning?"

"Of course, at the ass-crack of dawn." She turns to face Hayden and narrows her gaze. "Take good care of our girl or I'm coming after you."

Hayden quirks a brow. "Two death threats in less than twenty-four hours, Miss Flynn? That's a record for me."

"I'm about to make it three, if you don't promise me you'll take things at her pace." She plants a hand on her hip while using the other to point to her face. "Eyes of a killer, remember?"

"Of course," Hayden says. "You have my word that I'll take very good care of Calista."

Harper's face splits with a grin. "Okie dokie. Let me know if you need bail money or an alibi. You two have a good night."

A secret smile curves his lips. "We will."

~

I GLANCE AT HAYDEN SITTING IN THE DRIVER'S SEAT, TAKING IN the look of concentration on his face. "Where are you taking me?"

"I made reservations for Le Boudoir tonight."

"That's one of the nicest restaurants in the city. I've heard it has amazing French cuisine, but the wait-list is more than six months out." I pause. "Don't tell me you made this reservation for someone else, and I just happen to be filling in for her."

"I haven't even so much as looked at another woman since I met you."

My eyebrows shoot up. "You're just saying that."

"I never say things I don't mean, Callie."

"So you're not trying to persuade me?"

"I didn't say that. However, I also want you to have the best of everything."

I bite my lip. Until he sucks in a breath and his gaze darkens. "If you do that again, I'll pull this car over so I can have a taste."

"Sorry," I mumble.

The rest of the drive is both long and short with Hayden's sensual threat hanging over me. However, once we get to our destination, I'm more at ease. It's hard not to give in to temptation with this man, but being in a public place will cure me of that.

Le Boudoir is everything I imagined and more.

Dark wood panels line the walls that are lit by the golden glow of crystal chandeliers positioned above each table. The employees, wearing crisp black suits, glide between the tables, and speak in hushed tones to preserve the peaceful ambience. The place is elegant with hints of intimacy in the darker corners of the room, its tables filled with couples who provide a constant hum of conversation.

"It's so beautiful," I whisper, not wanting to disrupt anyone's meal.

"Yes, it is."

I turn to look at him with a smile on my face, only to find him already staring at me. "This way," he says.

Hayden places his hand on the small of my back, his fingertips gripping me securely. The protective gesture has tendrils of warmth shooting through my whole body. He leads me to a section in the back, one that's obviously reserved for very special diners who have large bank accounts. I want to protest against the extravagance, but when he glances at me as if I'm his reason for breathing...

I can't deny this man anything.

He pulls out my chair, and I sit down, immediately nervous to have him across from me. I won't be able to hide from his scrutiny. "Why did you bring me here?" I ask.

"I wanted to go somewhere where we could enjoy a leisurely dinner with minimal interruptions."

"So this whole thing isn't a ploy to convince me to move in with you?"

He lifts his water glass. "I never said that."

"Fair." I smooth the napkin over my lap with trembling fingers. "It's been so long since I've been anywhere this nice. I have to admit, I kind of feel out of my element."

"I want you to listen closely," he says, fixing me with a hard look. "You belong anywhere I bring you. No exceptions."

A blush heats my cheeks and I pick up my water, partially obscuring my face behind the glass. "Thank you."

The waiter stops by our table a few seconds later and I use his welcome interruption to gather my composure. It's fleeting. After taking our orders, the man leaves to retrieve our wine, quickly returning. He sets the glasses in front of us and excuses himself until our meal is ready.

The air between Hayden and me takes on an electrical charge once we're alone.

I smooth out my hair, trying to hide my fidgeting by wrapping a long curl around my finger. He watches me with an intensity that makes it nearly impossible to breathe properly. I reach for my wineglass and take a sip, hoping the alcohol will relax me a little.

Hayden tilts his head. "You're nervous." It's not a question.

"Yes."

"Why?"

"Why is a mouse nervous around a cat?"

He smirks at me, making my heart flip in my chest. "I prefer to think of you as a little bird. *My* little bird."

"Either way, you're the predator in this simile." I shrug. "I just hope you don't plan on putting me in a cage."

"It's for your safety. And others'."

"Others?"

He nods. "If they touch you, I'll...Let's just say, I'd rather they didn't."

"This conversation isn't convincing me to agree to your terms." I take another sip of my wine. Okay, it's almost a gulp. When dealing with Hayden, I find that liquid courage helps me be more bold. "Maybe you should take me to my apartment after dinner."

"I could, but none of your things are there."

"What the hell?"

His lips thin with displeasure. "Language, Calista."

"What did you do?"

"Your personal effects are at my home. The furniture was donated to the shelter you used to volunteer at. Hopeful Hearts, right?" When I nod, still fuming, he continues. "If you decide to return to your apartment, it'll be a new one in a different location, and it'll be fully furnished."

I down the contents of my glass and set it on the table with a quiet thud. Leaning forward, I glare at him. "I appreciate you wanting to keep me safe, but this is *my* life, Hayden. You can't control every aspect of it."

His hand shoots out and grasps mine where it rests on the table. It's so quick I don't have time to react before he's tightening his fingers and bringing my knuckles to his mouth, never breaking eye contact with me. He presses a kiss to each one and then a final one on the palm of my hand, letting his lips linger until I'm squirming in my chair.

"Your life is all I care about, and I'll do whatever it takes to preserve it, Callie. Even if that means pissing you off."

"But what about the agreement?"

"The seventy-two hours was an excuse to give you time to come to terms with everything. Because you are going to give me what I want. I won't leave you alone until I know you're protected."

I try to jerk my hand back, but he maintains possession of me by gripping me tighter. As if to soothe my temper, he strokes my knuckles with his thumb. Leisurely. Back and forth until I stop fighting him.

"Give in, little bird. Let me take care of you."

I swallow hard, captured by his gaze. The determination in his voice. "I let my father take care of me and then I was destroyed when he died. Don't you see how risky this is for me?"

"I'll give you financial security, if that's what it'll take to get you to say yes."

"I don't want to be a charity case," I say between clenched teeth.

"That's not how I see you, and you know it."

He releases me when the waiter arrives with our food. I fold my hands in my lap and bow my head, keeping my attention on the delicious meal sitting in front of me. My stomach grumbles softly, and I pick up my fork to eat, praying I don't stab Hayden with it for driving me crazy. The fact that I'm having these types of thoughts might be a direct result of being Harper's best friend.

And I love her for it.

"Please, eat, Callie."

When I jerk up my head, I find Hayden watching me with curiosity swimming in his gaze. We eat in silence for a few moments, the tension between us palpable.

I know he means well, but why can't he understand how much his proposal scares me? Maybe he does see it and doesn't care since it interferes with my safety. However, the thought of relying completely on another person and giving them power over my happiness and security again is terrifying.

Yet Hayden sees his actions as him protecting me, his way of caring for what he considers to be already his. Me. His need to possess and control everything around him will either break me or give me freedom in his embrace.

I take a deep breath and lift my gaze to his. "We want the same thing, but your methods need adjustment if this is going to work."

His brow furrows. "How so?"

"If you want me to be in your life, this thing between us has to be a partnership, not you dictating my every move." I set down my fork and hold his stare. "I can accept your financial security, but only if you promise to keep it in an account that's separate from mine. I only want it there as a fail-safe and nothing else. As far as living with you, I can agree to the bodyguard, but I want to continue working. And lastly, I want to schedule an end date."

"End date?" he repeats, the words clipped. He tightens his grip on his fork until his knuckles lose their color. "What do you mean?"

"I don't expect you to let me live with you forever, so we'll treat our contract like a lease agreement. I'll agree to stay for a certain amount of time and then at the end, I'll have access to the trust fund you set up for me. That way I'm earning the money and not a handout."

Hayden leans forward, his gaze narrowing infinitesimally. "Are you saying that you want me to pay you for living with me?" When I nod, he clenches his jaw. "That'd make you no better than a whore."

The words hit me like a cold wind, knocking the breath out of me. His accusation lingers in the air, and I resist the urge to rub the chill from my arms. The anger in his eyes flickers when I bite my lip, quickly morphing into lust.

I shake my head. "I didn't mean to imply our agreement is purely transactional or that I see myself as a whore. It's more about finding a sense of security that ensures we both have a future beyond this temporary agreement."

"There is no future without you in it."

"Hayden..."

"You're my life. That won't change."

I twist my hands in my lap. "What if it does?"

"You're mine in life and death. There is no end when it comes to us."

"I don't believe that."

He shrugs. "You don't have to. I know it to be true. You're looking for security in material things, so ask for what you want. Money, done. Abstinence, done. Only for a time anyway. A marriage certificate where you'd be my wife and therefore entitled to all my assets? Done. I'd marry you tonight if that's what you wanted. Whatever it takes to get you to finally understand that you're everything to me."

I stare at Hayden, stunned into silence by his passionate declaration. Marriage and money? Just to prove his devotion and commitment to me? I don't know whether to be flattered or frightened by the intensity of his feelings. They have always bordered on obsession, burning so fiercely they in turn consume everything in their path. There are times when I worried they'd destroy me too, but now I'm wondering if the flames will keep me warm and ward off predators that are hunting me.

Perhaps I've been afraid of the wrong person. Hayden knows the darkest stains on my soul and still wants me. If this same man would move heaven and earth for me, how can that devotion be anything other than a gift?

He searches my gaze, taking in the look on my face, and blows out a sharp breath. He runs his fingers through his hair, finally letting me see the uncertainty beneath his cool exterior. This man has always been sure of himself and me.

I don't want that to ever change.

"What are you thinking?" he asks. "Talk to me."

"Yes," I say softly.

"What?"

"I'm saying yes."

"To marriage?" When I shake my head, he jerks back. "Then what?"

"I'm saying yes to *you*, Hayden."

His brows snap together. "What about my conditions?"

"I don't care about proposals, a seventy-two-hour waiting period, or marriage. I don't care about the physical or monetary things you can give me, but if that's what you want, then I'll find a way to accept it. I've used everything as an excuse because I was scared, but I'm putting off the inevitable. All I want is you. So, yes."

He stands abruptly and his chair teeters before landing with a loud thud. I stare up at him with wide eyes as he rounds the table to stand in front of me. "What are you doing?" I ask.

"When the woman of your darkest fantasies says she wants you, you don't let anything get in the way of her changing her mind."

CHAPTER 39

C alista

The car ride back to Hayden's place is electric.

Energy fizzes along my nerves, igniting my skin and making it sensitive, but he has yet to touch me. If not for the dangerous glint in his eyes, I'd think he was unaffected by my presence.

And the fact I'm giving myself to him.

Hayden is the perfect gentleman the entire time and it drives me insane. He opens my car door and escorts me to the foyer, all without skin-to-skin contact. As usual he places his hand on the small of my back, guiding me to our destination, but there's nothing more than that. My nervousness grows the closer we get to his penthouse.

I step into the elevator with him behind me, and the doors shut, leaving Hayden and me alone. The air is heavy with anticipation, the pull between us undeniable.

He stands behind me and I can feel the heat emanating

from his body. Butterflies take flight in my stomach when he leans forward, his lips just beside my ear. His breath tickles my neck as he reaches out to punch in the code giving us access to his floor.

I frown when he steps back and leans against the far wall, putting as much distance between us as the enclosed space will allow. He stands with his hands in his pockets, his gaze unreadable. Except there's a narrowing of his eyes whenever he looks at me.

I turn my head and try to focus on the floor numbers slowly climbing, but I'm acutely aware of Hayden. Every part of me longs to turn and kiss him, to give in to this tension that threatens to swallow me whole.

The charged silence hangs between us, weighted with unspoken truths and wants. I lean against the wall, feigning nonchalance. Until he whispers my name. The sound is desperate and full of agony.

I flick my gaze to him and my breath hitches. Fists clenched at his sides, he takes a step toward me and stops, uncertainty etched into the set of his jaw. My heart stutters at this uncharacteristic indecision, a crack in his impenetrable facade. I sway toward him without thought, longing for the familiar heat of his skin on mine. He stares at me, his gaze traveling over every inch of my body as if he can't decide where to touch me.

"Fuck it," he says, his breath ragged. "I can't wait anymore."

He backs me into the wall, his mouth trailing fire down my throat as fingers grip the hem of my skirt. Then he claims me for a kiss. It turns ravenous, all lips and teeth and edges softened in the space between frantic heartbeats, until I'm trembling from the sensual onslaught.

I cling to his shoulders as he glides his hands over my

fevered skin, rough and impatient yet somehow reverent in their rediscovery of every curve. Then he abruptly breaks the kiss to drop to his knees before me. And lifts my skirt to my waist.

"Let me see that pretty pussy."

A growl rumbles from deep in Hayden's chest before he yanks my panties down to my ankles in one swift movement. With a fierce hunger, he watches when I spread my legs, giving him access to the intimate part of me. His eyes drink me in, as if he can't get enough.

"You better come before we reach my floor," he says.

His stubble scrapes against tender skin when he grips the backs of my legs and buries his face between my thighs. His mouth on me is like a wildfire—hot and insistent, leaving sparks of pleasure beneath his touch. His tongue circles and teases until I'm panting, my breathing short puffs of air that fog up the mirrors on either side of me. Before I close my eyes, I look at my reflection. Hayden's head is between my legs and I'm clinging to him, my eyes bright with the pleasure he's giving me.

I thread my fingers through his hair as I rock against him, aching for release. His fingers dig into my skin, keeping me immobile while I writhe beneath his skillful tongue and lips. The moan that escapes me spurs him on. He devours me until I'm mumbling incoherent things, every sound sheer desperation.

Just when I think I can't take anymore, he drives me over the brink with one final stroke of his tongue. My body shakes uncontrollably as ecstasy slams into me. I cry out his name, the sound ricocheting off the walls and echoing in the small space.

"That's my good girl," he whispers against my sensitive flesh, his breath skimming my clit.

He doesn't let up, continuing to lap and suck until my orgasm has long since faded. He pulls away slowly, licking his lips as he looks up at me with a smirk. His eyes are filled with satisfaction, the hue like aquamarines.

"You taste even better than I imagined," he murmurs.

Before I can respond, he stands up, his focus centered on my mouth. I watch him as he lowers his head and claims it for a kiss. I taste myself on his tongue, immediately groaning at the eroticism of it.

When he pulls away, the side of his mouth lifts. "See what I mean?"

I nod, still high from what he did to me. My legs are weak and unsteady, but somehow I manage to stay upright as he straightens my skirt. My eyes widen when he removes my panties from my ankles and pockets the material with a wink. Then he takes my hand in his before we walk down the hallway toward the door, not saying a word until we reach it and step inside.

Hayden locks the door and spins to face me. His eyes gleam with a longing that sears me where I stand. Before my next breath, he pins me against the wall, his lips crashing into mine. I melt into him, kissing him back with everything I have. Weeks of suppressed desire are finally released at this moment.

He tangles his fingers in my hair while I clutch at his back, pulling him closer. He deepens the kiss and winds his arm around my waist, lifting me off the ground. I wrap my legs around him as he conquers my mouth with every sweep of his tongue and the pressure of his lips on mine.

Only when my lungs spasm does he break the kiss. I suck in a breath as he drags his mouth along my jaw and down my neck, stopping at the sensitive spot just below my ear. At my shiver, he smiles against my skin, knowing the power he has over me. To unravel me completely.

And then rearrange me. To be whatever he needs.

My fingers tremble with excitement as I fumble with the buttons of his shirt, wanting to feel his bare skin against mine. He assists me and tosses the shirt, giving me an unobstructed view of his body. I trail my fingers over the contours of sculpted muscle until he groans and moves my hands to the side.

He grips my shirt by the collar and rips it down the middle. Eyes wide, I blink at the sound of material being shredded. But I revel in the savagery, in his desperation to have me.

To fuck me.

With my blouse and bra discarded on the floor, he palms my breast and claims my lips once more. I sigh into his mouth as he caresses me, tweaking my nipple, one then the other. I revel in the feel of his skin on mine and the solidness of his body pressing into me. Heat radiates off of him and there's a transference of energy and urgency as he halts the kiss to undo and remove his pants.

"I'm going to wreck that pretty pussy of yours," he says on a groan.

I look down. And almost wish I hadn't. Hayden's cock is huge. He's going to more than wreck me. He's going to kill me. But what a way to die.

He reaches between our bodies, stroking me, and his breath hisses between his teeth. "Fuck. You're dripping for me."

Our eyes meet and I'm lost in his gaze, the way it burns with the intensity of his lust for me. He's set me ablaze, igniting a fever that only he can sate, the same fire that's going to consume us both in an inferno that'll leave nothing behind but ashes.

The tip of his cock leaks pre-cum onto my belly and I pull him closer, needing the friction and heat of his body. His eyes drop to my lips, swollen from the violence of our kisses, and the blue darkens with desire.

"This is how I like seeing you," he says. "All fucked up from *my* hands and mouth on your body. Keep your eyes on me. I want to watch your face as I fuck you."

After lifting me by the waist, he positions his cock at my entrance and thrusts his hips forward, steadily easing inside me. The pressure increases rapidly as does my breathing. When it becomes too much, I squeeze my eyes closed at the prick of pain.

"Eyes on me," he snaps.

I obey without hesitation. "It hurts."

"It better." He continues filling me, one inch at a time, until I'm panting and tears sting my eyes. "That's it, baby," he murmurs. "Almost there. Fuck, you're perfect. Better than I imagined."

The tenderness in his voice mixes with the raw need pouring off of his body. With one hand gripping the back of my neck, the other grabs my hip firmly, keeping me in place until I've taken all of him.

He pulls almost all the way out before driving back inside me. I swear he's deeper than before. But the pain is gone. It's been replaced with a delicious sensation that lights up every nerve ending in my body.

"Tell me you're okay," he says. "Because I can't stop, baby. This is what you do to me."

"I want it harder."

"Fuck, you're such a good girl."

He withdraws to thrust back inside me, each time

deeper than before, wrenching a gasp from me. His experienced body creates a punishing rhythm, hips crashing against mine, his hold on my neck tight.

"I'm not going to stop until you're ruined for anyone else."

I grip him tight as he drives harder, slamming me against the wall with his rough movements. They become even more urgent and intense until he's fucking me without restraint.

Unhinged and primal.

"The way you take my cock," he says. "It's so fucking good."

I take it all. Everything he gives me. And I still want more.

Of him.

Hayden yanks me away from the wall and stalks over to the couch. He lays me on my back while remaining inside my body, but is quick to sink back into me fully. I sigh when he buries his face in the curve of my neck, breathing my name like a prayer as he begins to worship me again. I cling to him, desperate to keep this moment alive, desperate to maintain this connection between us. Not only one that's physical, but emotional as well.

"That's it, baby," he says when I dig my nails into his skin. "Use me. Take what you need."

We're both reckless, drunk on this explosive passion. The tension within me builds until I'm hovering between insanity and complete bliss. He fucks me relentlessly, throwing me into ecstasy. I come, and his lips claim mine, leaving me to cry his name in his mouth.

"Fuck, Callie."

He withdraws and grips his cock, jerking it roughly as if he's angry at the idea of withdrawing from me. I watch him unabashedly. He's masculine beauty and sex all in one as he fucks himself, his fist working his cock with hard, fast strokes. Before he comes all over my chest, the warm liquid clinging to my skin.

His chest and mine collide when he collapses on top of me, our bodies slick with sweat and cum. His heart pounds against mine, grounding me, reminding me he's human. Even if he does fuck like a god.

He takes my jaw in hand, lifting my gaze until it meets his. I stare up at him, silently expressing what words fail to do. I'm falling for him.

If I haven't already.

He kisses me softly now, ever so slowly. The urgency has faded but the passion remains. The intense attraction that goes beyond sex. It scares the shit out of me.

But I'm not going anywhere.

CHAPTER 40

H ayden

CALISTA BELONGS TO ME.

She always has in my mind, but now I have her body. I've marked and claimed it, indicated by the cum on her skin and the splotches of red blooming along her neck and chest. The only thing that I've yet to possess is her heart. I need that as well.

More than anything.

She trembles underneath me, staring up at me, her face stained with tears. Using the back of my hand, I brush away the dampness and study her response to my touch. She leans into me and closes her eyes, a gentle sigh sweeping past her lips.

No one else has been there for Calista like I have. It's only fitting that I be the one to comfort her.

"Are you all right?" I ask. When she nods, I narrow my gaze. "Don't lie to me."

"I'm fine, Hayden. I'm just...tired."

"Tired?"

She gives me a smile meant to reassure me, but it doesn't quite penetrate the worry gathering at the back of my mind. "You kind of wore me out," she says. Despite her cheeks being flushed from exertion, she blushes. "It's never been this way for me."

"Me either."

The truth is out in the open before I can think to recall it. Any regret I had at exposing my innermost thoughts evaporates at the warmth brightening her hazel eyes. Calista gazes up at me as though I'm her savior. I suppose that's true.

But I'm also her enemy, the man who killed her father.

Any feelings she's developed for me would wither and die if she were to learn about that. Even for the sake of the truth, I can't tell her. Losing Calista isn't worth the risk. Nothing is.

"Hayden, please don't say things unless you mean them. You don't need to protect my feelings."

She has no idea how false that statement is.

I lift a brow. "I'm telling the truth."

"But you've been with so many women." She shakes her head, drawing my gaze to the dark strands. "It's hard to believe that sex with me is different."

"*Everything* is different with you."

For starters, I never became obsessed with or stalked other women. I didn't have to chase them either. But most importantly, no one else has made me *feel*. With Calista, I'm beginning to experience the full spectrum of emotion. It's unnerving yet I'm powerless to stop it.

"That's sweet of you to say," she whispers. "I appreciate it."

I scoff. "I'm not trying to be sweet. I always mean what I say or else I wouldn't bother saying it to begin with. So believe me when I tell you that I've never met anyone like you."

This woman affects me in ways I couldn't predict. Even now, I'm surprised by my behavior and thoughts when it comes to her. And I hate surprises. I suppose Calista's presence in my life is the only one I haven't minded. I did in the beginning, but now?

I can't imagine living without her.

"Honestly, I can say the same thing about you," she says. "Harper thinks you're crazy."

I might be. "What do you think?"

She scrunches up her face in a way I find endearing. "I think you're insane, but if that's the case, then I'm crazy too because I like it."

If you only knew the things I've done...and will do for you.

"Your opinion is the only one that matters," I say. She beams up at me and that familiar ache in my chest returns. The one that only happens because of Calista. "Let's get you to bed."

She nods, but when I lift my torso she goes completely still and squeezes her thighs. A wince has her brow wrinkling and I immediately stop moving.

"Callie?"

"It's fine."

"Look at me." She flicks her gaze to mine and I search it, finding unease and needing to reassure her. "You shouldn't be sore for very long."

"It's not like I'm a virgin, but I—"

I slam my mouth to hers, smothering the words that could send me into a rage. Calista yields to me, her lips parting and her body softening underneath mine. I kiss her until she wraps her arms around my neck, any lingering discomfort far from her mind.

"If you say another man's name while wearing my cum on your skin, I'll kill him," I say. *I might anyway since he had the privilege of your body before I did.* "One thing's for certain, I'll be the last person to fuck you."

"Hayden." My name is a gasp. Or perhaps a wheeze.

"Good girl. That's the only thing I want to hear from you."

"Oh, my God." Calista's gaze bounces back and forth between my cock and her cunt. It makes me hard. Then her chest starts heaving with her jagged breaths, bringing my attention to her beautiful tits. Now I'm ready to fuck her again.

"Did we stain the couch?" she whispers.

Amusement comes barreling up my chest. It catches me off guard, but at the look of exasperation on Calista's face, I don't stop it. My laughter rings out in the open room. I can't remember the last time I laughed like this.

She slaps my arm playfully. "I'm being serious, Hayden."

It takes me a minute to get myself under control. For once, Calista has made me lose myself, but I can embrace it. "Nothing's wrong. I told you I'd wreck you. Now let's get you cleaned up."

Her bewildered expression morphs into horror when I pull her into my arms, ready to carry her to the bathroom. "The couch," she wails softly. "I've ruined it with our...sex."

I laugh again, louder and longer than before. "It's not ruined, it's improved."

"Ew, Hayden. Just ew."

"We'll have to agree to disagree."

"I need some sanitizer or you're going to have to get rid of the couch. And that woman's picture," she mutters.

I almost laugh for a third time. The photograph in my room is of Calista. One day I'll tell her, but not tonight.

After setting Calista on her feet in the shower, I angle the spray away from her until it's the right temperature. Then I wash her from head to toe. Enjoying every fucking second of it.

She blushes furiously the entire time, but that only adds to my pleasure. I haven't taken care of a woman like this since my mother, and it's soothing in a way I didn't expect. Maybe because my mother was drugged out of her mind when I looked after her. Memories surface, disturbing the serenity I've found with Calista and I'm quick to dismiss them, but it's not without effort.

"Thank you," Calista says, once she's dressed in my t-shirt and lying in my bed. "You didn't have to do all that."

"Yes, I did. I take care of what belongs to me."

"Including me."

"*Especially* you," I say.

She mocks me with a frown, but it melts away the second I climb onto the bed and pull her to me. Contentment like I've never known surrounds me like a blanket, offering warmth and peace. All because of the woman in my arms.

"Go to sleep, Callie."

She salutes me with a yawn. "No problem, sir."

"We need to discuss your flippant behavior at some point."

"Yup."

I grin. "You think I don't hear the 'fuck you' when you do that?"

"Yup."

With a laugh, I swat her ass, making her yelp. I massage

her skin while using my other arm to keep her in place. "I think you enjoy testing my patience."

"Yu—erm, yes, I do."

My smile widens. "Sleep now."

"I can't when my ass is on fire."

"Language, Miss Green."

Calista lifts her head from my chest and kisses me, startling me with her uncharacteristic display of affection. Now I'm the one who's been wrecked. My heart, wherever that fucker might be, bleeds for her.

"Good night, Mr. Bennett."

"Good night, baby."

CHAPTER 41

C alista

"It's been three days," I say.

Harper looks at me with a confused expression twisting her lips. "Three days since what?"

I lower my voice, my gaze darting around the Sugar Cube before I answer in a whisper. "Since Hayden and I had sex. Why hasn't he initiated anything?"

"I don't know." Harper taps her chin. "That doesn't sound normal for someone like him. Maybe he's waiting for your vagina to heal? I mean he did dig into it like he was searching for gold or some shit."

My face heats up and I press my hands to my cheeks. "Sometimes I can't handle your honesty."

"But you love me for it."

"I do."

"If he's worried about you, then you could give him the signal that it's go time." She waggles her brows at me. "I have plenty of ideas which involve you being naked, a fondue machine, and chocolate. Or cheese."

I scrunch my face. "No, thank you, but I can get behind the gist of the plan."

"Can't go wrong with being naked," she says with a shrug.

"I suppose. I just need the balls to do it."

"More like the ovaries. I wouldn't worry about it though because the pheromones coming off you two could fog up bulletproof glass. So, how's everything else going? Besides the non-sex after the mind-blowing sex." She plants a hand on her hip. "You seem happy."

"I am happy." I bite my lip in thought. "Probably the happiest I've been since my dad's funeral."

Harper nods with a knowing look. "Good dick will do that to a girl."

"It's more than that. I feel safe. It took Hayden two days to identify my stalker and get rid of him. If that's not reassuring, I don't know what is."

Harper's gaze narrows. "That was really fast. I guess with his access to certain resources it wouldn't be hard. I'm just glad you're not in danger anymore."

"Me too."

"Then what's the look for?"

"What look?"

"That one." She gestures to my face with a circling motion. "Why was there a funny sound in your voice just now?"

"What sound?"

"Something's up." She turns to look over her shoulder and raises her voice. "Welcome to the Sugar Cube. I'll be right with you." Then she faces me, rolling her eyes. "I hate how customers get in the way of our girl talk. I expect an answer once I fill their order."

I handle the transaction and as soon as I give the customer their coffee, Harper's on me. She hands me a cake pop as though to placate me for the interrogation she's about to initiate. I take the dessert with a sigh.

"All right, girl," she says. "Give me the deets."

"What if Hayden's too good to be true? He's handsome, wealthy, and treats me like I'm his reason for living. That has to be a red flag, right?"

Harper's lips pull to the side. "Red's my favorite color."

I bite back a laugh. "Be serious."

"I am." She takes my shoulders and stares at me, her green eyes scrutinizing my face. "Look, you've been through a lot in the past year and it's probably got you in survival state of mind. No one can blame you for that, but you don't want to ruin the happiness you've found just because of your past trauma. If Mr. Bend-me-over Bennett is the real deal, you'll regret pushing him away to protect yourself."

"And if he's not good for me?"

After a quick squeeze, my friend releases my shoulders. "If he's a piece of shit, then you'll find out soon enough and dump his ass. Don't be overly cynical until he gives you a reason. You deserve to be happy, okay?"

I smile at her. "Okay."

She flicks her gaze to the door and does nothing to stifle her loud groan. "It's time for the brunch rush. Hold on to your butts. Do you know that movie reference?"

"Yes," I say with a laugh.

The familiar work calms my mind even as my body moves on autopilot. Thankfully, the line of customers moves quickly without any incident and the time passes even faster. My mind drifts to Hayden and I lean against the counter before squirting hand sanitizer on my palms. Once it dries, I check my phone. The lack of messages from him has my lips pulling into a frown.

> Calista: Hey.

> Hayden: Are you all right?

> Calista: Yes. I was just wondering what time I'll see you tonight?

> Hayden: The case I'm working requires more attention than I'd like. I'll be home a little later than usual.

> Calista: Oh, okay. Well, good luck. See you later.

> Hayden: Thank you. You too.

With a sigh, I put the phone in my apron pocket. Maybe I need to follow Harper's advice and tell Hayden I'm interested in sex. My plan won't involve a fondue machine, but my friend has the right idea. With Hayden working late, I'll have plenty of time to freshen up and put on something enticing.

I walk over to the now empty tables and wipe them down. A flash of color catches my eye and I pause, lifting my head to peer out the window. A small girl in a magenta jacket walks down the sidewalk with an older woman that I know to be her mother.

"I'll be right back," I call to Harper.

My co-worker nods at me and I grin as I dash outside. My assigned bodyguard, a bald man who's over six feet tall and built like a mountain, steps forward the minute my feet hit the pavement. I wave at Sebastian—who may or may not be part of the Russian mob—and point to the child to indicate my intention. Before I can second-guess myself, I call out the girl's name.

"Erika!"

The girl and her mother turn around, eyes widening in surprise. Erika's face splits into a toothless grin at seeing me and my heart expands in my chest. I kneel down and hold my arms out.

"Miss Calista!" Erika tugs her hand from her mother's to launch herself at me.

I meet Sebastian's gaze and he gives me a quick nod. Now that any potential issues have been averted, I look at Erika, willing myself not to cry. "How are you, sweet girl? It's so good to see you. I've missed you like crazy."

Erika beams at me. "I'm doing good. Mama got a new job so we got our own apartment now."

I release the little girl and look up at her mother. "That's wonderful, Alice. I'm so happy for the two of you."

"We couldn't have done it without your support, Miss Green," Alice says. "You helped me with my resume and talked to the boss. I'm convinced you putting in a good word for me got me the job. Although we'll miss seeing you at the shelter."

"I appreciate that." I hug Erika again, tighter this time. "I'll miss seeing you too. I've been busy so I haven't been volunteering at the shelter, but hopefully I can after the holidays."

The lie chills my bones faster than the winter afternoon. The very idea of stepping into that place makes me want to throw up. My stomach begins to churn and I push away the thoughts of my assault.

"You should go back to volunteering," Alice says. "You made such a difference. Not just in our lives, but for other families as well."

I dip my head in acknowledgment. "Thank you."

"Well, we better get going. It was so great to see you, Miss Green."

"Please call me Calista." I look at Erika. "I'm going to miss you most of all. Don't tell the others, but you've always been my favorite."

~

I'M NAKED.

With step one complete, I walk into Hayden's closet, looking for something to wear as a surprise for when he comes home. I've already reapplied my makeup and run a brush through my hair, leaving the long tresses unbound the way he likes them. Hopefully this plan will "encourage" him. I think about having sex with him all the time and I can't believe it. I was never this way with my ex. I may not have been a virgin when I met Hayden, but he's definitely ruined me for any other man.

Just like he wanted.

I sift through the different articles of clothing, undecided if I should wear one of his dress shirts, his jacket, or his trench coat. I could also choose something from my new wardrobe, but in the end it won't matter. If he's not interested in the fact that I'm completely nude underneath, then nothing else will get his attention.

My gaze lands on his favorite suede jacket hanging neatly on a hanger. I visualize myself wearing it for him and enjoying his smile of approval. Decision made, I slip my arms into the buttery-soft sleeves. The hem brushes my knees and the garment immediately swallows my petite frame, which is perfect for the reveal I have in mind.

A sigh escapes me as I run my hands over the supple

leather and leisurely trace the fine stitching. My fingers encounter strange lumpy objects deep in the right pocket and I purse my lips at the discovery. I insert my hand into the opening and nearly yank it right back out when I feel the smooth texture of the objects inside.

With my heart galloping in my chest, I grab a handful of the items and withdraw my fist. I stare at it, watching my knuckles begin to lose their color and feeling the first tremors streaking through my forearm from my tight grip. Trepidation fills me until my breathing thins and becomes difficult, my body acknowledging what my brain is refusing to.

With aching slowness, I uncurl my fingers, revealing the small, round objects resting on my palm. Over half a dozen loose pearls sit in my hand, with several more still resting in Hayden's pocket. I stare at them until my eyes dry out and force me to blink.

My blood runs cold as the horrifying truth hits me like a bolt of lightning. How else would he have gotten these pearls if he wasn't the one who took them? Hayden, the man who claims to want me safe, is in fact the stalker who terrorized me for months. Revulsion courses through me as I picture him stealing the necklace, breaking it, and then leaving a single pearl for me to find.

Tears blur my vision and sobs wrack my body as I sink to the floor, clutching the pieces of jewelry. The man I thought cared about me violated my trust. And for what? To manipulate me into being with him? This entire charade was unnecessary.

I would've been with Hayden because I'm already falling in love with him.

My heart pumps harder with every beat until I worry it'll explode inside my chest. Given the pain zipping through my body, I almost wish it would. If only to stop the agony. I gave Hayden everything and he made me question my sanity while taking away my sense of security.

I knew he was too good to be true.

I just wish I understood why he did all of this when we could've had an honest relationship; why he chose obsession over love.

Taking a deep breath, I roughly wipe my eyes. The sadness churning within me hardens into icy resolve, a cold wall that's impenetrable, similar to the one I created when my father died. Except this one's more fortified. When Hayden gets home and walks through that door, the fantasy of him ends. And the real man—the stalker—has much to answer for.

I invited a genuine monster into my life. The only thing left to do is face him and hope I make it out with my sanity intact.

Because my heart is definitely a goner.

CHAPTER 42

H ayden

I slam my fist on the office desk with a curse.

Calista is my only priority yet I'm no closer to finding the person responsible for her assault. Even with access to government databases, I can't find anything that'll point me in the direction of a guilty party.

At the idea of not enacting justice on her behalf, a growl rushes between my clenched teeth. I've already failed my mother on that front. I can't do the same with Calista. It could send me over the edge and into the pool of insanity churning in the recesses of my psyche.

I retrieve the pill that caused my mother's overdose from the drawer and set it before me. The starburst symbol in the middle is worn from the number of times I've touched it. For reasons I can't explain, staring at it helps me center my thoughts.

If only it wasn't a tangible reminder of my shortcomings: first to protect my mother, then to avenge her.

I pick up the pill and roll it between my fingers, the action soothing to the tumultuous energy coursing through me. The symbol and composition were the only clues I had to go on after my mother's death, but no amount of research provided answers as to where it came from. The police wrote it off as another illicit street drug. I didn't give up then, and I won't now.

It's not an option. Not when Calista is counting on me. Maybe I'm the one who needs this absolution, this chance at redemption as much as she needs the closure.

Setting down the pill, I start a new search. The cursor blinks accusingly as I hover over the keyboard. There has to be something I'm missing, a small detail that'll provide a breakthrough on this case. With that in mind, I start at the beginning, recalling my conversation with Calista.

My skin grows heated as my anger rises. The mere thought of her assault has me sweeping my arm over the desk's surface, tossing and scattering every scrap of paper to the floor. With the area bare, I retrieve a legal pad from the drawer and write down everything.

WHERE: HOPEFUL HEARTS CHILDREN'S SHELTER

WHEN: JUNE 24TH
WHO: CALISTA GREEN
WHAT: VICTIM WAS PRESENT AT THE LOCATION AROUND 4PM, BUT THE TIMESTAMP OF THE PHOTO SHOWCASING HER INJURIES WAS 8:30PM. BY THAT TIME, THE BRUISES WERE PLAIN TO SEE ON HER IVORY SKIN AND SHE WAS CONSCIOUS.

I squeeze the pen until my fist shakes. What possibly happened in those unaccounted for hours has my stomach heaving. Calista was hesitant to talk about that night and there are times I wish I hadn't pushed her, but I needed to know everything. And now that I do, blood will flow.

The law has limits. I don't.

Not when it comes to protecting the woman I...

My breathing halts. I'm not sure how to finish that thought. The only thing I know for certain is Calista's mine. Forever.

I return my gaze to the legal pad, taking in the sharp lines and bold strokes of my writing. It taunts me, provokes me. There's still another question to be written, the one that haunts me: Why would someone hurt Calista?

MOTIVE: AN INDIRECT ATTACK ON HER FATHER? LUST? MENTAL INSTABILITY? OPPORTUNITY?

With a loud exhale, I push back in my chair and retrieve the papers from the floor. After placing her medical record front and center, I go over the contents. Calista was physically assaulted. There's no disputing that. However, the sexual assault examination was inconclusive, despite the drug in her system.

I frown at the description.

A depressant with an unknown compound that results in behavior similar to a "date-rape" drug.

The phrasing tugs at my memory, forcing my brain to sort through the years' worth of information I've stored during my career. I snatch up the coroner's report for Kristen Hall, Senator Green's secretary. The phrasing in her record isn't identical to Calista's, but it's close. Too fucking close.

My gaze darts between the words on the page and the pill sitting off to the side. Back and forth, again and again as my mind creates a connection, one that has my chest painfully tightening.

This is merely a coincidence.

Or is it?

What are the chances that the drug that killed my mother, and was found in Kristen Hall's bloodstream, is the same drug that was used to incapacitate Calista?

If I look at the common denominator in the fucked-up equation—this drug with a mysterious compound—that makes the entire scenario way more feasible. I'll have to look at this case and its victims as a whole. The connections are there in the evidence.

Now that I've seen it, I can't unsee it.

My gut twists until I'm gritting my teeth against the discomfort. Two out of the three women involved in this situation are dead. Does that mean Calista's next?

Whoever's behind this better fucking kill me if they think they're going to hurt her.

I RACE THROUGH THE CITY WHILE TRYING TO CONTROL MY panic before it interferes with my faculties and I crash my car. My need to be with Calista has never been stronger, my obsession with her safety has never been more urgent.

I've never been one for dramatics, but I might fucking die if I don't touch her soon. Even if it's only to reassure myself that she's alive.

My thoughts have plagued me since my discovery of the cases' connection to one another and they continue to, driving me closer to insanity. So close I'm beginning to worry I've already gone past my limits and crossed over into dangerous territory where my instincts guide my actions.

Right now those instincts want to protect and fuck Calista.

I shake my head at my thoughts, but that doesn't stop me from running through the lobby and cursing while I wait for the elevator to reach my floor. My ragged breaths only become more uneven when I reach the door to my penthouse.

I'm inside within seconds and stalking through the living room toward the bedroom. Until I spot Calista by the windows, peering out. The tightness in my chest loosens when she turns to look at me over her shoulder. The woman I've killed for—would again without question—is alive.

And stares at me with the eyes of a wounded animal.

My steps falter as I come to an abrupt halt. I run my gaze over her, from head to foot, only to return my attention to her face. The skin around her mouth is tight and her bottom lip trembles enough for me to see it from where I stand.

"Callie?"

She holds up a hand when I start to walk toward her. "Don't, Hayden."

"Fuck that."

I stride up to her and with every step her body goes more rigid. Ignoring the strange behavior, I peer down at Calista, clenching my fists to keep from grabbing her. She holds her ground with a lifted chin.

"If I ask you a question, will you promise not to lie to me?" Her voice quivers during the delivery. Is she apprehensive because of me or the answer I might give? "I have to know the truth," she says in a whisper.

I dip my head in acknowledgment, not acquiescence. It's

enough. Calista parts her lips to inhale deeply, drawing my gaze to her lush mouth. God, how I want to fuck it.

She raises her fisted hand and slowly unfurls her fingers, giving me an unobstructed view of the pearls resting on her palm.

"Where did you get these, Hayden?"

ALTERNATE POV
BONUS CHAPTER

H ayden

> Hayden: Enjoying your night out, Miss Green?

> Calista: Yup.

I 'm not sure if I want to spank Calista or fuck the ever-loving shit out of her.

Both. Definitely, unequivocally both.

I stare down at my phone in my hands, gripping the piece of technology as though it's a lifeline to the woman driving me insane. Actually, I'm past the edge of insanity. I've become *unhinged* in the hours it's taken for Calista to respond to me. At first I thought something had happened to her, but once I discovered she was ignoring me, the only danger to her now is me.

> Hayden: This conversation is not over, Miss Green. Who are you with?

I wait, my pulse ratcheting with every second I don't receive a response from her. She's doing it again: dismissing me as though I'm of no consequence to her. In contrast, I'm willing to burn down the city in order to find her. Luckily for the citizens of New York, I put a tracker in the cell phone I bought for Calista.

My patience—what little I had—is gone. I've given her an opportunity to come to her senses, but she's refusing to. *Time's up, Miss Green.*

> Hayden: I'm coming to get you.

I stop pacing the floor of my living room and pivot toward the front door, snatching my keys on the way out. My phone vibrates in my hand. I look down at the screen, but my stride doesn't falter as I read the messages. It quickens.

> Calista: First of all, Mr. Bennett, you shouldn't know where I am. And if you do, we need to talk about fucking boundaries. Second, I'm busy, so this conversation can wait until toomorrrow.

> Calista: tomorrow* whoops.

> Hayden: First of all, language. Second, boundaries don't exist between us. Third, stop drinking.

> Calista: *orders another motherfucking drink* 🍸

Calista's defiance has a reluctant smile tugging at my lips. Our clash of wills can only end with me as the victor, but I admire her having the courage to push back. Every time she's disobedient, a spark of anger flares to life inside me. It combines with the tiniest thrill, heating my blood in an entirely different way.

> Hayden: That better be a glass of motherfucking water. I don't want you throwing up in my car when I take you home.

> Calista: I'm not going anywhere, so leave me alone. Unlike you, there's a man here who's actually interested in me.

I halt in the middle of the foyer on the ground floor of my building, blinking at my phone again and again. Another man? *What the actual fuck?* Is she joking with me? For both their sakes, I hope so.

> Hayden: If he touches you, what I did last time will seem like a joke in comparison.

> Calista: 🤚 I'm not answering you anymore tonight. Kindly fuck off, Mr. Bennett.

> Hayden: I'm definitely fucking something, Miss Green.

I shove my phone in my pocket and climb into my vehicle. The time for discussion has passed. All that's left is for me to take action, to claim what's mine while reminding Calista I always mean what I say.

After careening down the streets, I park my car and walk into the club, my steps purposeful. The room buzzes with conversation around me, the occupants oblivious to the storm brewing inside my chest. I scan the area. It doesn't take long to find my target.

Calista—looking so beautiful it fucking guts me—is actually with another man, his hands sliding a bit too confidently over her curves as they sway to the music. Each touch sends a spike of fury racing through my veins. It's irrational, I know, but I can't help it.

The stranger whispers something in her ear, and she laughs, throwing her head back in genuine amusement. Her smile, something I have yet to experience more than once, is now on display for everyone to see. Especially that asshole she's dancing with.

I fucked up the guy at the bar for touching her hair... what does she think I'll do to the man who dares to touch her body?

I take a picture of the man's face and send it to Zack. I need the hacker to identify the man I'm trying not to kill. Hopefully he's of no importance to society, but even if he is, I'm not sure it'll stay my hand.

The DJ shifts the music, and the beat drops heavier, more insistent. The man's hands roam lower, and Calista doesn't stop him. My jaw clenches as I watch his fingers explore territory that I've fiercely guarded from others. Even from myself.

Until now.

I head in their direction, my legs carrying me toward Calista before my mind fully catches up with the decision. Fuck this man's identity. I don't need to know who he is. Not when he's touching Calista in ways I've only dreamed of.

The crowd parts quickly, as though sensing the danger coating me like a second skin. I walk up to the couple, my gaze locked on the woman I'm obsessed with.

"Can I kiss you, Calista?"

The stranger's request has my muscles going taut, but it's Calista's nod that has my blood boiling. This man's life is forfeit. Last time I killed for Calista, but tonight it'll be for me.

Like her smile, she's giving him her kiss. Those are *mine*.

As I step closer, our eyes meet, blue colliding with hazel. There's a flicker of surprise in her gaze, a question perhaps, or a challenge. Does she see the violence in my eyes? Does she understand the fury and the forbidden desire battling within me?

The man leans in, and something inside me snaps.

The world narrows to the two of them, and an infernal heat kindles within me, my vision tinged with a wrathful blaze. In an instant, I'm moving, propelled by a force I can't control.

I reach them just as his lips are about to meet Calista's. My hand lands heavily on the man's shoulder, and I yank him back with all the strength I can muster. The shock on their faces might have satisfied me under different circumstances, but all I feel now is a searing, possessive anger.

Calista has never been mine in the way a lover is, but in this moment as I confront them, I'm acting like an enraged husband defending his wife. It's irrational to feel this way about someone who I've never even kissed. Yet here I am, acting on impulses I'm unable to reign in.

Harper appears beside Calista, her presence adding to the havoc I've unleashed. I'm like a hurricane, a destructive force about to tear through everything with reckless abandon.

"What's going on?" Harper's voice cuts through the tension, but I barely hear her. My focus is on the man. My eyes burn into his, daring him to challenge me so I can hit him.

"What the fuck, man?" he shouts, his voice edged with both surprise and anger.

At his question, I shift my gaze to Calista, the intensity of the moment sharpening every sense. "Would you like to explain it to him, Miss Green?" My voice is easily heard through the pounding music, unnaturally calm, a contrast to the chaos of emotions swirling inside me.

Calista shakes her head, her eyes wide, telling me everything I need to know without a word spoken.

"Is this the brother you were talking about?" The man's question slices into the conversation, his tone dripping with disdain. "I can see why you think he's an overbearing prick."

I raise an eyebrow at Calista, and she flinches. "Brother?" I repeat, letting the word hang heavily between us. With a click of my tongue, a sound more of chastisement than anger, I continue, "Miss Green, I thought you were above lying."

Turning to the man, my gaze hardens. "If I'm her brother, then the things I want to do to her are beyond incestuous."

Harper hisses in Calista's ear, her grip tight on Calista's arm, mirroring the tension rising around us. When I drag my fingers down to adjust my cuff link, a subtle signal of my intent to destroy this man, Harper and Calista stiffen.

"Oh, fuck," Harper murmurs, echoing the sentiment I can barely keep contained. I've been here before, ready to fight, to protect, driven by a fury that doesn't care for reasons or provocations. Or even the law. Unless it's my personal sense of justice.

"I warned you," I say directly to Calista, my voice low but fierce. The memory of my previous threats looms between us, a stark reminder of my resolve.

The fear in Calista's eyes spurs her into action. She rips her arm from Harper's grasp and positions herself between the stranger and me, her hands outstretched in a plea. "Please," she says. "Don't do this."

I drop the serpent-shaped cuff link into her upturned palm, the ruby eye gleaming ominously under the club lights. She closes her fist around it, stepping closer, her desperation palpable.

"You're so beautiful when you beg," I murmur, the words slipping out, raw and honest. I reach for my other cuff link, my movements deliberate, each action underlining my intent. Handing it to her, I begin to roll up my sleeve, signaling that I'm not backing down, that I'm too far gone.

Panic flares in Calista's eyes, a vivid, electric fear that seems to charge the air between us. She grabs the fabric of my shirt, pulling herself up on her tiptoes, still barely reaching my height even in heels.

Then, in a move that catches me entirely off guard, she kisses me.

My focus narrows down to the press of her lips against mine, a desperate, searing connection that floods my senses with heat. Every fiber of my being focuses on this contact, this unexpected surrender that feels both like a victory and a profound complication to everything I am trying to control.

I've always kept my distance when it comes to kissing women—it's too intimate, too revealing of the emotions I've carefully guarded. But as Calista kisses me, everything I've held back crashes down like a dam bursting under the pressure of unfulfilled desire. In that single, electrifying moment, the walls I've built around myself don't just crack; they shatter completely. The flood of emotions, long suppressed, surges through me with overwhelming force.

Her lips against mine feel like the first real breath after years of suffocation. It's terrifying and exhilarating all at once. Each caress of her tongue against my mouth sends shock waves of need through my body, awakening parts of me I had resigned to darkness.

The intimacy of the kiss, something I've always avoided, now feels like the only truth I know. It's a revelation, opening my eyes to how much I've starved myself of this genuine human connection, how much I've denied myself the warmth of closeness.

As Calista deepens the kiss, my hands instinctively pull her closer, desperate to feel more of her, to reduce the space between us to nothing. This kiss isn't just an act of passion— it's an act of liberation from my self-imposed restraints. I'm not just kissing her; I'm reclaiming the parts of myself I thought were lost to the shadows.

The raw power of the moment is humbling. The careful control I always pride myself on slips away as if it were nothing more than a thin veil, easily torn apart by the strength of what I feel for Calista. I'm vulnerable, exposed in ways I've never allowed myself to be, and yet I don't want to retreat back to safety. Not now, not when she is so close, when she is right here offering me the taste of her.

I groan, the sound more surrender than lust. Although there's an overwhelming amount of that as well. This woman could bring me to my knees if she'd only ask.

I deepen the kiss, relinquishing to my need for her, drawing out the seconds into a slow, torturous eternity where only Calista and I exist. Her lips move against mine with an urgency that seizes my soul, wrenching it with a mixture of elation and fear. This isn't how I imagined our first kiss—fraught with tension, anger, and jealousy, yet here we are, and it's as if all the pent-up longing and hidden feelings have found their escape in this one reckless moment.

Her hands shift from gripping my shirt to winding around my neck, pulling me closer, as if she could meld us together and erase the barriers I've so carefully constructed between us. My hands act of their own accord, settling on her waist, holding her to me with a possessiveness that is second nature to me. The heat from her body, the pressure of her fingers against my skin, and the intoxicating scent of her hair all conspire to drown my senses in her.

I devour her in a way that leaves no room for hesitation. Or retreat. This woman is mine and has been since the day I met her. The day that her hazel eyes gazed at me as though I was the only man in the world worthy of her.

Suddenly, reality snaps back as the music thumps around us and the murmurs of the crowd seep into my consciousness. I pull back, breathless, unable to stop my hands from shaking. Calista's eyes are wide, shimmering with a mix of emotions that mirror my own confusion and burgeoning hope.

"You're full of surprises," I manage to say, my voice a mix of awe and something deeper, something like worship. Or perhaps fear, at the depth of my feelings for her.

Calista Green owns me body and soul, with my heart not far behind.

**Keep reading for a glimpse of the next book
in the Possessing Her duet.**

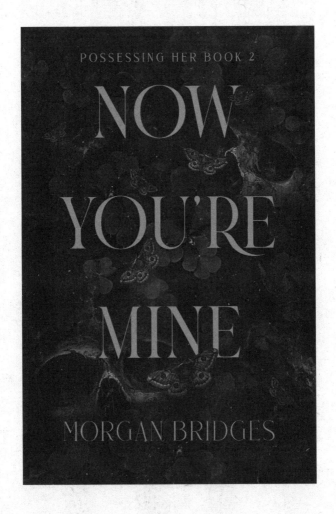

POSSESSING HER BOOK 2

NOW
YOU'RE
MINE

MORGAN BRIDGES

CHAPTER 1

C alista

I CAN'T DO THIS.

The emotional pain of Hayden's betrayal streaks through me, causing tremors to wrack my body and the pearls in my hand to clink against one another. The tiny sound is like the banging of a drum. Or is that my heart? I could've sworn it stopped beating the minute he entered the penthouse.

And looked desperate to touch me.

I take a fortifying breath and lift my chin. If I don't confront him now, I never will.

"Where did you get these, Hayden?" I repeat the question I asked a moment ago, my voice still shaking but my resolve firmly in place. "I need to know."

He holds my gaze, the detachment in his eyes gutting me. "You already do."

I shake my head, either in denial or as a response, I'm

not sure. "No, what I have is a suspicion that needs to be confirmed."

"What do you want me to say, Calista?"

His use of my full name has me wincing. I quickly school my features and fist the pearls to place my hand on my hip. "The truth. That's all I want from you."

"You don't know what you want." He averts his gaze in a rare show of uncertainty. "And it doesn't matter until I find out who's behind your assault."

From one blink to the next my agony morphs into anger. "*What?*"

Hayden brings his attention to me and this time it's with the full weight of his stare. It settles on me, pressing in from all sides until I'm hunching my shoulders. The unspoken thoughts running through his mind are loud in the silence and I almost wish I hadn't confronted him.

"Never mind," he says, squeezing the bridge of his nose. "Keeping you safe is the only thing that's important."

"How can I be safe with you when *you're* the one who's been stalking me?"

"I did it to protect you. Whether or not you choose to accept that is your prerogative."

I huff. "Explain how scaring the shit out of me was for my protection."

"Language, Cal—"

"Fuck language and fuck these roundabout answers," I say, my words one decibel away from a shout. "Tell me how someone can justify breaking into my apartment, stealing my shit, and then have the fucking nerve to say it was for my own good."

Hayden's gaze flashes right before he grabs me by the shoulders and yanks me to him. "Don't you realize how vulnerable you were walking in the city at night? Do you know what could've happened if I hadn't been there to watch over you? Or is that a truth you don't want to acknowledge?"

I shove at his chest. It's as effective as pushing a mountain, and I drop my arms in defeat, still clutching the pearls. "I didn't have a choice. However, I'm sure it's easy to pass judgment from your penthouse. You can say whatever you want, but I don't believe my safety is the only issue here."

He lowers his head until our faces are mere inches from one another, our breaths mingling. "I wanted to fuck you," he says, his tone guttural and deep. "I wanted you more than I'd ever wanted a woman in my life. I broke into your apartment and took your necklace to stop myself from taking your body. So yes, I wanted to keep you safe from the world, but also from myself and what I would do to you."

"And now that you've fucked me? Is your obsession gone?"

He releases a sardonic laugh that has my skin prickling. "Gone? Oh no, my sweet little bird, my obsession with you has only gotten worse."

His words kickstart my heart like I've been given a shot of adrenaline. The idea of Hayden watching over me like a deranged bodyguard gives way to an incessant throbbing at my temples, one that has me gritting my teeth and sucking in a breath. With my entire body rigid, except for the rise and fall of my chest, I stand there, unable to do anything except feel overwhelmed.

By Hayden's desire for me.

And my fear of him.

I don't think he'd hurt me physically. The things that scare me are the depth and intensity of his commitment. Do I have it in me to embrace this side of him? Do I even want to?

"Were you ever going to tell me?" I whisper.

"No."

The truth of his response is like a smack to the face, and I rear back in his hold. "How can I trust you when I know you'll lie to me?"

"I will lie, cheat, steal, and kill if that's what it takes to keep you. You're all that matters to me."

"Even if I hate you for it?"

He flinches at the question, as if taking a bullet to the chest. "You can hate me for now but not forever."

"You can't control that, Hayden."

"True," he says between clenched teeth. "But I can control everything else."

I drop my gaze, not wanting him to see the agony that's sure to be in my eyes. This man admitted that he wanted to possess me and I ran. Do I have the strength to try again? Does it matter when my chances of success are minimal and part of me doesn't want to leave in the first place?

I've never understood how you could love and hate someone simultaneously, but Hayden has enlightened me.

"Let go of me," I say, my voice calm despite my inner turmoil.

Hayden places his index finger under my chin to lift my head. "Never."

I stare up at him, not bothering to conceal my fury. "I don't want you touching me right now."

"Miss Green, I wish you would try to stop me."

The futility of my situation rises like steam to heat me all over. I shrug from his hold, but his grip is too strong, frustrating me all the more. In one last-ditch effort to get free, I fling the pearls at him. The iridescent orbs hit him in the face and his chest, bouncing off to clink on the floor.

He releases me. I press my lips together to keep my jaw from dropping, unable to believe that worked. Without his hands on me, my thoughts clear, putting this fucked-up situation into perspective.

"Hayden, I care about you, more than I want to admit right now." When he quirks a brow in disapproval, my stomach dips. "But you have to see this from my point of view. How would you like it if someone violated your trust and invaded your privacy?"

"Everything is about motivation. If a mother kills someone for hurting her child, would you condemn her?"

I shake my head. "That's different, because she didn't hurt the person she loved."

He stiffens.

"Regardless if you want to admit it or not, you've hurt me with your actions. I need time to…"

"To. What?" he asks, the words clipped.

"To figure out if I can move past this."

Hayden smirks and the mocking expression has the hairs on my arms lifting. "And if you can't?"

"I—I don't know."

"Let me be clear, Miss Green. That's *not* an option." He leans forward, placing his lips by ear. "You can run, but I'll *always* chase you."

I take a step back and he lifts his head, his gaze trailing my every movement as I cross my arms. The action is nothing more than an attempt to put a barrier between us, but I need distance from him in any way I can.

"You can come after me physically, but here?" I say, pointing to my temple. "This is a place you can't follow me, no matter what you do."

He frowns, his confident air disappearing. The blue of his eyes glitters with uncertainty and something I've never seen: fear. It stabs me, cracking the facade of bravery I'm shielding myself with.

"Hayden," I say, struggling to keep my voice stern, "there's nothing left to talk about. We're at an impasse."

He doesn't move, not even to acknowledge what I've said. Or maybe that's on purpose to show he disagrees.

"I'm going to call it a night," I say.

"But you haven't eaten."

I shrug. "I can't when I'm upset."

"Upset" might be the understatement of the year. My brain is so muddled I don't know if I can chew and swallow food without choking. And from the way my thoughts are buzzing in my skull, I doubt that I'll sleep tonight.

"You're going to eat, even if I have to force feed you," he says, his tone leaving no room for argument. "Now, you can either walk into the kitchen or I can carry you there, but either way, you're going."

Righteous indignation causes me to lift my chin with a dainty sniff. "Fine."

I don't wait for him. My bare feet sink into the plush carpet with every step until I reach the cold tile in the kitchen. The stark change in temperature against my soles sends a chill through me, but not more than the predatory man trailing me. Although I can't hear him walking, I can sense him.

I always do.

"Do you have a preference tonight?" he asks.

After turning to look at him, I shake my head. "It doesn't matter what you give me, I won't enjoy it."

"Miss Green, you'll enjoy *anything* I stick in that pretty mouth." When I press my lips together, he smirks at me. "Have a seat."

My pride, already raw from his lies, chafes at the

command. I cross my arms and give him a pointed stare. His gaze narrows to little more than slits.

"Sit. Down."

I continue holding his stare, begging my inner fortitude to remain strong. Backing down is not an option. Not when this man has taken possession of me in more ways than I care to admit.

He's on me from one blink to the next, moving too fast for my brain to process. I let out a shriek at the feel of his hands grabbing my waist. He lifts me onto the island, his fingertips digging into the fabric of my jeans. I chose to wear them and a plain blouse instead of Hayden's clothes. Once I found the pearls in his pocket, I couldn't get the coat off fast enough.

I glare up at him, unable to keep my breathing even while agitation rushes through me. My chest heaves with every inhale and he drops his attention to the hint of cleavage my top displays. I resist the urge to pull the neckline up.

"My eyes are up here."

His lips twitch. "I'm not going to apologize."

"Then what are you doing?"

"Making sure you stay put."

I huff. "I'm not going anywhere."

"It's good to hear you accept the inevitable," he says, "because now you're mine."

CHAPTER 2

C alista

HAYDEN'S WORDS WRAP AROUND ME LIKE A RIBBON, SILKY, YET restrictive and binding.

He watches me for a moment as if challenging me to jump off the island. I've already fucked around and found out. I'm not interested in another lesson.

Before I can think of a response, he walks over to the refrigerator and removes a tray laden with fruit, cheese, and crackers. The bright colors are too cheerful for the tension-filled atmosphere. Like the black-and-white decor all around us, Hayden and I are complete opposites. While he's domineering and severe, I'm caring and tender-hearted.

In a perfect world, we'd complement one another.

In a fucked-up world, we'd devastate each other.

He places the food next to me and I eye it dispassionately. I wasn't lying when I said it's difficult for me to eat when I'm stressed. Between losing my father and my recent financial situation, I'm thinner than I've ever been in my life. You'd never know it from the way Hayden stares at me.

Like he's doing now.

After reaching for a cracker and placing a slice of cheese on top, he offers it to me. I shake my head. Vigorously. Everything he does—except being a deceitful asshole—is sexy. I'll be damned before I let him seduce me with a fucking piece of cheese. Not to mention, accepting anything from him would feel like an act of surrender.

"I can do it myself."

"I know."

"Hayden…" I warn.

"It's either this," he says, lifting the food, "or my cock. Your choice."

My jaw drops. He's quick to take advantage of my bewildered state and plops the cracker into my mouth. While giving him a death glare, I chew, silently appreciating the sharp flavor coating my tongue.

"Good girl," he murmurs.

I choke, my eyes widening. After forcing myself to swallow the food, I resume squinting at him. Hayden picks up a strawberry and bites into it slowly, his eyes never leaving mine. Juice drips down his long fingers and my mouth goes dry at the memory of what he's done to me with them.

"My eyes are up here," he says in a lazy drawl.

I stiffen at having been caught ogling him and avert my gaze. He's quick to place a finger under my chin and guide my head back toward him.

"Open for me," he says. When I part my lips, his pupils contract. "Such a good girl."

Heat sweeps through me at the praise. Arousal and anger combine, leaving me hot and shaky. I clench my thighs and focus my thoughts on anything except the man in front of me, but he keeps bringing my attention back to him with every touch and every spoken word.

I force myself to remain still until I've consumed a fair amount of food, and then I hop down before Hayden can stop me. After racing to the other side and putting the island between us, I shake my head.

"I'm full."

He sets down the piece of pineapple in his hand and reaches for a napkin to wipe his fingers. "Then it's time for bed."

"I'm not sleeping with you."

His head snaps up. "Care to repeat that?"

"Nope."

Amusement flickers in his eyes. "I didn't think so."

"I'm serious. I need time to think."

"You can. In my bed. With me."

I come close to stomping my foot like a petulant child. "You're not listening to me."

"I'm definitely hearing you. I'm just denying your suggestion."

"It isn't a suggestion or request or anything that fucking requires permission."

"Language, Miss Green."

I let out an honest-to-goodness scream. The sound bounces off the walls and furniture, piercing my eardrums hard enough for me to stop. When I clamp my lips together, Hayden tilts his head.

"Feel better?" he asks, his tone chiding and unfazed.

"Not really."

"Come here."

It's not a request.

I eye him with suspicion. "Why?"

"You look exhausted."

"I've had a pretty exciting day." I don't bother hiding my sarcastic undertone. "How often does a girl find out that the man she's living with is her stalker?"

"How often does a man find a woman he'd destroy the world for?"

I bow my head and release a sigh of defeat while briefly closing my eyes, ignoring the way my heart lurches in my chest. "Stop. I can't do this with you right now."

"Come here, Callie."

His tone is soft and gentle, soothing to my wounded soul. I slap my palms against the island to keep from going to him. To keep from accepting the comfort of a monster.

"I need to be alone," I say, my voice small and weak. Every time I deny Hayden it adds another crack to my defense against him. When he's domineering I can patch the holes in my armor, but this tender side of him?

It wrecks me.

"Please." My supplication is a mere whisper, the last of my rebellion a monosyllable of both weakness and desperation.

Hayden stares at me from across the island, so close physically, but very distant emotionally. The chasm between us is a third party, a looming presence in our relationship. Whatever's left of it.

The beautiful man in front of me swallows hard, right before blowing out a harsh breath. "Very well."

I don't ask him what he means. Instead, I take the brief reprieve and edge around the island. And him. Once my feet meet the carpet, I head in the direction of the guest room located a few doors down from Hayden's bedroom.

My spine tingles the entire way and my senses strain to pick up on any trace of him following me. When I reach the hallway, I stop and chance a look over my shoulder.

Hayden's exactly where I left him in the kitchen. His entire frame is lined with tension and he's completely still, but that's not what steals my breath. The man grips the countertop with his head bowed, his body in a position of defeat and utter despair.

I bite the inside of my cheek to refrain from calling him. Or worse, returning to his side. I might care for Hayden, but this issue between us won't be resolved unless he can see how his behavior hurt me.

It takes every ounce of my willpower to turn back around and take a step. Once I'm in motion, I pick up the pace until I'm in the empty bedroom with the door shut and locked behind me.

A grim smile tweaks my mouth as I lean heavily against the door. Hayden might get upset because I've secured myself inside the room, but he's left me no choice. I need a moment of peace.

Not that I believe a simple metal mechanism would keep him from getting to me. It certainly didn't work at my apartment.

With a groan, I slide down until my butt hits the floor. Bringing my knees to my chest, I rest my forehead on them and wrap my arms around my legs. Curled in a tight ball, I let the tears flow.

I cry over my battered heart.

I weep over my broken trust.

I mourn over my bleak future.

How am I supposed to move past Hayden's lies? Is that even possible? I have no idea. The frightful unknown mixes with agony to create an unbearable anxiety that has my sobs growing. My entire body is nothing more than a collection of skin and bones held firmly together while I feel like I'm falling apart on the inside.

How can one person be responsible for so much pain?

My shuddering causes my spine to rap against the wooden surface behind me, the staccato tapping out the soundtrack of my misery. Every tremor and every tear, a manifestation of my bleeding heart that struggles to beat despite me drawing breath.

I can feel Hayden's presence before I hear him speak. "Baby?"

The term of endearment has my soul wailing. I bite down on my fist until the tang of blood hits my tongue. I can't go to him, not when I'm the one who asked for space. But hearing his voice and the concern underlying it? I'm like an addict wanting a drug, knowing it'll just hurt me.

The silence is charged, becoming heavier with every second I refuse to speak. My sobs immediately quiet with Hayden standing on the other side of the door. I don't stifle them for his benefit. I do it for mine.

I won't give him a reason to break the lock, as well as the remaining shreds of my dignity.

At the sound of his footsteps receding, I release a sigh of relief. I might've held my breath when there was a mere three inches between us, but my tears continued to stream down my face. Sometimes I think they'll never stop. But like all things, they come to an end.

I lie down on the floor, uncaring about comfort or anything else while chasing the blissful reprieve found in sleep. Closing my eyes, I concentrate on my heartbeats instead of the man down the hall. Except my brain refuses to cooperate. I might've told Hayden he'll never invade my mind, but I lied.

The man follows me into my dreams.

Turning them into nightmares.

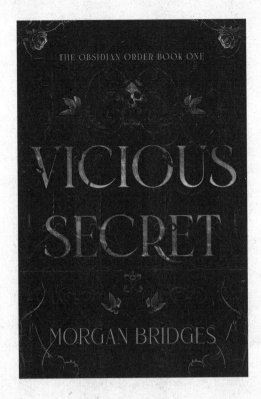

THE OBSIDIAN ORDER BOOK ONE

VICIOUS SECRET

MORGAN BRIDGES

Mors solum initium

Death is only the beginning.

The Recruit

The Obsidian Order only cares about three things: secrecy, loyalty, and power. Every man born to the founding families is bred for this purpose, to serve the society and its objectives.

As a result, we are the elite. Untouchable. Unbreakable. If we make it through the Trials. I will, as long as my obsession doesn't get the best of me. This girl…

If the Order doesn't kill me, she'll be the death of me. Because I won't give her up. She's mine.

The Bride

All I want is my freedom and some coffee. And to find my foster brother. Every clue that leads me closer to Ben only frightens me more.

Something dark and dangerous rules this campus. Similar to the stranger I keep running into. The one I can't stop thinking about. Xavier tells me to stay away from him, but then I'm snared in a game of shadows and savagery.

Now the only way to survive lies in the arms of a man I once tried to kill. The same one who's made me his property. His bride.

ABOUT THE AUTHOR

Morgan Bridges is a lover of anti-heroes, deep and thought-provoking books with beautifully written words, romance that's sigh-worthy, scenes that are so hot she blushes, and heroines that inspire her to the point she wants to take their place.

You can find out more at:
authormbridges.com
TikTok @morganbridgesauthor
Instagram @mbridges_author
Facebook @MorganBridgesAuthor